Forgotten

Book #1

The Fate Trilogy

Sarah J. Pepper

Forgotten
Published by Neximus Publishing
ISBN-13: 978-0988246904
Copyright © Sarah J. Pepper 2014

Photography: Josh Wilcoxon of Wilcoxon Photography
Hair/Makeup: Angelique Verver of Platinum Imagination

Novels by Sarah J. Pepper

Devil's Lullaby – Ringer's Masquerade Series #1

Death's Melody – Ringer's Masquerade Series #2

Angel's Requiem – Ringer's Masquerade Series #3

Forgotten – The Fate Trilogy #1

Twisted Games – The Fate Trilogy #2

Fallen Tears

Death of the Mad Hatter

Locks: Rapunzel Unhinged

My death granted immortality.
With one look, I knew he'd be my undoing…

Chapter One

His chocolate brown eyes didn't radiate with vengeance as he pressed a knife to my chest. They glistened with tears. His dark brown hair shimmered, like golden fibers had been melted into each strand. The sight would've been utterly breathtaking if sand and sweat hadn't dried into his hair. A bloody gash under his left eye interrupted his otherwise perfectly tanned skin.

Burnt oranges, soft yellows, and deep reds surrounded the sun as it neared the horizon. My time was quickly slipping away. A hint of scorched wood piggybacked the wind while smoke crawled over the blood-soaked dirt.

I reached up with my gnarled, weathered hand and gently stroked his face. Hiding in the sheer beauty of his eyes rested his tortured soul—screaming for forgiveness. His tears trickled onto my aged skin as he shoved the blade deeper through my chest. I struggled to breathe. My vision darkened at the edges.

The vision of my death unfolded so many times that it felt like a memory rather than a glimpse of the future. Judging from my saggy skin, I'd live a long life only to be killed by the most delicious eye candy I'd ever seen—a cheery ending to my derailed existence. Peachy.

I hated knowing the future. I couldn't do anything but wait for the inevitable. Why such a pleasant outlook on life? Being a blind, orphaned, clairvoyant freak hadn't provided me with much normality in my life. Not that I was bitter. I considered myself a realist—no matter what my shrink said.

Clearing my head of the nightmarish vision, I rubbed my temples and wished for the impossible. I wished for the *Happily Ever After* that I would clearly never have, not even when I'm old. Perhaps a miracle would occur and I'd be able to make out more than just a gray abyss. I mean, I saw the future clearly. Thus, at some point my sight had to return. Right? Until then, I'd live in a world of shadows. My sight was comparable to wearing night vision goggles, I was left up a creek in determining color, depth, and definition. In my world of gray, people and objects appeared to be shadows instead of colorful, three-dimensional shapes.

My optometrist dubbed my legal-blindness an unfortunate side-effect of my past. Even though I couldn't recall the murderous night that ended with my one-way ticket to Orphanville, it was enough to cause physiological problems. I was thereby sentenced to a life of blindness. I guess that watching a sister die does that. My psychiatrist told me it was because I couldn't handle the reality that my sister Lily was dead, as well as my parents. I was pretty sure that was a load of BS, but I didn't have a PhD to back me up.

"Not you again," Ryker groaned, sitting down next to me, obligated to *act nice* in public. Annoyance rolled off him like the stench of his potent cologne. I swear he bathed in it. "When will you get the hint that we don't want you here, Winnie?"

I cringed. Even the cracking from the popcorn machine, screeches from excited players striking out, and rattling pins couldn't drown out his obnoxious voice.

"If I'm not welcome, why did Bree invite me to Strikers?" I asked, trying to put up a confident front.

"Because she pities you," he retorted. "Though you have some guts. Not many people *fake* being blind."

I rolled my eyes—my first line of defense against morons. "It is girls' night. *You're* crashing it, not me. And I play bumper ball."

"Get a clue! Bree tells her mom that she's going out with you only because she wants some time alone with me *outside* the parental supervision. She doesn't care about you—not really," Ryker said and leaned in close. "No one really wants to hang around a charity case like you. For that matter, no guy will touch you. You aren't really the dinner and movie type."

I didn't know which was worse—that I detested that my best friend Bree repeatedly shoved her tongue down his throat or that he could actually make me second-guess my friendship with her. The truth was, Ryker was right. I didn't have a lot of friends. People just didn't get me.

He leaned in close like he was going to reveal a secret. I sat still in the plastic chair, making no move to get any closer to him. Ryker was as likely to spit on me as he was to share gossip. "You're not exactly normal, Winnie," he whispered, like it was the darkest secret known to man.

"Just for one night, can you act like an actual human being and be nice, even when Bree isn't within hearing distance?" I begged, tucking my hair behind my face.

"*Humans* can be pretty evil."

Something about the way he phrased his comeback bothered me. Yet, I shrugged it off. *Everything* about Ryker bothered me.

"You're proof of that," I said, stiffly. I was *so* tempted to knee him in the groin and act like he spontaneously racked himself.

"I'm going to go see if *my girlfriend* needs help carrying our drinks. My prayers would be answered if you weren't here when we returned. Go find someone else to annoy," Ryker said, and then walked away like he sensed his manhood was endangered.

I should have kicked his man-bits.

Since Ryker had inadvertently stink-bombed me, I was in some desperate need of fresh air. Besides, deep down, I knew Bree wouldn't be disappointed in having a little alone time with Ryker. I unfolded my walking stick and made myself scarce.

The notorious tapping of my walking stick was drowned out by the noise, making my disability less obvious. Here's to happy coincidences. I made my way to the side door in the hopes that there would be less people coming and going. I seriously needed a few moments to myself. I hesitated by the girls' bathroom, thinking that it might provide better privacy, but kept heading for the door. Bathrooms echo…and if I had to hear myself cry, I didn't need my sorrow amplified. I pushed open the back door and let myself out. It was dark outside, which only made it more difficult to determine the amount of people nearby. I couldn't see them, but I heard a few coughs from around the corner. Guessing by the smell, I'd stumbled upon a few smokers who weren't smoking cigs. Great, second-hand-high.

I leaned against the brick building facing away from the smokers and took a few deep breaths. At the very least, the marijuana scent put out some of Ryker's cologne that was burned into my nostrils. Rain drizzled lazily from the sky, just like the police reports stated it had on October third, almost sixteen years ago. Dreary days symbolized the upcoming anniversary of their deaths. I tried not to think about my late parents or sister—not in public anyway. It was a losing battle to fight away the tears. I didn't know if it was Ryker's comments, the anniversary of their deaths approaching, or that I was having some cruel PMS side-effect, but I was seriously losing my cool. It wasn't long before the cold raindrops trickled down my cheeks, camouflaging my tears.

I gripped the cold, metal railing by the steps and wished that I could melt into the shadows. Ignoring everyone around me, I pressed my lips together, and screamed out in my mind. Not a peep came from my mouth, but the frustration and anger brewing inside me exploded soundlessly. Why did life have to be so damn difficult?

"My boss will come looking if I'm not back to spray out the shoes with disinfectant," one of the smokers said.

By the sound of his voice, I knew him as Dillon, an employee at this fine establishment who hocked a loogie and then handed me a pair of stinky bowling shoes when I first got here. I wondered if his boss knew what he did on his break.

The other let out a cough and mumbled something about meeting up after his shift. After he departed, Dillon made his way toward me. His footsteps alerted me he was walking up the stairs. I prayed that he'd just keep walking by. My prayers were left unanswered. He stepped right in front of me like just because I was visually impaired meant that I no longer deserved a personal bubble.

"What's wrong with your eyes?" he asked. His boss had to be a moron if he didn't know what Dillon was doing on his breaks. I could smell the joint on his breath.

"It's called heterochromia. It's a mutation of the iris," I said dismissively and hoped he'd take the hint that I wasn't up for chit-chatting, nor did I want him to notice my tear-stained cheeks.

"You're the blind chick," he said like he'd deciphered some great mystery.

Duh! I was carrying a walking stick.

I didn't intentionally want to come off as rude, but I didn't want to make small talk in the mood I was in. He got the hint, because he started fumbling with his keys to open the back door when a boy called out.

"Hold the door!"

I immediately recognized his voice. He was one of my history classmates, Patrick.

"Better hurry, Patrick! Marcy was snuggling up to the quarterback before I left for break. What's his name? Greg? I guess it doesn't really matter. They probably are already officially dating. They're a match made in heaven if you ask me. Head cheerleader hooking up with the quarterback," Dillon taunted and slipped inside.

Dillon held the door open just enough for me to see shapes moving about inside. How could Patrick not know that the *Employee of the Month* was messing with him? Everyone and their dog knew Patrick had a wicked crush on Marcy since the ninth grade.

I hoped Marcy was worth the impromptu sprint workout because Patrick bolted up the stairs. He reached the top of the stairs victoriously just in time for Dillon to slam the door shut and lock it.

"Come on, man! Just let me in!" Patrick yelled.

Dillon's laughter resonated through the door. After a ridiculously long pause, Patrick had a brilliant idea to use the front door, instead of the side entrance to make his debut and sweep Marcy off her feet.

In his state of panic, he turned quickly and raced down the steps. All would have been just dandy if he hadn't slipped and grabbed at anything to break his fall. He caught my shirt. I braced myself against the railing, but I couldn't keep both of us from toppling over. Falling down the steps, I smacked my head on the asphalt and landed in a puddle. I inhaled a stupid amount of rainwater before the heavyset boy rolled off of me. Spitting up water only made the instant headache feel like my brain was splintering.

"Are you okay?" Patrick asked, pulling me up before I could tell him that standing wasn't a good idea.

I clutched my head, trying not to get wheezy when I found a conspicuous gash hidden along my hairline. I failed. The taste of copper filled my mouth. When had I bit my lip? Oh goodness, one of my eyes was swollen. Everything became even darker. Dizziness washed over me. Not sure where my walking stick had gone, I grabbed at the stair railing, but my hand slipped. I stumbled.

Patrick caught me awkwardly around the waist. "You don't look good," Patrick said apologetically.

"I'll be fi-ine." My words slurred.

"You need help." He pulled out a small gray object from his pocket, poked it a few times, and then held it up to his ear.

"I'll die if…" I took a deep breath and sat down on the bottom step. "…you're calling 911."

The operator's voice came on the line. "What is your emergency?"

Patrick mumbled, "I tripped and sort of fell on this girl—"

This girl? I wanted to inform him that we were in the same grade but the thought of talking made me queasier.

The shadows were already messing with my now half-as-good sight. One eye had entirely swollen shut. My lip was broken. And I couldn't be certain, but I'd bet that bumps and bruises covered my body. I put my head between my legs and focused on breathing when a shadowy figure caught my eye.

It wasn't so much of a shadow as it was the hazy outline of a colossal man. He seemingly materialized from the building's shadow. *That* wasn't abnormal. People were always sneaking up on me, appearing out of now where. What really freaked me out was that this man was gigantic. Like, eat your *Wheaties* wouldn't pile on the muscle that he had. He was a body builder for sure—or wearing some kind of massive backpack since I couldn't decipher his shape clearly. I was betting on the prior. Muscles grabbed Patrick by the shoulders, threw Patrick against the building, and held him by the throat. Patrick's feet no longer touched the ground.

"If she dies, I promise that you will suffer a slow, miserable death!" Muscles yelled, and he slammed Patrick's head against the bricks. Warm liquid hit my face; it was thicker than rain water. Blood.

"I think the girl just has a concussion," Patrick said.

"She's not just a meager girl, you naive twit!" Rage resonated from Muscles' voice. He effortlessly threw Patrick aside. The boy collided with the asphalt. Debris shot into the air. It looked like falling black snow in my sight.

I gasped. I didn't try to hide my astonishment or blatant fear. If I hadn't known that I would die an old woman, a part of me would be freaking-the-hell-out that I would bite the big one tonight! My mouth hung open. I could hardly fathom what had just happened, but I knew if I didn't high tail it out of there, mister nice man with the muscles would turn his attention on me. I'd always hoped that I'd be more defiant when danger presented, but instead I quivered like a scared little girl. My legs were weaker than I cared to admit, but their tremble was nothing compared to my shaky hands.

Berating myself that I was acting like a silly child, I grabbed at the ground, hoping to find something—anything—to distract Muscles. Instead, of an impressive weapon, I threw a rock, more like a pebble, at the building on the other side of the alley, expecting to draw Muscles' focus off the boy. It was a pitiful attempt, but he did turn his attention to me when he was finished with the boy.

In a couple steps, he was standing next to me. He bent over, picked up Patrick's phone and in a tone that my foster father would take with me when I was in deep trouble, addressed the operator.

"Sorry for the misunderstanding, my son missed a step and tumbled into a girl he's sweet on. I think he was simply trying to impress her by calling you," Muscles said and then waited for a response. A moment later he said, "Of course I'll bring the girl in if she shows signs of a concussion."

He groaned and knelt beside me. From what I could decipher, he held the phone against himself. "Tell the operator that you feel perfectly fine or they will dispatch emergency personnel."

I didn't have to ask what would happen if I didn't. I knew I would die, but there was a lot a person could survive through and *wish* they were dead. Besides, hadn't he yelled at Patrick for hurting me? Muscles had a twisted sense of heroism, but in my gut I figured my fate would be better if I obeyed.

In my perkiest imitation I said, "Hello?"

Speaking made my gums hurt, my *gums!* I didn't think it was possible to feel so rotten. I closed my eyes and focused on the series of questions the operator asked me. I lied through my teeth to keep Muscles, who was holding the phone to my ear, happy. After I promised to call if there was any trouble, Muscles ended the call and smashed the phone against the asphalt with his foot. I cringed and hoped that the crushed phone wasn't a sign of what was yet to come. I didn't know exactly what I expected, but what Muscles did next was totally out of the blue. He sniffed me. Yes, he *sniffed* me. Then his head twitched—a nervous tick.

"Jace!" Muscles called out.

Picture standing next to the bass speakers at a rock concert—Muscles yelled for reinforcement with as much power. It was deafening. The sense of urgency was immeasurable. I swear his cry echoed in my thoughts even after he stopped yelling.

My fight or flight response finally kicked in. I hadn't a lick of fight in me, but I wasn't going to stick around and see what happened this "lovely" rainy, dark night. I tried to stand but immediately lost my balance and fell backwards. It wasn't so much the indisputable concussion I suffered but rather what I saw next that put me on my butt.

In my world of darkness, a flash of light caught my eye—a white silhouetted man. He moved so quickly my eyes could hardly track him as he raced over to us. He didn't just appear out of thin air like Muscles seemingly did, but rather like he was running for his life. Just as quickly as he got here, he stopped abruptly at the sound of a whimper that had escaped my throat. I'd moved my head too quickly to follow his movements, resulting in a wave of nausea.

"She smells like *her*, Jace" Muscles said.

I couldn't be certain but I swear Jace, stared right through me. I gawked right back. Shame be damned. I couldn't tear my gaze away from him. Deep down, it felt like I was staring at a ghost.

My heart raced. My palms were instantly clammy. Running away wasn't exactly an option; my very being was unable to move under his scrutiny. I chalked up the physical ailments to being in the middle of a jacked-up assault, but something about him made it impossible for me to breathe. There was something devastatingly beautiful about him. It wasn't his appearance; looks hardly mattered to me. A euphoric feeling awakened in the depth of my soul.

I wasn't one to believe in love at first sight or any of that nonsense. Yet, I was irrefutably drawn to him; yet, I was tortured by his presence. Even so, I *knew* that I'd never met him before; I'd have remembered anyone who'd brought brightness to my gray world. Right? Even so, guilt struck me so hard my body ached. The way he caught his breath crushed my broken soul.

"I'm sorry," I whispered.

I didn't know why I had apologized. A tear slipped down my cheek. I promised myself it was only because looking at his blazing glow hurt my eyes.

"It's you," he gasped.

The torment in his voice was undeniable, as was the rapture. More importantly, his deep, otherworldly voice awakened at part of me that had been long dead—a part I hadn't known to exist. What seemed like lifetimes passed before he cautiously walked over to me. Normally, I would hear the crunch of the footsteps, but there was no sound when he advanced. My only clue he was coming closer was that his silhouette shined brighter. The closer he became, the more broken and beaten I felt. Tears dripped from my eyes as I gazed upon him. The unmistaken aroma of a rich, unlit cigar filled the air when he dropped to his knees in front of me. My headache pounded more ferociously when he neared. When he reached for me, nausea engulfed me. A cold chill slipped down my spine when he brushed my bloody hair away from my eyes.

"I've *finally* found you," he said affectionately.

The tension in my back grew when he caressed my temple. A chill flooded my bones. I couldn't even choke down a minuscule amount of spit when his warm hand touched the gash on my head.

"I'm going to throw up," I muttered as a vision robbed me from my reality.

A moonless night was illuminated by the fire crawling across a young man's bare back. He kneeled in the sand and faced the ocean. Blue hues danced from his skin, transforming into brilliant orange and yellow flames. Waves crashed against the shore, echoing in the night. He made no effort to run into the cool water; instead he picked up a stone half buried in the sand and threw it into the ocean. The longer it rippled in the water, the more clenched his fist became. His muscular arms glistened with blood and sweat, as if he'd just finished fighting, even though he bore no combat injuries.

Chapter Two

I came to in mid-vomit. The white silhouetted man, Jace, had moved to my side, but he made no attempt to move away. I *had* to have covered his shoes with my regurgitated lunch. But, it didn't bother him. In fact, he edged closer as if to comfort me, but he restrained from actually touching me again. As soon as I was sure that I wasn't going to hurl again, I brought my knees up to my chest, which put some distance between us. Pushing him away hurt my heart in a way it shouldn't. I knew nothing of this guy, yet felt obligated to him in some effed-up way.

The small amount of distance between us actually made me feel better. I could actually move without feeling achy all over. My headache had dimmed significantly. I actually felt like I could think somewhat logically. My fall had gotten the better of me. I actually was seeing this guy as a light instead of a shadow. Something in my noggin was seriously messed up. I gently touched my head where I'd broken my fall on the asphalt. I'd expected to feel the horrid gash but barely felt any injury at all.

Had I been given something for the pain that I hadn't remembered? How long had I blacked-out? Why did I feel so horrible around a person I'd never met?

14

I looked at Jace for answers. His shimmering reflection suggested that he was athletic, but I couldn't get a grasp on his actual physique. Some girls would have called it gawking; I called it assessing a potential stalker. Thus, I stared at the white figure where a normal dark shadow *should* have been, trying to collect as much possible information about him. He was freaking illuminated! Gazing at him was like staring at the sun.

He wiped away a rogue tear of mine. His touch made my skin burn…and a small part of me liked it. The other part wanted to drown myself in water. Even so, I couldn't convince my body to move. I liked his presence and that scared me. I didn't even know him; yet, I'd lost all sense of time when I looked at him.

"Your electric sea blue eyes are unique, even without the touch of hazel conquering your right eye," he said, describing my heterochromia mutation. His tantalizing voice sounded like dark chocolate—if candy could be consumed audibly. His European accent strongly hinted that he wasn't originally from Ashwick, or any other northern *Small Town USA.*

I focused at the place where his face would be. It was like looking into the sun. I blinked back tears. Unable to hold the gaze, I *closed* my eyes. I shouldn't have been able to see anything. However, in the exact spot where he knelt was a haze, like smoke. Opening my eyes, I frowned. I wanted to ask dozens of questions, not the least of which being why I could see his ghostly shape with closed eyes. But that would make *me* sound like a crazy person. My anxiety heightened. I told myself that there had to be a reasonable explanation. Right?

"I've missed gazing into your ocean eyes, Deino."

His deep, masculine voice drowned out the thunder. It soothed the buzz in my ears. It was as if his voice could caress me from the inside out. It sounded too good to be true. The deafening ring in my ears dwindled. The pounding in my head became a memory. My stomach eased.

I swallowed the lump in my throat. As much as I wanted to listen to him talk, I had to come clean and get out of here. I liked him far too much for not knowing who he was. He could be a murderer for all I knew and I was playing the part of the dumb blonde who didn't listen to logic.

"You have the wrong girl," I said and wished my voice hadn't cracked. "That's not my name."

"You fancy a different one?"

Oooh, his voice could end wars. It was so enthralling. *Stop going all gaga over him*, I chastised myself. Wishing my throat didn't burn, I licked my lips. They were smooth as ever. It was then that I realized my eye wasn't swollen. My body ached, but not as intense as before. Had I imagined all the injuries?

What other explanation was there?

I cleared my throat. "Listen mister–"

"Mister?" Jace scoffed. "It's been a long time since I've been a *mister* to you."

I wished I could swallow, but there wasn't enough saliva in my mouth to even spit. "Have we met before?"

"You don't remember me?" he asked. His concern mixed

16

with my anxious feelings. "My name is Jace—Jace Eatros."

He paused like it was my queue to say *Ahh, I remember you.* A twinge of guilt hit my stomach when he realized that I had no clue who he was.

"Tell me the name you go by, ocean eyes."

I knew I shouldn't tell him my name but... "Gwyneth."

Muscles coughed in a not-so-subtle way. He stood over the boy, kicked Patrick's leg, and waited for a reaction. The boy didn't move. "I hate to ruin the reunion, but unless you want a human casualty, you may want to check on this poor sap."

I'd completely forgotten about him…and Patrick! Immediately I was bombarded with several thoughts at once. Was Patrick okay? Was I drugged? Why was I acting so weird? Did concussions always make people sporadically ill one minute but fine the next? Was Bree worried? Where was she? Was she still with her douchebag boyfriend? Was I in danger? Had I missed curfew? Seriously, was Patrick okay?

Was I?

Jace didn't turn away from me but asked, "Is he a *Hunter?*"

"Just a human," Muscles grunted unceremoniously. His head twitched again.

Patrick had to be seriously injured. Although that wasn't a surprise since he'd been body slammed into the asphalt. I moved toward him, knowing deep down Patrick needed some medical attention, but Jace grabbed my wrist. It wasn't forceful by any means, but it stopped me nonetheless. Additionally, he didn't utter a word even though I half expected him to tell me to stay put. For no reason whatsoever, I knew Patrick would be fine…which made no sense at all.

How hard had I hit my head?

Without a word, Jace stood and walked over to Patrick, knelt beside him, and placed his hands on my classmate's chest. A few second passed and Patrick sat up, dazed and confused. He rubbed his head.

Patrick asked, "What happened?"

Muscles extended his hand to help the boy up. "You missed your step on the stairs, but I think you'll be just fine. Why don't you go home and get cleaned up? Most women go faint at the sight of blood. I doubt Marcy is any different."

Muscles knew about Marcy? Well, of course he did. Everyone did. But it still made me wonder how long he'd been around.

"What about her?" Patrick asked and nodded at me.

"She'll be fine, don't worry about her. She's in good hands," Muscles said like it was a joke. "Now, why don't you go home?"

Patrick obeyed like a drone. I gave him a little credit when he handed me my walking stick before vanishing into the night. I clutched it like it was my lifeline. When he was out of the picture, Muscles appeared beside me, towering over me like some *god*. I didn't know what unnerved me more: that I hadn't heard him approach or that he moved faster than anyone I'd ever known.

18

"What are you going to do to me?" I asked, not sure if I wanted to know the answer.

"You're the first of three," Muscles said, as if that should make all the sense in the world.

"Well the other two that I'm with tonight will be worried about me if I don't return soon," I said, hoping that I'd somehow be able to make a discreet getaway.

I should have known better. Muscles grabbed my arm and pushed me against the wall. He pinned me there. The suspicion that he only saved my life to torture me came to mind.

Muscles threatened, "You're not going anywhere without an escort, cupcake."

Jace jerked Muscles away from me. A tremendous amount of force had to be used because Muscles didn't back away willingly. Yet, Jace held his ground in front of me. The air shifted; a heat wave washed over me as the two stared each other down. Moments passed, but Muscles didn't try getting through Jace to terrorize me. I doubted there were many men who would stand up to Muscles and even fewer who'd he back away from. Apparently, Jace was one of the few.

"*She* is not herself," Jace said.

"*She* is playing games with you," Muscles yelled, pointing at me. "*She* is messing with you like she always does. How many times does *she* have to prove that before you understand that you will always been expendable to her?"

"She had her reasons," Jace growled, defending me in some jacked-up way.

19

"She will give you another reason to hate her, old friend," Muscles promised and then spit at me. "I never should have called you here tonight."

That comment didn't gain him any brownie-points with Jace. He took another step closer to me, shielding me from Muscles. "You had to call me. She was hurt."

"Hurt isn't dead."

I had the unexplainable urge to tell Muscles that he didn't know everything about death, but I bit my tongue. What had gotten into me?

Muscles swore and then disappeared in with the rest of the night's shadows in a blink of an eye. Jace took a few deep breaths before turning around to face me.

As much as I wanted to figure out what the hell was going on, I needed to get somewhere safe. Chilling out in a dark alley with a couple of strangers who had mixed agendas was just asking for trouble.

A wave of warmth washed over me when Jace turned and closed the distance between us.

"Don't mind him. He's been in a mood for as long as I can remember," Jace said, attempting to lighten the mood.

However, his abrupt proximity to me made my body ache again. Perhaps it was a symptom of a concussion. I dropped my walking stick and grabbed for the rail. My hand slipped. I damn near ate the asphalt again but Jace caught me; his hands were sure on my hips like he'd held me many times before. It weirded me out beyond belief, even though I didn't exactly hate the feel of him holding me. Neither he nor I moved. I just stood there, wrapped up in his arms, until my brain kicked in. Something was messing with me. Had he drugged me? Why was I acting so...love struck? This was unrealistic and absurd.

Sensing my uneasiness, Jace released me and backed away. "Sorry about the misunderstanding. I didn't mean to frighten you, but your appearance is uncanny to my...to a lady I once knew."

He might have spoken casually, but I could sense his curiosity and concern. It made no sense, but nevertheless I was somehow able to pick up on his feelings. Oh hell! I was *delirious*. That explained everything. Whew!

"What are you thinking, Gwyneth?" Jace asked, jarring me from my thoughts. The way my name rolled of his tongue gave me shivers—shivers in places that I'd never had before. In places that liked the shiver...

It took me two attempts to speak and I wasn't about to indulge in the fantasies playing out in my mind at that particular moment. "I'm just shaken up and want to go back to the Thompson's."

"Thompsons? Not your home?" he questioned.

I clenched my teeth. I was *so* not going to discuss my foster care situation with a perfect stranger for whom I already had inappropriate feelings.

"I could give you a ride, Gwyneth. I'd take you anywhere you want. Any place you want no matter how far-fetched," he whispered. "I can take you to a place humans can only imagine."

A place humans can only imagine? What did he think he was? It was time to get out of the here. "That's okay. I came with a friend… and her boyfriend."

I dug in my jeans and instructed my phone to *call Bree*. Her voice came over the speaker a moment later.

"Where did you go?" she asked. "Ryker and I had to start the game without you, or we were going to lose our lane."

"I wanted a little downtime, but that's not really important, not anymore. Something's happened," I said and then waited for her immediate demand to know why I was bailing. "Will you drive me back to the Thompsons? I had a little fall—"

"If you want her to come quickly then tell her you were attacked," Jace suggested a little-too-loudly to be accidental.

"Attacked? Are you alright? Who are you with?" Bree asked.

"No one important," I replied.

"No one important?" Jace repeated. He spoke lightly but there was a hint of irritation lingering in his question.

"OMG! You're with a *guy*?" Bree squealed.

I could overhear Ryker telling her that I was probably making up this story because I was bored but didn't want to go home.

I sighed, "Just come get me."

"You're seriously with a guy, like a real-life *guy*?" Bree asked like Ryker's comment got her thinking that it would be something I might do.

"Just because I'm not into dating doesn't mean I can't converse with the opposite sex, Bree," I said.

"I figured the boys would be looking for any reason to talk to you," Jace said loud enough for Bree to eavesdrop.

"But I can hear him. She's not making him up, Ryker," Bree whispered. It was muffled, like she'd covered the phone to converse with her boyfriend. Half a second later she spoke, more clearly this time and into the phone. "He sounds stupidly hot, like so hot that girls sound moronic when they talk to him!"

"Can you just come outside, *please*?" I asked.

"I'll be there in two shakes," Bree said and then hung up.

Wishing that there was a way to speed up time, I shoved my phone back into my pocket. It didn't take Bree very long to race outside, probably because the mere thought that there was a guy with me, piqued her interest. A curvaceous, obscure figure walked out of Strikers door. I could tell it was Bree by her ballerina-like grace.

"What happened, Winnie!" she said, racing to me. She gave me a hug and then inspected me like she was a certified nurse. Bree said, and then reached for my head where I thought a gash should have been. "Your clothes are soaked with blood. Your hair looks like you've gotten a bad dye job."

I shrugged my shoulders. "I tripped."

Jace didn't remark about my little white lie, or complete lack of details, which I found interesting. Either he figured out that I didn't want to make a big deal about the incident, or he had his own motives for not mentioning it.

"You tripped," she repeated. Clearly she wanted more details.

I gestured to the stairs. "Down the stairs, luckily for me I landed on my head. Jace came to my aid."

"Gwyneth has a small cut on her head. They tend to be quite grisly, but she should be ok," Jace said, distracting Bree from the obvious holes in my story.

Bree nudged me and then squealed, "You told him to call you *Gwyneth?*"

I shrugged my shoulders. My cheeks burned from embarrassment. I'd gone by my child-hood nickname *Winnie* since grade-school, so I wasn't sure why I told Jace to call me by my actual name, Gwyneth. Nevertheless, Bree was making a much bigger deal about my name request than necessary. It didn't mean anything…

Jace extended his hand. "My friends call me Jace."

Bree shook it. "And what should Winnie call you?"

Insert awkward silence. I wanted to bury my head in the asphalt or at the very least now would be a good time to black out.

"She may address me however she likes," Jace said in a tone that suggested I should call upon him often.

Bree giggled, "I'd say you're quite lucky to have such a fine-looking gentleman come to your aid."

"*Gwyneth* doesn't owe *me* anything," Jace said, like mentioning it in the first place was hilarious.

"Bree? Are you coming back?" Ryker called out, standing in the doorway. I could smell him from the bottom of the stairs. "Or should I cancel our game?"

"Can we just get out of here?" I whispered to Bree. "I don't really feel like being in public right now."

"Totally," Bree agreed. "Game over, Ryker. Winnie is in no shape to toss around balls."

I envisioned Ryker looking Jace up and down because what he said next was for Bree's benefit—not mine. I saw through his little act. "Are you okay, Winnie?"

Jace answered, "She is a little confused but should be fine."

I could feel the weight of Ryker's gaze on me. I knew, without a doubt, that he was assessing the situation. "I haven't seen you around Ashwick before," Ryker said. I bet he was stalling just to annoy me. "Are you new to these parts?"

"You could say I haven't been in this part of the country for quite some time," Jace said, chuckling like he'd made a joke.

I tried to keep from biting my lip. If a voice could be lickable, Jace's voice was exactly that. I wasn't the only one who was thinking dirty thoughts. Bree squeezed my hand and giggled approvingly.

"Are you going to be attending McKesson High, like the rest of us?" Ryker asked.

"I'll check out a few schools that have open enrollment," Jace said. "I usually don't enroll in public schools."

"Yeah, I pegged you for a private school kind of guy," Ryker said. Jace had to be eloquent if he'd impressed Ryker.

"So it was nice meeting you and all, but I *really* need a shower," I said, hoping to get out of here—stat.

Jace didn't so much as comment about me in the shower, but a moan slipped from his throat, hyphening his enthusiasm. "Then we shouldn't keep you waiting. Goodnight, Gwyneth."

Bree took my hand. I was grateful not to have to use my walking stick. She led me to her pickup while Ryker went and closed out their game.

"Betty is just a few parking spots down."

For all intents and purposes, Bree named her grandfather's hand-me-down pickup Betty. To her, all cars, boats, and canes should be given a distinguished name. She'd even named my walking stick Stella. I found the name juvenile, but like most nicknames, it stuck.

A whine resonated from the passenger door when I opened it. The stench of cow manure was still prominent even though the truck hadn't been used on a farm for over a decade. Bree helped me inside the pickup and set my backpack by my feet. Then she subtly glanced over her shoulder—a guy-scouting pro. She had her talents, none of which I possessed.

"There are times I swear you're faking this whole blind bit," she squealed as soon as the doors were shut. "Mister tall, dark, and handsome looks so delicious I could just eat him up. Even his burly friend next to him is a hottie!"

"Jace's friend?"

I caught a glimpse of Muscles under a street light, a few feet away from Jace. There was that nervous tick again. I'd thought that he'd left. The beam of light highlighted more characteristics of his dark frame. He looked like he came from a family history of lumberjacks. His arms appeared to be as wide as my legs. He was as thick as a football player, *with* pads on. Even his neck was absurdly pronounced.

"I usually don't go for gingers," Bree continued. "But for him I'd make an exception. He has the body of a lineman—the kind that you can tell is all hard muscle and not just extra padding around the midsection."

"I don't care how they look," I whispered, and hoped she heard the alarm in my voice. A little part of me regretted leaving out the details that Patrick got his butt handed to him by Muscles and that Jace was the very definition of a total creeper even if he could charm the pants off of me. "Are they watching me?"

"Yep, the *Abercrombie and Fitch Underwear Models* are totally checking you out! Like staring you down, checking you out! Winnie, I think you might have some not-so-secret-admirers."

I wiped my clammy hands on my pants. For some reason I couldn't tell her that they were more interested in me than what was normal. Saying it out loud would make it real. I just wanted to forget this whole evening.

"There's more fat in a Hersey's kiss than on Jace's body.

Speaking of kissing, he looks like the type who's had *lots* of practice. You know I have a thing for chiseled eye candy, especially brown haired, brown-eyed ones. Ugh! If Ryker and I weren't together I'd totally call dibs on him or his red-headed friend."

"You can have them both," I muttered.

"Maybe I will," she giggled.

I couldn't imagine what fantasy was playing out in her mind. "Can we *please* get out of here? I feel disgusting and feel like a vamp that buffeted on some unsuspecting humans."

"Ryker just came back outside. I'm going to say goodbye, and then I'll call my mom and make sure it's okay for you to stay overnight," she said, taking my hand. She got suddenly serious. "Are you sure you're okay? It's just you and me now, so you can drop the show. You look awful!"

"I'm fine, really," I said.

She climbed out of the pickup and gave me the once over. "We are going to have to burn your clothes, Winnie."

"No arguments there."

Once alone, I willed my nagging headache to pass. It didn't work. I wished it wasn't such a long, sloppy ordeal to "say goodbye" to Ryker. They were in their own little world when they kissed, oblivious to the entire human race. I made a mental note to have a serious talk with Bree about acceptable PDAs.

After what seemed like forever, I unrolled the window to let in some fresh air. Ryker and Bree had apparently come up for air, and were now discussing, with Jace, his romantic future. I wasn't trying to eavesdrop, but Bree's voice carried. I buried my face in my hands when Bree *subtly hinted* that I was without male companionship.

"For years I've been looking for a lady who meets Gwyneth's description," Jace said, boldly.

"Single?" Bree asked, elated.

"Not exactly."

Chapter Three

I would've flunked out of art class if it weren't for ceramics. Mrs. Briggs insisted on my ability to describe primary colors, complete sketches, and paint like everyone else in the room. Since I was only "legally blind," she demanded my participation in class. Tell me, *please,* how a blind person was supposed to do all that? Granted I saw depth, definition, and color in my visions. However, I wanted to keep up the façade that I was blind like every other vision-impaired person.

Covered in dirty water and spatter, I molded the wet ball of clay. It was my second perfected attempt at creating a bowl. I'd make kitchen utensils all day if it upped my grade a notch.

"Your bowl is lopsided," Ryker said.

He sat across the same table as me. I swore that he signed up for the same classes as I purely to annoy me. Why else would he choose the exact table I sat at when there was an abundance of other seating options?

When I didn't acknowledge his remark, Ryker flicked a piece of clay in my direction. It wedged onto my school uniform. Wiping it off, I stuck my tongue out at Ryker. It was a little childish, but I feared that a string of obscenities might spill out of my mouth if I opened it.

It hardly registered when someone knocked on the art class door, but I smelled Jace's otherworldly scent as soon as he walked into the room. My skin tingled. High-pitched giggles echoed around the room when the girls, and a couple homophile guys, got a good look at him. From where I was sitting, he left something to be desired—like my stomach not being tied in knots. I had assumed my negative reactions had been due to my attack, so why had I suddenly become uneasy? I'd chalked up the odd night due to a state-of-deliriousness, resulting from my palpable concussion. So why was I still physically ill around *him*? At least I wasn't overcome with guilt like I had been the first time we met.

"This is Jace Eatros, a transfer student. Please make him feel welcome," Mrs. Briggs stated, after reading a note he handed her.

Was he following me? That night at Strikers had been so utterly confusing; I truly didn't know what happened. What was real? What had I imagined? I never thought I'd ever run into him again or I'd have come up with a plan for when our paths crossed. Not knowing how to react, I sat utterly still, praying that Jace couldn't see me if I didn't move—like a tyrannosaurus rex and his prey.

He waved to me.

I shouldn't have been surprised that a defensive mechanism

rooted from the cretaceous period didn't work. If I could just sink down in my chair far enough he might not notice me…

"Is this seat taken?" Jace asked. His hand was on the back of the empty chair beside me.

I shook my head and concentrated on my ceramic project. I wanted to demand to know why he was following me, but I kept my lips sealed. It wasn't like I could prove it; it was just a feeling I had. Long ago, I learned to trust my instincts.

"If I didn't know better, I'd say that you are following me," I said, hoping to sound good-natured, but I was sure I had failed.

"I figured that I'd give McKesson High a shot," Jace said. "And would it be so terrible if I found you particularly captivating?"

Ummm, maybe? We didn't even know each other!

"Don't mind her, Jace," Ryker said. "I've been working on Winnie for years now. My best bet is that she's missing the girlie parts that make women enjoyable to be around."

"Shove it, Ryker!" I said, flicking my dirty fingers in his direction.

"Thanks for the advice," Jace chuckled and reached for the ball of clay I was kneading.

My skin burned when he reached for me. I dropped the clay before his hand grazed mine. A headache began to throb. I forced myself to relax when every muscle in my body wanted to clench tight. There was no denying the ill-effects. Jace literally agitated me.

"You're pale," Jace said.

"I've never felt better," I lied.

He set my clay ball back down in front of me. After wiping his hands on a towel, he draped his arm across the back of my chair. An imaginary clasp tightened around my throat. I tried to remember how to breathe. My chest refused to let air into my lungs.

"You play ball?" Ryker asked. "Football is over but we're always looking for talent on the basketball court."

"I prefer hand-to-hand combat," Jace said heedlessly.

As soon as Jace spoke, my lungs finally began to fill. I swallowed the lump in my throat. What was going on?! How could anyone trigger this kind of a reaction? I wanted to push Jace's hand off the chair; however, I had an unexplainable urge *never* to touch him. It was like some primitive instinct had taken over my body and refused to be anywhere near him, but just as strongly, I refused to move away. My arms and legs froze. It took an act of God to even lean away. My anxiety peaked. I swallowed again and breathed through my nose, hoping no one had noticed my awkward, clipped movements.

"Like MMA?" Ryker asked in an octave lower than what he normally spoke. I wanted to say that it was pathetic that he had developed a bro-mance, but I couldn't unclench my jaw.

"Yeah, something like that," Jace said.

My brain felt like it was going through a shredder when his finger trailed against the back of my shirt. My eardrums split, and a loud ringing from his finger running over the fabric in my shirt drowned out everything else in the room. The harder he pressed against my back, the more my stomach twisted. My back spasmed. It took all of my self-control not to cry out when he flicked his finger across my neck.

Just as quickly as I froze, my limbs obeyed me once again; I could move freely and seized the opportunity. Stumbling out of my seat, I mumbled that I needed a glass of water. Gravity shifted under my feet. I stumbled onto the floor. Maybe he stuck his leg out and tripped me; I wasn't sure, but I knew Jace had done it somehow.

I glared up at him, only to gasp. For a moment the definition in his face formed. Most of his facial features were still muddy, except for two perfectly formed lips. He spoke in a foreign language—one that I'd never recalled hearing but was familiar with all the same. However, that wasn't what struck me dumb. His lips— his perfectly shaped, full lips—didn't move when he spoke. I blinked, attempting to clear my vision. I *had* to be seeing things.

His voice boomed in my mind the longer he spoke. The words I couldn't understand echoed an unrelenting ringing in my ears. I couldn't look away from his white silhouette. I distantly heard Ryker talking, but whatever he said wasn't nearly as important as what Jace was saying—even though I didn't understand a single word.

"What do you want?" I whispered, unsure if I actually wanted to know. I focused on his lips and watched intensively.

"*You*," he said crystal clear and then spoke in the language I didn't understand. His voice tasted like syrup on my tongue, but his lips never moved.

Mrs. Brigg's shoes clicked sharply against the tile as she walked towards me. A girl, Kayla, helped me back into my chair while everyone else gawked. The teacher demanded to know why I was laying on the floor.

"My vertigo is off. I think I'm getting a migraine," I said, trying to think of any logical reason why I had suddenly gotten ill. I certainly wasn't going to take the opportunity and point a finger at Jace. They'd assume I was crazy; I wasn't so sure they'd be wrong. I tried to stand, but the world shifted under me again. It forced me back on my knees. I covered my mouth and hoped not to vomit.

"I'll call the nurse and let her know you're on your way. Kayla, can you escort Winnie?" Mrs. Briggs said.

"I'll be fine by myself," I said, irritated that I'd been assigned a babysitter, even if I wasn't exactly in top-notch shape.

My stomach instantly eased when Jace muttered another incomprehensible comment in the language I didn't understand. The sound of his voice calmed me, which bothered me at the same time. Kayla released her grasp when I promised not to move without her. She left to grab her things when Jace piped up.

"Mrs. Briggs, I'm not feeling the greatest either—a little nausea. May I be excused as well?" Under his breath, Jace admitted that his nerves getting the best of him from being in a new school.

"I suppose. Could you escort Gwyneth?" she asked.

"I'll be fine," I said, failing at my attempt to stand.

Jace grabbed my arm, stabilizing me. A heat wave radiated off of him and crawled over my skin. A blazing light scorched my sight, but I couldn't look away. What was worse was that I couldn't figure out what to do. Stare him down in what little defiance I had? Bust out my t-rex moves and stand utterly still? I wanted to pass out, but I refused to have any rumors start that I fainted in Jace's arms, or worse—find out a classmate had recorded it on their cell and uploaded it to *YouTube*.

Mrs. Briggs said, "I think it's best if you have—"

"I can walk…" I said a little louder than intended. The edges of my sight darkened. I lost my footing, slipping deeper into Jace's embrace. His hot skin warmed mine. He held me tight against his hardened body. I'd never felt safer in my life. "…by myself," I finished stubbornly, after realizing that his muscular body had distracted me from finishing my outburst.

"Winnie swooning into the new guy's arms," Ryker snickered. "Bree will be furious she missed it!"

Pushing away from Jace, I thought briefly that perhaps the best place to throw up would be on Ryker. It took every molecule in my being to stand upright. I swayed but kept my balance.

Jace commented under his breath about me being more stubborn than he remembered. The moment his breath hit my skin, my blood boiled. A whimper escaped my throat, but I knew Jace heard it because the intensity of his silhouette brightened. I clenched my teeth together to prevent any other signs of defeat from slipping out of my mouth in the form of a gasp.

"Kicking or screaming, I won't let her out of my sight," Jace promised Mrs. Briggs, ignoring my protests.

I objected, but he silenced me in his own special way. He

36

grabbed my arm, holding me with a grip I couldn't shake. Heat radiated off him. My chest clamped so tight I couldn't breathe. My back stiffened. His white silhouette flared, and the pounding in my head felt like all its hairs were being ripped out in chunks. Tears felt like acid on my eyes. I thought I saw red in my sight. Liquid seeped from my ears as the dull ring progressed into a fierce shriek.

My world darkened as my legs gave out under me.

***

I awoke on a hard mattress. A young man was threading together a mess of sounds into a song. The longer I listened the louder it became and the more relaxed I'd gotten. The thread of words formed a melody strangely memorable yet ghostly unfamiliar.

Disinfectant dominated my sense of smell. However, a smoky scent, faint but ethereal, lingered in the air. My damp school uniform clung to me, encasing me in my sweat. Tissue paper shifted under me as I sat up and swung my legs over the side. My feet didn't come close to touching the floor. I rubbed my hands together and listened for any sound that would indicate the nurse was nearby. Nothing. There wasn't a sound, except for the background noise. Wishing I had a glass of water, I licked my desiccated lips.

"Do you feel any better?" Jace asked. The organized thread of jumbled words ceased to resonate.

A trickle of heat crawled up my spine as he sat down next to me. The tissue paper didn't make a sound like it had when I moved.

"Is the nurse here?" I asked, ignoring his question.

"She'll be back soon," Jace said. His mood was light, but I

could feel his eyes taking me in, analyzing my actions, my appearance, and whatever he deemed important. "You have nothing to fear from me."

"I'm not afraid of you." My stomach knotted.

"Then why are you trembling?"

"I'm not." I clutched my shaking hands.

He chuckled. The low tones in his laugh were hazardously appealing. A voice that was as deep as his should have personality to match. Of course, I hadn't actually met many creepers—were they all so appealing?

"What do you want with me?"

"Many things," he answered. Warmth flooded from him, wrapping me in heat. It had a nauseating effect, while being simultaneously pleasing. "But it's obvious you need more exposure to others like us."

"I'm grateful you saved me in the back alley, but I think you got the wrong impression. There's no *you and me*. There's never going to be an *us*."

He nudged my shoulder. Muscle spasms erupted in my arm and upper body. I put my head between my knees to keep my dizziness at bay. Covering my eyes with my hands, I focused on breathing evenly.

"It'll get easier to be near me with more exposure," he said. "I'll grow on you."

"You're not doing anything *on* me," I retorted.

"I don't recall you being so feisty… I like it."

"I don't want anything to do with you," I said, hoping not to come off as a complete witch, but he just wasn't getting a clue. "I'm not interested in you—at all!"

"Right," Jace laughed.

"I'm not playing hard to get."

He leaned in close and called me a liar. Before I could deny it, he started rubbing my back. He worked on the knots, but his touch only made me tenser. My clammy elbows slipped off my legs. Sweat dripped from my brow.

What I wanted to ask would sound crazy, like lock me up insane-crazy, but the question begged to be asked since it was clear, to me anyway, that he was following me. "Are you going to kidnap me or something?"

"I'd rather not," he said. "But I wouldn't put it past Marco. He is quite…*infatuated* with you."

"Muscles? Your friend from the alleyway?" I asked, looking up at him. I thought about my hazy recollection from that night. I cringed at the thought of that beastly man watching me.

"You remember?" Jace said like he was surprised at my recollection.

"Of course I do," I said. "Muscles damn near killed Patrick!"

There was a long pause and then Jace laughed, "You hit your head harder than I thought. Maybe you should tell the nurse you're hallucinating."

I frowned. "What are you talking about?"

"I was the only one who witnessed your fall, Gwyneth. Marco and I were just going to hang out and bowl a few rounds Saturday night. Marco was on the phone when I heard your cries from the alleyway. I was the only one there. He showed up *after* you called your friends to take you home," Jace said. "Ask Bree what happened. She'd tell you the same thing *and* that you were acting really confused."

That wasn't the truth. It couldn't be. However, it would make more sense than what I recalled. "You're lying."

He didn't deny it. He just sat there, immobile. A part of me suspected that he was hoping I'd challenge him. I didn't. I couldn't prove it; people would never believe me. I *had* gotten a concussion. Maybe he was telling the truth. Perhaps I'd be completely delirious and made up the whole thing. Even so, I couldn't shake the feeling that I was missing something—something important, something obvious, something dangerous.

"Am I in danger?"

He didn't answer.

I swallowed a lump in my throat. I imagined the worst. "Are you going to kill me?"

Utter silence. The tension in my stomach tightened, but it wasn't from whatever sickening effect he had on me. That should have been an easy answer—right? *No, I'm not going to kill you.* Why would there be any reason to hesitate?

My apprehension suddenly eased—which made no sense. Shouldn't my anxiety have heightened? Instead, calmness passed over me; was Jace behind it? I no longer felt like ripping out my stomach and stomping on it. My head no longer pounded. My trembling hands dried.

A small part of my subconscious didn't want him to leave. Regardless of my conflicting feelings, he hadn't moved. His white silhouette still glowed, but it wasn't as bright. He whispered words that I didn't understand. Time passed as I listened to every enchanting syllable. Eventually, he got around to speaking English.

"I can't," he said, and then spoke an afterthought. It was almost undecipherable. "Not again."

I imagined that my jaw hit the floor. However, my lips scarcely parted. My mouth dried, and all the air had been sucked from my lungs. It took several attempts to take a breath.

A sharp sound of heels clicked on the tile floor. Walking into the room, a nurse said, "Good, you're awake."

"I believe Miss Thompson could use a glass of water," Jace said suddenly cheerful and hopped off the mattress.

"It's *Patterson*," I said.

"Of course," he said. A hint of amusement lingered in his voice. Now he knew my first and last name. Super.

"Watch your mouth," the nurse warned.

After Jace left, Martha raced into the nurse's office. Long ago she tried convincing me she was as skinny as she wanted to be, (which meant she never dieted and hated exercising but kept herself trim). She had long, flowing brunette hair that retreated in length over the years (meaning that she continued to let Bree come near her with a pair of scissors to practice trimming it) and claimed she wore magnifying glasses to hide her bland green eyes. (There are times that I've considered my sight to be better than hers, even when she wears her thick-rimmed glasses.)

The sixth-period bell chimed just as Martha escorted me into the hallway. There was nothing like having my foster mother rescue me to cap off a horrendous day.

Squeezing my hand in hers, Martha led me to her '91 *Ford* minivan. In the past twenty years, the vehicle taxied seventeen kids, but I was the only long-term and current resident.

An oversized shadow was leaning against the outside wall of McKesson High, watching Martha and me pull out of the parking lot. It wasn't until his head twitched that I recognized him as Jace's friend. Was Muscles conducting surveillance on me too?

I might have been slightly paranoid.

"Martha, does the big guy leaning against the building have red hair?" I asked, remembering that Bree had mentioned his ginger roots.

"Winnie, there's nobody out here."

Chapter Four

Martha's husband, John, showed up after she watched me sip down two bowls of chicken broth that evening. After reassuring his wife that we would call her if anything happened to me, John helped me escape to the sanctuary of my bedroom. He was the father I never had, or rather the one that had been stolen from me.

Serving the Missoula area, John was one of the greatest lawyers that Ashwick employed. Then again, I might have been a touch biased. From what Bree told me, he looked like any dark haired, tired, crusty lawyer off of *Law and Order,* but he had a smile to die for.

My golden retriever's pitter-patter on the oak floor warned me that my eighty pound attention-hog-dog would become a moving obstacle at my feet. The school's policy allowed for my pooch to join me in my eight hours of suffering. However, after a particularly horrific episode when I forgot to give him enough potty-breaks cut his guide dog career short. Holding a squeak toy in his mouth, Max followed us as we walked up the stairs to my second floor bedroom. Safely inside, I breathed a sigh of relief. In the entire world, my bedroom was my sanctuary.

"Are you okay?" John asked, closing my bedroom door behind us.

"Pretty sure I just ate something that disagreed with me, that's all."

Since I'd slipped into a pair of flannel shorts and a purple colored t-shirt as soon as I got home, I was all ready for bed. I crawled onto the mattress. I patted the pillow top so Max knew he was welcome onboard. The entire bed swayed when he wagged his tail.

John loosened his tie and sat down on the edge. "An orphan runaway might be bedding down here for a bit, but you never know how long kids like that will stick around, so prepare yourself, okay, munchkin?"

"You know I'm not a little girl anymore," I said, just as I hoped he'd never drop his personal nickname for me. In his eyes, I'd always be the lost little nine-year-old who showed up on his door one snowy evening.

"Of course," John said as he tucked me in. "Are you still up for watching the game with me Thursday night?"

"I'd never miss a kickoff."

With that, he kissed me good-night, leaving me alone with my thoughts. Sleep evaded me—which wasn't completely horrible since it was hours before I normally went to bed. My mind kept drifting to the vision of my demise. I'd be an old woman when death would take me. I wasn't wishing my life away, but I was desperate to know the reason why the young man would kill me. I recalled the regret in his eyes made my chest hurt. It was clear he didn't want my death, so how could he go through with it? It'd take a lifetime for the answer to unravel, but my intuition screamed that it was imperative.

My mind wandered to Jace. He wouldn't kill me again. Had he meant that people like *us* was some code for *clairvoyants?* I'm sorry, but people didn't die more than once, unless reincarnation was real. My theory didn't feel right but what could he have been hinting at?

As slowly as sleep took me, I was jolted awake. I was suddenly free-falling. I collided with the ground. It felt like my body was being torn into pieces. My skin seemed to melt away from my bones as they crushed under unexplainable pressure. I retched and gagged, fighting the urge to expel everything in my stomach. I held my head. It felt like my skull was being pulverized. A blast exploded in my ears.

Just as quickly as I was torn apart, my body pieced itself back together. I screamed into the night sky with the first breath I could take. Gasping for air, I tried to relax, which was exactly the opposite of what my body had planned. My muscles tightened and relaxed like they weren't sure how to properly work. I kneeled on my hands and knees, struggling to breathe.

A tear escaped my eye and ran down my cheek while I trembled on the ground. Horror erupted within me, but my fear brought on the tears—had I just died?

"She isn't meant for travel like this." It was Jace's would-be-friend Marco.

I couldn't bring myself to search for him. My head felt like a hundred pounds. Gravity crushed down on me. Had I traveled to another world?

"Which is why *I'm* here. She *needs* to remember. She has to if we have any hope," Jace said. His sexy voice was burned into my memory.

"She wanted to forget," Marco warned.

"That may be, but we need her to remember if we have any hope of finding the others. Or do you want to search aimlessly for the sisters? How has that worked for you this last century?"

Marco growled, "Just call me when you are ready to bring her back."

He vanished without a trace, leaving Jace alone with me. *I had to be dreaming.* It must have been one of those weird dreams where you know you're asleep but couldn't wake up. And I so wanted to wake up. My body hurt in places that it never had before. Hell, even my hair hurt!

"Just breathe," Jace said in a strained voice. "As long as I'm nearby, you'll be okay."

I choked on the air. I couldn't. My lungs wouldn't work properly. Sensing my distress, he began to sing in a foreign language.

My anxiety lessened. When breathing became natural again, my awareness of my surroundings heightened. A moonless night revealed little of my surroundings. Shadows played in the twilight. A light breeze twirled my hair around itself. The air was cooler than it should have been. I shivered. My shorts and thin cotton shirt weren't much help. Crushed flower petals cushioned my knees and palms. Their refreshing scent complimented the appealing aroma of the young man behind me.

Jace worked knots from my back as I straightened up into a kneeling position. His hand rolled over my back in the same way they had in the nurse's station. However, this time it didn't make me ill. Soon, I was able to sit upright. Anticipating my movements, he moved with me and situated himself snuggly behind me. His hips molded perfectly against my backside. I convinced myself that if I wasn't so confused and shaken, I would push him away and demand answers.

I closed my eyes, concentrating on the aromas around me: burnt wood, flowers, grain… and a hint of Jace's smoky scent hung in the air as well. His hot breath hit my neck when he whispered the name he'd spoken the night we first met echoed in my mind. Deino.

He slipped his hands lower on my back; a warm rush flowed over me, soothing me from the outside in. I fought the good feeling it brought. Given that I'd fallen asleep in my bed and had awakened outside, I had to be sleeping; it was the only logical answer. This place didn't feel real; it couldn't be real. It had to be some kind of nightmare with a twisted happy ending.

"Don't fight me, not here, dearest."

His command suggested that he'd man-handle me until I behaved like he wanted. However, his firm hands trembled when I turned to meet his gaze. I planned on telling him to back off but was taken back when I saw a shadow instead of a glowing silhouette. His dark figure barely showed in the dark night. He looked like every other dark figure in my life. A part of me was disappointed.

47

Jace confused me, in my reality and in my dreams… My subconscious was working overtime to come up with a dream based on my *minor* attraction to him. My mouth parted when his grip tightened around my waist. Okay, so it might have been a *major* attraction, but it still didn't mean that I was going to act on those feelings.

"You need more exposure to us, but you also need to remember…remember everything, including me and who I was to you," Jace said, picking up on my confusion.

I couldn't see what his expression was, read a thought in his eyes, but I felt exactly what he wanted me to as his warm hands caressed me. A passion burned within him—one I'd lose my breath denying. I felt it too. If this was some kind of joke, we'd both be the butt of it. I fought an internal battle. I wanted to push him, slap him across his face right after I kissed him.

How could one man be so utterly confusing? He was so unforgettable that apparently even my subliminal thoughts wanted a piece of him. In reality, I'd never give him a chance.

His hand slid down to the top of my waist band, interrupting my thoughts. I wasn't sure if my voice would obey me because the primal language our bodies spoke was so extreme I could hardly think straight.

"If I was *dreaming*, you'd be shirtless," I said.

Without saying a word, he leaned closer against me. His bare chest pressed against my back, warming me with his body heat. It was in that moment, I let myself dream freely instead of fighting it. My shirt was taut. Sliding his hands under the thin fabric, he rubbed his thumbs over my stomach, while he pressed his hips against me. My skin tingled against his touch. I squirmed. He gripped me tighter, keeping me still.

Grasping my hands in his, he moved them over my stomach, like he didn't trust himself to touch me the way he wanted. With my hands acting as a barrier, he held me tight. He pressed his fingers into mine and guided them. My hands drifted over my ribs while his fingertips barely caressed my skin. The faint touch teased me. I moved my hands out from under his so he could do what he wanted. His entire body flexed against me as he tightened his grip around my waist. He took a deep breath of my hair as he pulled me tighter against him with one hand while the other slipped lower over my shorts. Catching my breath, I leaned hard against him.

"You make it difficult for me to concentrate when you gasp like that," Jace whispered like it was a dark secret.

He kissed my neck. It was so feather-like I wasn't sure if his lips actually brushed my skin. His nose trailed up my neck, reaching the bottom of my ear. He rested his forehead against my temple and breathed slow and steady.

"Escape from reality, Gwyneth," Jace whispered in my dream. His heat, power, and fervor encased us. His lips hovered above mine, waiting for me to close the gap. "Sometimes it can be too painful to live in, even for immortals."

Trouble would certainly find me if I got involved with a guy like Jace: unhinged, rebellious—insanely addictive. But dreams were supposed to be an escape from reality; this wasn't real.

"I've been imagining your kiss since I found you, Gwyneth."

Since this was a dream there was no harm in admitting the embarrassing truth. "I've never actually kissed anyone before."

Every.Single.One.Of.His.Muscles.Tightened. It was like he was waging a war with himself. My confession excited him, yet he was trying to stay in control...

He pushed his hips against mine while keeping me molded against him, trapping me. He shivered when I spoke his name. Moving faster than humanly possible, he swung my legs out from under me. Laying me down on the crushed flowers, he leaned over me only to pull away. It was as if he suddenly changed his mind that he had enough self-control to caress me and not lose it. Without his body over mine, his warmth left.

I closed my eyes, hoping to see him better in my mind's eye. "What do you look like?" I asked, craving to know if he was as perfect as I imagined his hazy outline to be.

"Skinny, blond, blue eyes," Jace rattled off quickly.

It was the opposite of Bree's description of him being tall, dark, and candy-de-lious. I said, "Liar."

Instead of denying it, he cautiously reached for me and caressed my cheek. He kept his hand there and gradually slid his body next to mine. He slipped his hand across my bare stomach where my shirt had come up. My body burned where his thumb stroked my skin. I caught my breath. His electrifying touch awakened my skin, sending a tingling sensation around my body.

He was relaxed, or so I thought until I reached for him. Every muscle my fingers ran across was taut. I explored his rock-hard chest. I gained confidence the longer he held me. His physique wasn't

50

enormous, but his muscular frame was still intimidating as well as desirable.

His smooth skin burned hot under my touch. He slid over me without further hesitation and then positioned himself just close enough to be daunting. Confidence radiated from him. He knew exactly what he was doing. Bree was right; he had a lot of practice in the art of seduction.

"My eyes are brown," he whispered. "They match my hair."

I moved my hands up his chest, under his arms, and around his back, seeking out every unblemished feature of his body. My hands found his carved stomach that rippled like water. A small treasure trail led to his pants.

I swallowed and then did something I'd never have the coolness to do in real life. I used his jeans as leverage to pull him down on me.

"You'll be the end of me, Gwyneth."

He cupped my face, gently tilting my chin upward. He whispered that the beauty of an entire ocean could not compare to the exquisiteness of my eyes. He closed the gap when a gasp slipped from my throat. A deep groan rose in his chest as his tongue rolled over mine. My passion awoke as I devoured his kiss in my dream.

Chapter Five

I woke on the bedroom floor, tangled up in my sheets. Even though I slept through the night, I felt drained. It wasn't until I rubbed the sleep from my eyes that I recalled the dream: Jace, the heat, the kiss. I pressed my lips together and tightly wrapped the covers around me.

"It was just a dream," I assured myself. I hadn't actually made myself available to Jace. I hadn't wasted my first kiss on him…even if it did taste sinfully delectable.

Footsteps on the first floor brought me back into the present. I dragged myself off of the floor and was careful not to make too much noise. No matter how tired, I wasn't going to hang out with Martha all day. I hardly survived the afternoon after she picked me up from school. My world had become entirely too warped when I chose McKesson High over solitary confinement in the Thompson residence.

Dialing Bree, I zipped up my khakis and shrugged on my uniform shirt. She agreed to pick me up one block from my place.

After sneaking out of the house, I walked down the sidewalk and waited for Bree. She arrived in a few minutes. I'd just swung the pickup's door open when I got a text from Martha telling me to call at the first sign of an upset stomach.

"JJ's?" Bree suggested as soon as she took a good look at me.

"Definitely." My stomach was growling like a rabid animal.

"Rough night?"

I nodded and looked out the window to hide my grin with my hand. My lips were swollen. I tried not to think about what I'd done to my pillows. I opted not to tell Bree about my dream because she was the type of person to look too deeply into it. Yes, I indulged in a happy fantasy with Jace in my sleep. No harm done. However, it didn't mean I even remotely wanted him in real life; Bree didn't need to overanalyze it. I didn't need to over think it either…so why was he still invading my thoughts? Jace's demeanor, conceit, and attitude screamed player. He'd walk all over my heart if I let him.

"You know I'm not going to let you wander around like that," Bree said as she pulled away from the curb.

"You know the rules. No make-up at school."

She scoffed like I didn't have a choice. "*Minimal* concealer today, Winnie. You've got a wicked case of eye-bags."

"No eye-liner."

"No liner, but then you have to let me tackle your hair."

I nodded, secretly grateful that there was someone in my life who'd tell me if I looked like a slob even if I wasn't big into the whole appearance bit. She tossed me a brush that she kept in her backpack, along with an emergency stash of make-up.

"You're going to give yourself split ends yanking at your hair like that," Bree warned. On the down-stroke, she grabbed my hand and pried my brush from my fingers. "Blondes show splits much more than brunettes like me."

"Lucky you," I said.

"Quit smiling like this was your plan all along. You know I can't stand the sound of you shredding your hair."

"If I had your curls, I wouldn't look like I just walked through a hurricane, and then I wouldn't have to worry about looking like a train-wreck," I said, knowing the general appearance of her shadow since she had allowed me to feel her face and hair years ago.

"Like you'd use the products needed to make my locks look fabulous," Bree said.

"I might."

"Right, so why is there dust taking up permanent residency on the hair gel I gave you last spring?"

I sighed, "You know I hate your so called *donations*."

"You know you look amazing when you let me do your hair

and make-up. But no, instead you run around like the natural look is what boys want to see nowadays. I swear you're terrified to be pretty," she said, fussing with my hair long enough to make it lay flat across the middle of my back. "That's your plan, isn't it—to hide behind this mess of hair? Heaven forbid you actually talk civilly to a guy."

"If you mention Jace, I'll freak."

I envisioned Bree rolling her eyes. I heard her dig through a pocket where she kept bobby-pins. She pulled half my hair back; I never said a word. It was a fight we repeated too many times to count. I'd eventually give in and regret bringing *appearances* up. They didn't matter; why should they? I couldn't see. Nevertheless, I knew she was looking out for me in her own way.

After finishing, she drove the rest of the way to JJ's. The small coffee bistro smelled like its walls were coated with coffee beans and flavored syrup. The waitress finished a texting-convo before she wrote down our order that included a much needed double shot of espresso.

We'd just ordered our drinks when I heard a person shuffle across the tile behind us. Without having to look, I knew who it was. Like the Thompsons and Max, Hector was a part of my makeshift family. He hobbled due to an old fighting injury that had shattered his right kneecap. Boxing was a big part of his life, and mine too. Knocking me on my butt in the ring, Hector literally helped me overcome some hard knocks in my life.

Hector grabbed my shoulders firmly and briefly held me tight, instigating a playful fight. If I wasn't so hungry, I would have socked him in the gut when he first gripped my shoulders.

Even though he had six inches on me, I proved myself in the ring. He couldn't match my agility, even if he could obliterate me with a few solid hits.

"I'm surprised to see you here," Hector said.

Since I could smell coffee on his breath, I knew he wasn't here to get his first shot of caffeine of the day. Martha must have sent him to check up on me. That she knew exactly where I went after leaving the house meant I was all too predictable. I made a mental note to address that issue.

"You need to brush up on your spy skills, *Mr. Coffee Breath.*"

He raised his hands in the air as if to say *I surrender.* "You caught me, Winnie."

"Are you going to hit some bags with me later today?" I asked, not wanting to talk about my over-protective foster mother.

"Only if Bree joins you," Hector said.

"And show you up in the ring? I don't think you want the humiliation," Bree teased, and grabbed the drinks that our waitress finally got around to making. "Better get going, Winnie. At this rate, we'll get there just in time to miss first period. As enticing as detention sounds, I'd rather spend my afternoon with Ryker. He's taking me on a secret date—mission impossible style. Parents aren't cleared to know the classified details."

"Let me guess, he's taking you to a movie?" I asked.

"Hush! You'll blow our cover!" she giggled.

"See you tonight then?" I asked, reconfirming my workout date with Hector.

"Like I'd stand up a gorgeous gal like you," Hector said, bidding us goodbye.

Once outside, Bree nudged my shoulder. "If he weren't like, old enough to be—"

"—he's only twenty-two. It's not like that's ancient," I said, and took my drink. Pulling the lid off, I let the drink cool before I climbed into the pickup. "And no, I'm not interested. It'd be like kissing my brother."

"He's good looking, in great shape, considering his limp, and his light brown hair shimmers perfectly in the right lighting," Bree continued like my rapport meant little to nothing.

"Maybe you and Ryker should give it a rest. You seem to be rather hung up on brown-haired guys lately," I said, thinking about the color of Jace's hair.

"Not loving Hector's sickly green eyes," Bree said, ignoring my comment. For a moment, I thought she might actually consider pursuing a date with Hector. "But then again, I'd hold out too if the hottest new guy in school was chasing my tail. Ryker mentioned that things got a bit hot in art class between you and Jace, and then he said that you faked an illness. He sent me a picture message of him carrying you in his arms."

I didn't want to tell her that I literally had adverse effects to being near Jace. She'd think I lost my marbles. Pronouncing every word crystal clear, I said, "I'm *not* holding out."

"Admit it! He swept you off your feet, Winnie!"

"Only because I tripped first."

***

Standing in the art classroom doorway, I closed my eyes, turned my head, and then looked around the room. Jace's smoky outline was the only figure that showed in the cloak of darkness. He was in the far back corner of the room—sitting in my spot to be exact.

He leaned back in my chair. Considering that I couldn't see much definition in his hazy shadow, I couldn't help but notice how effortlessly he moved. I hated that my heart picked up its beat. The simple act of watching him lean back in a chair shouldn't make my pulse race. Pressing my lips tight together, I tried—unsuccessfully—not to think about how his lips had felt on mine. Only in dreams did guys do and say everything perfectly; in reality, they were the complete opposite.

I opened my eyes and almost brought my hand over my eyes to block his blazing glow. I didn't recall his silhouette being this bright yesterday. I walked confidently to *my* spot.

I made it halfway across the room before a nauseating heat wave hit me. How was he doing this? Jace had another thing coming if he thought he was going to win a battle of the wills with me. I mentally patted myself on the back once more for not telling Bree about the dream. I knew she'd never purposely "out" me, but a few secrets have slipped from her mouth before. If it got out that I actually dreamed about Jace, not only would I be absolutely mortified, but he might actually believe he has some kind of influence over me. Pressing my hand against the wall, I steadied myself and hoped the nausea would pass, when a vision hijacked my concentration.

Warm, brilliant red liquid seeped into my pink blanket. I was a young child, an infant. Lightning flashed across the night sky while rain pelted the roof only to stream down the window beside me. My screams competed with the thunder. But no one listened to me, not even the wrinkled old man who held a bloody knife in one hand and a cane in the other. Blood gushed from a young girl next to me. My pink blanket turned red. Colors blurred until everything melted into a shade of gray.

I stifled a whimper when the vision faded away. Only in my visions did color arise and this one ended with darkness. Also, I was always older in my all my visions—my future. If I wasn't mistaken, the vision marked the day in the past—the day I lost my family and my sight. Tears quickly gathered in my eyes. I lowered my head, wiped them away, and hoped no one had noticed. I clenched my teeth and willed the world to stop spinning in a spiral of gray. I leaned against the wall in attempt to keep my balance. I closed my eyes together as tightly as I could, willing more tears not to escape. Keep yourself untouchable, I thought, because only the weak cried. I refused to shed another tear for their deaths. Nothing I could do would bring my family back. Revenge dug its cold claws into my soul long ago. I forced my misery down deep. I needed to be strong.

My future always unraveled before me as broken pieces of visions, randomly throughout the day—but not my past. It'd been dormant, until now. I wanted to scream out in fury thinking of my sister's pointless death. The man who murdered her and my parents was old, near the last days of his life. I always imagined him being middle aged, not elderly. That he might already have died a peaceful death wasn't something I was willing to accept. I wanted him to suffer for his crimes; I yearned for justice. It was ghastly enough that he stole my parents' life, but my sister was as defenseless as I had been. It was unacceptable.

"Winnie?" Mrs. Brigg asked, bringing me back into my pathetic existence. "Are you still not feeling well?"

"I'm just dandy," I lied, stifling my grief.

She hesitated, expecting me to change my mind. When I didn't, she continued her lecture. I needed a punching bag and then a pillow. Seeing my sister's murderer in my visions wasn't something I was prepared to tackle in school. I needed a distraction.

Pressing my lips tight together, I glanced at my spot that Jace had so kindly occupied. I smiled spitefully, pleased to take my anger out on someone so delightfully aggravating.

I took one step forward and nearly fell. His blazing white silhouette dimmed as I gathered my bearings. I tried to shake the absurdity that he could control my physical well-being, even though a part of me still suspected he could. I took a deep breath and continued to my table. I passed one table before I nearly dropped Stella because my hands were drenched with sweat. Again, I paused and closed my eyes and looked upon his hazy figure.

Jace nodded, encouraging me to come closer. With a frown plastered on my face, I passed by another table. After bumping into one, I apologized and opened my eyes. Everyone else's dark shadows stayed the same shade of utter darkness, but Jace's white abyss dramatically darkened. I seriously needed a doctor check-up. Occasionally, my eyes played tricks on me but not this extreme.

"You're in my spot," I glowered, standing a few paces away.

"If you want it, you're going to have to take it," Jace said, tossing what appeared to be a ball of clay in the air.

"Winnie's known to throw a wicked right hook; I wouldn't intentionally annoy her unless you're looking for a black eye," Ryker chimed in.

"Is that so?" Jace asked, intrigued.

"I've been training for years," I replied.

Jace wasn't going to let it go. "Why?"

Oh hell, I didn't know! Maybe because I fell off too many treadmills or that I wanted to work out in an unconventional way. Traditional gyms bored me.

"Because sword fighting wasn't being offered," I joked.

"Have you?" Jace asked a little too quickly.

I frowned. "No."

Folding my walking stick together, I tried to keep my voice at a reasonable volume which was incredibly difficult. Putting up with the two most confusing males in history was a feat I hadn't the energy to deal with today.

"She doesn't look like much of a fighter," Jace chuckled and rocked back into his chair. "Being passive-aggressive suits her."

Why did his voice have to sound so enticing? I dug my nails into my palm, using the pain to think clearly. "Please move."

"Don't want to sit by your dream boat, dearest?" Jace said. "Your cheeks are a little rosy. Flustered about anything in particular?"

My dream with Jace blitz-attacked my thoughts. It wasn't real, I reassured myself. I was in bed making out with my pillows, not with Jace in the middle of a field. Besides, in my dream he looked like a dark shadow, instead of the irritating white abyss like he did now.

"Nope," I said, dismissing my dream as some kind of subliminal joke my hormones had played on me.

Jace casually threw the clay in the air. He was baiting me, assuming I'd bite. He waited for a come-back, or any remark, but what he didn't know was that I'd lived with my fair share of bullies. I stood silently, calculating the rhythm in which he threw the clay ball. At the point where it was the highest, he looked up, and I gave the chair's leg a swift kick. Jace collided into the floor and then stood up faster than I could follow. He seized my arms. His touch practically burned my skin! My feet wanted to give out when another vision raided my consciousness.

Standing above me as I clutched my blanket was the old man, holding a bloody knife in one hand. He was scarred and wrinkled. His hands were wrinkled, weathered. Time hadn't been good to him. He grabbed my arm and cut it. My blood seeped from my skin. The old man leaned in close, smelling me. The smell of fresh rain filled the air. But what scared me was the look in his eye when he smiled at me. It was pure evil.

The vision ceased to play out when Jace tightened his grip on my arms. Rattling off commentary in his language, he acted like he wanted to strangle me. Struggling to keep himself dimmed, his anger spread over me in a heat wave. I was sure he'd send himself into a blazing white figure again. Conversely, just as quickly as the warmth

62

passed over my body, it was replaced by a tingling sensation that crawled over my skin, energizing me.

I pictured him glowering down at me while he lost his cool. It filled me with a sick sense of gratification knowing that I got under his skin too. Jace mumbled a few words in his cryptic language, and as if on cue, a headache formed at the base of my skull when his figure brightened, but I'd come equipped with a few tried and true items from Martha's medicine cabinet. A container full of *Ibuprofen* rested nicely inside my backpack, along with a bottle of *Pepto-Bismol* and even a few *Benadryl* pills.

"I asked nicely for you to move," I stated, defending myself to whatever sting of obscenities he cursed.

Just as I prepared to make some snide remark about his secret language, the definition in his white figure brightened. My head pounded, my eyes filled with tears, and I forgot how to breathe. We stood facing each other; two insults away from throwing punches when he subtly leaned closer to me; the space between us was suddenly too narrow and entirely too wide; the mood between us shifted. I waged a war with myself. Lured by Jace, I was simply exasperated. The thought of slapping him was tempting, but the idea of doing other vigorous activities distracted me as well. I swallowed and held onto my anger instead of focusing on his magnetism.

The definition in his face chipped away from the shapeless abyss into a more precise shape. His mouth formed in my sight, which was impossible. My mouth watered eagerly when he parted his lips slightly as he breathed deep—methodically. The clasp on my lungs loosened just enough for me to catch my breath. A moan resonated in his throat, after the gasp escaped mine. His plush lips promised lucrative activities that made me squirm. I clenched my teeth, promising myself not to act like a giddy school girl—no matter how lickable his lips looked.

The black water hid everything under its surface. Nothing showed through, except for the faint outline of a calloused hand. Just when I was about to look away, a single blue flame sparked just below a ripple of water. The flame danced and flickered like it would have in the wind.

The brilliant blue hue had been embedded to memory. It was the first time that I'd seen the vision, yet it felt oddly familiar.

"You test my patience, dearest," Jace sneered.

He lifted me. My feet still touched the floor, but it was an illusion. He supported my body weight. I twisted in his grasp. It didn't faze him. I swallowed hard, not exactly hating his abundance of upper body strength. A prickle flowed from his hands; I sensed that he was enjoying my vulnerability. I bit my lip to keep me from saying something regrettable. I only spoke after I convinced myself that it didn't sound idiotic.

"You test mine." My defiance wasn't exactly profound.

"She tests all our patience," Ryker said, adding his two cents.

"Winnie! Jace!" Mrs. Briggs said, spotlighting our improper behavior. "Sit down and be quiet."

He slowly lowered me, like it took no effort. I held back a squeal. Placing my hand on the table in front of my usual spot, I reached for the chair. Jace side-stepped behind me and pulled out the seat in front of him. I was about to sit when he kicked my leg. I fell clumsily into the chair that he conveniently pushed out next to my spot. Sliding me over, he sat down in the vacant chair my backside had been aiming for all along.

Mrs. Briggs continued with her lecture and left us to achieve whatever it was we were supposed to be accomplishing with the clay. I crossed my arms, seething about how I was going to counter-attack. Not just because Jace stole my chair but because he somehow made a mess of my intentions.

"You just declared war, Jace," Ryker warned.

"You know nothing of war, do you, Gwyneth?" Jace said. When I couldn't think of anything to say or do, he continued. "No, you're just a little girl, mad at the world."

"Little girl now?" I asked smugly. Reaching for my old ball of clay, I re-formed the edges so it began to resemble a bowl. "I've been demoted from *dearest?* Have you finally gotten the hint that you shouldn't be gunning for the role of my boyfriend, because you're definitely not my type."

Despite everything that just happened, Jace grinned. I don't know how I knew he was smirking at me, I just did.

Jace said, "In all the years I've searched for a woman like you, there's one thing I've learned. The ones who fight the hardest are worth the chase."

"This is not a challenge."

With everything that just happened, I wanted him to read the metaphorical, flashing neon sign above my head that read *not interested.*

"Riddle me this, Jace. Why go through this whole charade to

get my chair if you don't want a war between us?"

"It's closer to the door."

"Meaning?"

"That he's got a fast escape route," Ryker chimed.

"You're not a part of this conversation," I said, wishing Bree would get a clue and ditch him so he wouldn't find a reason to be around me all the time.

"Meaning if anyone comes through, I will stand between you and them."

"So you want to be my protector? From who? Marco?"

Can anyone say possessive?

"Everyone," He said, "And I prefer to be addressed as a guardian."

"Let's set some ground rules, I do not want you, need you, or request your *unwanted* services of protection," I jeered. "I take care of myself."

"If only," Jace sighed, losing himself in his thoughts. "If only…"

Chapter Six

Bakker's Cemetery was a thirty-minute bus ride, so I packed enough treats for my fur buddy and a blanket. Max sniffed out everyone on the bus who came close enough. I assumed he was blinking up at them with his puppy dog eyes, begging to be petted.

The bus screeched to a stop half an hour later, we got off and walked down the familiar sidewalk that I'd taken many times. The bus stop was only one block from the church and vast yard. Max led the way. Finding our old oak tree in front of three old stones, I threw the blanket down. My parents rested by my sister, Lily. Snuggled against the stump and using the surface roots for an arm rest, I dug in my bag and popped out a treat for Max. He gobbled it up eagerly.

"I thought I'd find you here."

John was leaning against an old fence a few paces away. I'd been too consumed with being the worst investigator ever to notice him. He pushed off the fence and walked over to me. I scooted over so he could sit down beside me.

"October third," he muttered and kissed my forehead. "You know I wouldn't be a very good lawyer if I forgot dates."

I sighed, not wanting to talk about it. I knew he'd drive me, but visiting my family's burial place was something I wanted to do alone; thus, we sat in silence. Max enjoyed himself since John and I both decided the awkward silence was best filled by petting him.

I broke the silence first. "What did you think of Martha when you first met her?"

John let out a laugh and said that was the last question he'd expected me to ask. "The woman drove me nuts. I couldn't stand her. She was a barista at JJ's when we first met. She actually spilled coffee all over me. I'd be lying if I hadn't thought about suing her, but then she had grabbed half a dozen towels. She dabbed the drink off my lap and saying sorry like she had some form of apologetic tourettes. I was a goner."

"What are you talking about?" I asked, not following his train of thought.

"She ruined my suit by spilling coffee on it; I was the one who acted like it was the end of the world; still, I refused to get my morning coffee anywhere else. I'd convinced myself it was because their brews were the best, but if I'd have been honest with myself, I would have known it was because of Martha. Her eyes lit up when she looked at me. It scared me," John said, and put his arm around me. "My life was planned out perfectly. I was on the fast track to becoming partners in a corporate firm. Good looking ladies chased me. It was only a matter of time before I asked one of them out, settled down and got married, but then Martha came along and made a mess of my life."

"But you have the perfect life," I said. "Don't get me wrong, Martha's great—a little crazy, and extremely disorganized—but great."

"Life is messy. If I wanted to live a life where I'd know exactly how everything would play out, I wouldn't have settled down with someone who didn't know how expensive a handmade Italian suit was. Love isn't something you chose, Winnie. It picks you when you aren't looking. And love isn't just between two people; it makes a family," John said, squeezing me tight. "Just because someone isn't flawless doesn't mean he's not ideal. Martha isn't perfect, but she's the best fit for me. Nothing you find on the internet can explain love like that."

We spent the rest of the morning in the graveyard. John wasn't my biological father, but he fit the bill. It couldn't have been a better way to spend the anniversary of my family's death. He left before I was ready, which was okay with me. I stayed a bit longer and just enjoyed the time I had with my family. I tended to their graves. The stones were rough and cold under my fingertips. It felt good to make sure every weed was pulled and that the tombstones were clean of debris. When I came to my sister's grave, my fingers brushed against something that felt nothing like a weed. Silk petals caressed my skin. I held it up to the sun; the light gave way to three lilies that were woven together with a thin thread. I smiled and pressed the flowers to my chest, right above my heart. Hector remembered! In honor of my sister, he decorated her gravesite with the flower of her namesake. Whatever happened, that he always had an eye out for me.

I pulled out my phone and instructed it to *call Hector*. He'd be at the library at this hour in the day. It took a few rings before he answered.

"You remembered," I said, clutching the lilies.

There was a long pause before he replied. When he did I swore I heard his voice catch. He never knew my parents or Lily, but he carried their loss with me nevertheless.

"I'd never forget."

***

Leaning against the brick wall outside McKesson High stood Jace's oversized comrade. Every so often Marco's head would twitch. A steady stream of students walked past me as I held onto the cold metal railing and watched him. The afternoon sun shimmered against his figure enough that I knew that even if he wasn't very strong, he had enough sheer body weight to throw around. He was the type of guy who probably had a few fights under his belt. Closing my eyes, I looked in the general direction of where he stood. I saw nothing until I started to open my eyes. His silver outline dissolved into nothing.

"Why do you close your eyes when you look at us?" Jace asked, standing a couple steps above me.

Stalk much? "Who do you mean by us?"

"I can't say."

Well, if he wasn't going to share his secrets…"Then neither can I."

Even though Jace refused to move onto his next conquest, he

did have the sexiest voice on Earth. I had to give him that. Taking in a deep breath, I took in his otherworldly scent blowing in the breeze, when a vision ripped me from reality.

"You wish for my immortality," I said, stroking his thumb with my gnarled hand. My old body scarcely obeyed my command. I wanted to rest, needed it. The thread of my life was unraveling while his was as strong and youthful as ever. It was cruel in more ways than one.

He held my face in his hand, comforting me. "I want your immortality and for you to have what you and the humans used to have."

"You only get one request, and you have to be willing to kill me for it," I said, and guided his hand over my chest. The knife skimmed my skin, but it was enough to tear it open.

"Living as an immortal in this body would be more like a curse than a gift," he said. The regret in his eyes was already evident. "I want you to have the opportunity to be what you once were, before she took it."

"Immortal?" I gasped, not believing what'd I'd just seen.

I clutched my chest. I could hardly breathe, barely stand, and scarcely think. My life didn't make any sense before, and now I was certifiable. Murder, betrayal, and death encompassed my entire existence. Now I was to believe that there was no ending to all my suffering? I didn't want to live forever, not like this. There was just too much pain in my life. I didn't even feel like a whole person. My soul was ripped to shreds. And then there was Jace…

He actually gave me a sense of hope in my dark existence. Yet, the trust between us just wasn't there. I was positively star-struck by his presence. I wanted him to be mine and no one else's, but I couldn't get over the fact that I knew nothing about him—other than he was seriously smitten with Deino…and I wasn't her. So all the hope he gave me was a falsehood. Falling for him would only end in my heartache when he figured out I wasn't the girl he loved.

"What happened just now, Gwyneth?" Jace asked. Concern clung to his question. "You seemed extremely distracted just now. And you…"

"I what?"

"Were you thinking about me just now? Your fragrance…you smell like me."

I needed to snap out of this. Granted, I had a lot of practice pretending to be normal after getting futuristic visions, but their frequency was increasing lately. I took a deep breath and focused on being my usual stubborn self.

"Smell like you? And what's scent like? A cigar like spice that sends subliminal sex messages to the carnal part of every freaking woman in a ten foot radius?" I retorted and then pressed my lips together. *Oh-mah-gawd* I just admitted that his scent was like aphrodisiac cologne.

"Finally, the truth comes out."

Shaking my head, I opened my eyes and walked away without so much of a reply. He reached for me. I missed my footing when his hand grazed my jacket, just above my hips. I gradually faced him, keeping a hand on the rail. If my balance faltered, he might not notice. His brilliant outline offset the sea of dark shadows passing by.

"In all seriousness, what happened? I know you're shaken up

about something."

"You wouldn't understa—"

He silenced me unexpectedly. Not by clenching my arm, arguing with me, or making me sick. He gently tucked my hair behind my ear, careful not to actually touch my skin.

"Tell me what just happened, Gwyneth. I *know* something happened. I can sense it."

"You can pick up on my feelings?"

"You can't deny the attraction between us, Gwyneth. You make it out to be this ethereal sense. But the truth is that people who have strong feelings for each other pick up on subtleties that others cannot."

We had chemistry—that was for sure. I just didn't know if I wanted to kill Jace more than I wanted to kiss him. His perseverance unnerved me, scrutinizing my every move like a twisted guardian angel. He waited patiently for me to join him. Like he knew my defiance would crumble under his intense gaze. Standing so close to Jace without actually touching him, made me want to crumble into his arms, but I wouldn't do it—no matter how inviting.

"You act like you're not human."

"I've been called worse," he said.

Chapter Seven

The smell of sweat comforted me, wrapping its glorious stench around me. KnockOuts was my home away from home. Normally it wasn't hopping with a lot of girls my age, or any females for that matter, but it didn't stop me from clocking in workout hours. Of course, I was the only person in the place that wore perfume on a regular basis so the new guys would gravitate to me, trying to impress me with their muscles. However, when they realized I wasn't into looks and winning a popularity contest wasn't my thing, they left me alone. Thank god. Thus, I wasn't very popular with boys. Here or at school, minus Jace. So when I ran into a man walking out of the building I was taken completely off guard. It wasn't even so much that my thoughts had distracted me; it was that I should have seen his bright figure—warning me that he must have been associated with Jace. That and that I suddenly had the urge to vomit all over him.

He walked through the door and stopped a few feet away from me. I was grateful for the distance because my stomach eased.

"It's been far too long since I've seen those hypnotic eyes of yours," he said.

My skin tingled as the air vibrations hit me. I became nauseated. The last thing I wanted to do was touch him.

"Do I know you?" I asked.

Brown curls twisted over his pale blue eyes as he laughed. My aging skin crawled as he wrapped his hand around my wrist. He was taller than me but only by a few inches. Another woman with tanned skin and coffee brown hair watched as he lifted me from my seat on the grassy field. The sweet scent of lilies filled the air.

Three spears shone in the light. Their tips were thrown into the ground. The woman with wavy coffee-colored hair walked over and touched the spear. It disappeared instantly.

"You won't be threatening my sister with these, not yet Rippler," she said.

The athletic man danced me around the meadow. "You recall everyone's past, even the darkest parts?" he asked softly.

"I go by *Rippler* to people like us," he said like he knew I didn't know who the hell he was. It probably had something to do with my blatant frown and complete lack of recognition. "But infidels call me Zalen. Your tolerance has never been very good with me. At least Jace isn't lying about your nonresistant tolerance. I'm surprised he hasn't made you an *Addict* and forced you to do what he wants. But I suppose he's into free will and all that."

Yep, he was clearly a friend of Jace's. A: he made me ill. B: he looked different from all the other shadow people. And C: he thought I was some other girl.

"At least we know Jace isn't lying when he reports back and says that you're not ready to meet *her* or any of us yet."

"Who's her?"

"The *Master*. She's *dying* to meet you," he said.

Hearing *that* name—the Master—roll from his mouth instantly fueled a fury hiding within my soul that I didn't know existed. I didn't know what irritated me more—the instant rage against someone I'd never met or that he knew it would anger me.

He laughed. The vibrations of his voice echoed in my ears so loudly that I wanted to rip them off. "I'll let her know that you haven't forgiven her."

With that, he walked out of my life—for the time being. It took longer than I'd care to admit to put myself back together. His voice shook me up literally. My stomach was twisting into knots and I felt like my head was in a paint mixer. However, the more time that passed, the more my body settled down. Finally, I felt good enough to actually work out.

The manager pulled two leather gloves from the bin behind him. He was one of the only people who turned me down to feel his face—my way of picturing how people look. Charlie said he didn't want to ruin the illusion of the young, athletic man I imagined him being. I'd covered up my chuckle with a cough when he had made that comment. The husky, wide shadow gave me the impression that he used to be fit, but over the years his waist line grew with his age. His voice was rough and raspy from smoking too many cigarettes. Often, I caught him rubbing his face after taking off what looked like glasses. I sincerely doubted he had much hair since it would require him taking care of that too. Even though he kept the gym in decent condition, he slid me a few bucks to clean the place when it started to turn south.

Charlie bumped the counter with a pair of gloves before tossing them into the air. The counter bump was my warning. My depth perception was almost worthless, so I stood in defensive mode, protecting my face. One glove fell short and hit the ground a few feet from me, but the other grazed my shoulder.

"Speed bag is reserved for you, Winnie," Charlie hollered from the front desk.

"Thanks, Charles."

He groaned, "How many times have I told you to call me Charlie? You make me sound like an old man calling me Charles!"

"How many times have I told you I'll punch you in the face if you call me Winnie again?"

He chuckled until it turned into a cough. He spit a moment later. "One glove is two feet straight ahead of you and the other is about four paces over your right shoulder. Oh, Hector said that he'd be a few minutes late."

Following his instructions, I picked up the gloves and headed to the speed bag on the opposite side of the room from the front desk. Keeping my hand along the wall, I walked the perimeter of the room since there was a large boxing arena in the middle. My fingers traced the cracks along the cement bricks of the wall, leading me to the familiar worn leather where I'd lose time beating out my anger/frustration/irritation for years now. Reaching the corner, I took five steps forward. A speed bag grazed the top of my pony tail. I took a step backwards and began to punish the bag.

Finding a rhythm, I drummed it. My mind wandered immediately to the old man in my vision who defied the laws of nature and became younger. The blood dripping from his hands was so dark it appeared black. Was blood-lust the reason he broke through my parents' window, years ago? Had this man been a killer his entire life and that was what the vision indicated, because people just don't grow young? He killed with a knife—that much was obvious from the vision. I shouldn't have been able to recall so many details, because I still wore diapers. And until that moment, I'd only seen visions of my life when I was older. The laugh, his malevolent laugh, was so frighteningly familiar, like I heard it in another life perhaps; or was my imagination getting the best of me? Too many unanswered questions formed and my shoulders hurt badly enough that I couldn't keep them above my head any longer.

Even though Hector still had to show, I ditched the speed bags. Memory serving me, I counted ten paces back to where a skew of rolled up mats was stored. Flinging one in the air, I smoothed it out and laid down to get in a quick abs workout. Polishing off a series of different abdominal exercises to work the muscles, I moved into the plank position when someone pressed down on my shoulders, making the workout harder, by tenfold.

"It's about time, Hector!" I yelled, collapsing to the mat.

"You stink," Hector said, sitting down next to me.

"Well, I have been working out for like an hour now," I said, stretching out my abs.

"Not like sweat, Winnie. You smell like smoke," he said, like *I* was hiding something. The question was: where had *he* been?

He ducked as I pushed off the mat to tackle him. Pinning me against the floor, he laughed. I tapped out.

"Please tell me you're not sucking on cancer sticks," he said.

"I'm not that dumb," I said. "What was so important that you blew off our workout date?"

"If you must know, I was tying up a few loose ends at work," Hector said. The mat shifted under him. He moved into a hamstring stretch, groaning and complaining about the scar tissue in his knee. "Is there any particular reason why you're in such a foul mood today?"

"A weird dream kept me tossing and turning last night."

"Was it a good one?" Hector asked slyly.

"It was a weird dream because it involved this guy I can't stand," I admitted. Normally, I'd only tell Bree details about any guy problems I found myself in, but she was dead set on Jace and me hooking up. Her opinion would be biased. Besides, Hector was different than other guys. He wasn't dateable, filling the over protective brother role. "I know this is crazy, but I just sort of get ill when he's around."

"Lover's sickness," Hector teased, but was polite enough to hold in a chuckle when I scowled. "You used to get ill around me when we first started to hang out."

"Compliments to you teaching me how to fight," I said. "If I

79

wasn't puking from a minor concussion I was nursing my appendages with ice bags."

"Well, what do you think about him?" Hector said, seriously. "You've always claimed to have such good judgment in people. Do you need me to put—"

"Jace," I interrupted. "His name is Jace Eatros."

"Jace Eatros," Hector repeated.

The hostility in his voice was notable. Even though I was flattered Hector was taking his role as "big brother" to heart, I said, "And no, you don't need to put him in his place for me. I can handle him. I just don't know what he wants with me."

"He sounds like the stalker type."

No, that would be his weird, twitching giant friend who followed me around after school. Jace, at least, had the decency to make his presence known, no matter how unwanted.

***

From the smell of the house, John already had the wings drowned in BBQ sauce. Martha had pop chilling in the fridge. There were enough potato chips in their pantry to feed a small country.

I finished showering ten minutes before kickoff. Max barked eagerly as I changed into a pair of sweat pants and oversized football shirt John gave me from "the good old days" as the high school receiver. He told me it was royal blue and lined with gold edging.

"That jersey is falling apart!" Martha exclaimed as I made my way down the stairs.

"It's just getting broken in," I said, walking over to the couch.

John chuckled and handed me a plate of hot wings. I imagined him beaming with pride to see me wearing his old clothes. I made my way to the couch and waited to eat until he brought over the chips and pops. Max groaned when he realized, not only would I not be petting him, but I would not be playing with him anytime soon. Bringing over a squeak toy, he rested on my feet and proceeded to pout in a way only dogs can.

"I thought I threw that tattered old shirt away," Martha said after she joined us in the living room.

"You did, three times," John said, and scooted over next to me on the couch. "I rescued it from the trash."

Two minutes before halftime, the door bell rang. Martha got up, allowing her husband to swear under his breath after North Carolina tackled Duke's third-year quarterback for the umpteenth time. An authoritative woman at the door questioned Martha, but I couldn't make out any of the questions. Slamming his plate down on the end table, John stated that the defensive line wouldn't break five-hundred unless they started playing with their heads. Pop threatened to go up my nose when John growled about a bad call. Soon, he grumbled about his honey-do list and stomped off to the garage.

"She's here!" Martha said, walking quickly into the living room. She started to ask where John, was when a power tool sounded from the garage. "Get your father."

My father? My mouth dropped. "John?"

"That's what I said," Martha replied, acting like *I'd* said something odd before she raced back to the front door.

Absorbing what just happened, I sat there, stunned. I caught myself smiling, realizing that my place in the house had somehow changed when I wasn't paying attention. I was happy about the impromptu welcome into the family, but I was guarded. John wasn't my father. As much as I loved him, he couldn't fill those shoes. I shook my head, trying to clear it forcefully. I was probably reading too much into Martha's comment.

I pushed off the leather couch and let Max lead me to the garage door. Instead of opening it, I knocked twice and let John know that he was needed inside. After he assured me he'd be out after fixing something, I left for the front door and found myself looking down at a trembling, petite, dark shadow—a young girl, perhaps?

I walked slow, closer to them while Martha exchanged good-nights with the case manager. Ida Jenkins was a burly old woman, and, from what she'd told me, had worked in the foster system all of her working life. Years were sneaking up on her. She only had a few good ones left in her before she'd be forced into a retirement.

"You still like it here, Gwyneth?" she asked before leaving. She didn't check up on me often anymore, but it was still her duty to keep tabs on me even if I wasn't misbehaving anymore. I smiled; it was all the response Ida needed. She wasn't going to make a fuss about nothing and was probably hoping she wouldn't have to relocate me.

"John makes the best wings in town," I said, and offered her one for the road.

"Heartburn isn't worth it," Ida said and then excused herself.

Max wagged his tail forcefully enough that his body swayed, I knew he would topple the new girl the moment I let my guard down. After telling him to sit, I kneeled down in front of the foster child. I remember being in her place eight years ago: scared, cold, and utterly alone.

"Hello," I said, and extended my hand. The small girl timidly took it and muttered that her name was Elsie Yang. Her hands were frozen and boney. I highly suspected she was nothing but knees and elbows. "Elsie is a pretty name for an eight-year-old."

The girl said nothing. She looked like she was attempting to melt into the wall behind her. How did a girl so shy manage to be a runaway threat? Nix that—I knew firsthand how she could be a runner. I smiled brightly, hoping to win her over with pleasantries, even though I knew better. Assuming she was taking in the first sights of the house, I filled the space with rattling about how great the Thompsons were to live with, if you like heaps of laundry.

"What's wrong with your eyes?" Elsie asked. Her voice squeaked, almost surprised she spoke in the first place.

The soft click of the front door sounded. Elsie instantly stiffened. For all she knew, I was a mean, older kid who was just itching to lay down the rules, and the Thompsons were the people keeping her captive. John's footsteps sounded in the kitchen. If I didn't know better, I'd think he was waiting for Martha and me to finish introducing ourselves. Meeting everyone could be a bit overwhelming.

"It's okay to ask, Elsie. I'm blind," I said. I pictured her lips quivering as she tried to figure out what angle I was working.

"Blind?" she repeated.

"Yeah," I said. "It's kind of nice, actually. I don't have to spend hours in front of the mirror fussing about how I look because it doesn't matter, *and* I have really good hearing."

Her dark shadow got closer. She leaned forward to get a better look at my eyes. "How did you know how old I was?"

I told her it was a lucky guess and smiled brightly, even though I dislike it when people gawked at my eyes. It was extremely nerve-racking, but I wanted Elsie to feel safe. "Martha's husband, John, is in the kitchen, *hopefully* making dessert," I said a little louder, hoping he'd get the hint that a few wings and chips weren't going to fill me up.

Glancing toward the kitchen to see if John was going to make me a liar, I caught sight of a shimmery figure, glistening through the living room's window. I took a slow, deep breath and closed my eyes, hoping the orb would disappear. It didn't. My lungs fought to cooperate. My adrenaline spiked. Sensing my distress, Max scooted closer to me without actually moving out of his 'sit' position.

"Let's get you settled in first," Martha suggested as soon as she noticed my anxiety spike. "Your room is on the second floor, next to Winnie's."

When I looked back up, I saw Martha's and Elsie's shadow moving toward the stairs—their backs to the window. Another white figure moved alongside the first. Was it Jace and the Rippler? Abruptly, the two shapes vanished.

Chapter Eight

Sand shifted under my back, as the world threatened to spin out of control. I rolled onto my side, dry heaving. The fleeting sunset warmed my clammy skin. I felt like I was being torn apart and put back together but incorrectly. I took a deep breath in. The warm air burned my lungs. I screamed out in agony.

Only when I hoped someone would save me, did I realize *he* was already there, comforting me. Jace held me as if he was afraid to let go. His body was like a hardened boulder; it enforced the notion that he could protect me against anything; he could be my rock—solid ground.

He'd found me in my dreams again.

Gradually, I became whole again. My screams turned into sobs. His charismatic voice soothed me; it touched my soul in ways that shouldn't have been possible. His hazy outline was the definition of picturesque—in a blurred, vague way.

"I'm scared when you find out the truth about me, you'll leave," I said, wishing I had the guts to tell him I wasn't Deino.

"I'm afraid of the very same thing," he confessed.

I reached up to stroke his hair. Its shape became more defined as I ran my fingers through it. It flowed freely over his ears. The cut was styled, but no product clung to the locks. He leaned his face into my hand. I opened my eyes, taking in the surroundings. Jace's white silhouette was framed by dark ridges—cliffs. This time I hadn't gotten ill from his bright presence. The sound of waves crashing into the shoreline made me believe I'd been dreaming of the tropical island I'd heard on the television.

My fingers trailed along his cheekbone and the hard line of his jaw. He might have been clean-shaven earlier, but not now. I hesitated to slide my hand up under his eye. Bree mentioned him having a scar under his left eye. If my dreams were authentic, I'd feel a thin line interrupt his skin. He turned his head away before I could confirm.

"I want to know what you look like," I said.

"Why does it matter what I look like?" he asked. His silhouette flashed a fraction brighter. It made his figure clearer in my mind. The hazy outline sharpened but not enough to make out many distinctions in his appearance.

"I'm just trying to get an idea of how to picture you in my mind's eye." If I wasn't mistaken, he didn't want me to know his identity.

Gathering me in his arms, he lifted me from the sand. His muscles bulged, but he wasn't struggling to hold me up. I held on by wrapping my arms around his neck. When they rubbed against his bare collarbone, I realized I still wore my pajamas; he was, once again, shirtless.

Dreams could be so rewarding.

"How do you picture this?" Jace asked, and spun around before lowering me into the cool ocean's shore.

In contrast to the luminous water, the sand was as dark as night. The sun set on the ocean's horizon. I pretended to see the shimmering reds, yellows, and blues glowing over the waves. Polished gray and black rocks rubbed against my feet as each wave hit my knees. Jace moved to my side, taking in the view with me.

"My world is sketched in shades of gray," I said, not bothering to hide my frustration and disappointment.

He said nothing, considering my response. My skin tingled as his white silhouette flickered brighter, only to dim immediately. I reached for him. His hand was clenched tight. The longer I traced my fingers over his skin, the more relaxed he became. I waited for him to conquer whatever thought stole him away from me.

My lack of sight was a personal battle only I could fight. It wasn't anything anyone could restore. I should have known better—I shouldn't have known what I missed, since I'd been blind since I was a child. However, my visions teased me with the possibility of color and depth. Long ago, I'd fallen in love with facial expressions and subtle gestures. Nevertheless, I'd only see them in my mind, never in real life.

"Shall we add a little color then?" he asked as he took my

hand and led me deeper into the ocean.

The water darkened the farther we walked out. Only when the cold waves splashed over my stomach did we stop. He tightened his grip around my waist, keeping me steady against the force of the ocean's waves. When I didn't move away, his hands ventured farther until they slid along the backside of my legs. Effortlessly, he pulled me up against him, holding me just above the surface. Waves slapped noisily against the shore, but I swore his heart beat louder. He leaned close, but before his lips caressed mine, he pulled away. It made my mouth water for a taste of his kiss.

Tease.

"The hazel lingering in your eyes reminds me of the sand along this shoreline. The brilliant blues in them mimic the ocean itself—sea blue with a touch of hazel. Gazing into your eyes is like stealing a glimpse of heaven," Jace whispered as his lips brushed mine ever so slightly. "I find myself reminiscing of a time long lost when I look at you now, so full of youth and fight."

In the cool water, my leg suddenly warmed. A tiny flame danced just below the surface, just like it had in my vision. Jace raised his hand. The dark flame flickered. I didn't see the color; I didn't have to. In my heart, I knew it was blue, just like it was in my vision. Just like I didn't have to know what Jace looked like, I knew he understood the way I felt about him. Unable to stand the distance between us, I closed the gap between us. He kissed me like he was drowning in my fervor. I felt his enthusiasm. I craved the taste of it on my lips.

***

Fourth period literature was my one and only class with Bree. At least it was "Ryker-free." I know he tried to change his schedule to get into this class after Bree revealed our schedules. He confused me. If he hated me so much, wouldn't he try to get as few classes with me as possible?

Using Stella as my guide, I made my way to the last seat in the first row. Bree waved to me from the last chair in the second row and then returned to scribbling on a piece of paper—our homework. The five-question assignment took me nearly an hour to complete. Of course, I was somewhat distracted with finding excuses to look out every window in the house to see if anyone was still spying on me.

"Good morning, dearest."

I hadn't heard *him* walk up behind me, my stomach felt fine, my vertigo hadn't shifted, and I was still headache free. Cheers to small victories.

"Jace!" Bree squealed, completely forgetting about her assignment. "Switched schedules so you could suffer through Miss Conner's lectures with us?"

He shrugged his shoulders. "Happy coincidence?"

He spoke like he moved, effortlessly and hypnotically. He stood far enough away so our clothing wouldn't actually touch. His usual abyss wasn't blazing white; it was diminished significantly. Did that have anything to do with me not becoming physically ill?

Dismissing me, he leaned over the desk to talk to Bree, which bothered me more than I cared to admit. But, I'd already decided to barricade my heart from him, right? He was smitten with a girl he *thought* was me. I should be happy he was chatting it up with my best friend. Commandeering the desk in front of Jace, I dropped my backpack and slipped onto the hard seat.

"I'm in need of your personal assistance, Bree," Jace said loud enough for me to hear. If the morning sun wouldn't have reflected off of it just perfectly, I wouldn't have seen the paper he slipped to her in his hand. I clenched my teeth, determined not to overreact. I wasn't jealous. Jace rubbed his arm like he'd been suddenly chilled and turned back to me. If I wasn't mistaken, he blamed me for his sudden distress.

"Do you no longer want the seat closest to the door, or is your goal simply to annoy me?" I asked.

"We're on the second floor, dearest. Anyone threatening who comes through that door will have given me ample heads up." Jace said, and tilted his head to pick up the pencil that I knocked off. He picked it up but hesitated to return to a normal sitting position. His eyes were level with the back of my chair. "And the view is better from here anyway."

Every seat had a hole in the back. Prime viewing for perverts.

"You owe me an apology," he said.

I scooted away from the hole in the back of the chair. "For not having a tight enough ass?"

That caught him off guard. "I have no complaints about the tautness of your backside."

"Then why do I owe you an apology?"

90

"For starters, you ditched me after…"

His darkened figure slid deeper into the seat, distracting me with the smooth movement with which his body moved. He pushed his chest out slyly as he rested his hands on the back of his head. His movements were free flowing, but I knew they were perfectly calculated—they had to be. No one moved with such precision; it was like he expected a photographer to snap a photo of him at any moment.

His fluid movements reminded me of my dream—watching in awe as he moved smoothly over me. I swallowed the lump in my throat when I wondered what it was actually like to kiss him and then rolled my eyes because I allowed myself to remember a kiss that didn't actually happen. It was a dream, I told myself for the umpteenth time.

His voice—his insanely enrapturing voice—demanded the attention of anyone within hearing distance; yet, he spoke like he was talking only to me. The sentiment hiding in his voice, revealed hidden messages that only I could hear. It was like he was whispering promises in my ear instead of having a public conversation. Words jumped from his tongue in a way that made me suspect his lips were well practiced for more than listening to himself speak. I bit my lip as I lost myself in the dream. My first kiss was impossibly perfect; his lips felt like silk. Reality would surely never match; yet, I still shuddered recalling his embrace. It was just a dream, I told myself again. A moan grew from his chest. The sound made me want to lick the next words from his mouth.

He paused. "You didn't hear a single word I said, did you?"

I wanted to hide; he'd caught me daydreaming about him! I

couldn't just turn around and walk away like I had the other day after school, which I assumed was the incident for which he wanted an apology.

"You enjoy listening to me," he said as if it meant more than my school-girl attraction.

"You enjoy hearing yourself," I muttered. I turned to face him, bumping a pencil off his desk.

"Damn it Gwyneth!"

I raised my eyebrow. *He* was getting bothered by me? I couldn't see the thoughts running through his eyes, but deep down I knew there were dirty things he wanted to do with me that would probably get us expelled. Deep down, I wanted him to do those things. I bit my bottom lip, thinking about him sucking on it like he did in my dreams. Oh hell, he was right. Yes, I wanted to drag my nails over his skin as he put me on my back and—

"Stop," Jace moaned. He snapped the pencil he'd been holding in half. "Stop thinking whatever you're fantasizing about unless you want me to drag you out of the room and make them come true."

I mouthed, "No."

"Jace," Bree said, gaining his attention.

He sat up in his seat and leaned over to her, slowly taking a note from her. She giggled nervously. I scowled as they flirted with each other. For the first time in my life, I wished I shared just one more class with Ryker because Bree's flirting wouldn't be so obnoxious.

"Can you spare an extra pencil?" Jace whispered to her. "Mine's been decapitated."

She dug in her backpack and handed him one. I tried to ignore them both. They could pass notes to whomever they wanted; I had no claim to Jace and didn't want it. Jace was practically dangling a thread in front of me like I was a kitten, egging me to take it. Slowly but deliberately, I shook my head; I wasn't taking his bait. He chuckled, clearly not believing me. His laugh sounded like a hypnotic gong, ringing in my ears. He leaned forward to slip the note in his back pocket.

Sitting back in his chair, he tapped Bree's paper with his new pencil. He told her the answer to question five was on page seventy-eight, distracting her from our soundless conversation. Clearly he didn't know what was higher on Bree's agenda—flirting with the new guy or finishing homework.

Miss Conner closed the door to the classroom. The tardy bell rang at that precise moment.

"We will be discussing several of Shakespeare's classic tragedies," Miss Conner said. Her voice was high and exasperated. She acted like she'd been forced to teach for thirty-five years instead of it being her chosen profession. Whatever teaching passion Miss Conner thought she had her first few years as an educator had all but vanished at this point in her career.

Leaning forward in his desk, as much as it allowed, Jace brushed my hair away from my neck, which exposed my ear. Heat crept across my neck when he whispered how alluring my fragrance smelled. My pulse raced when a low moan rumbled in his throat.

"Sitting so close to you and not being able to touch you is pure torture," he said and then a searing pain shot down my spine instead of the warm tickle that had been there before.

We continued the hour-long lecture about *Romeo and Juliet* in silence while I tried to fathom in what universe an impromptu torture treatment from a guy would give any sane girl reason to swoon into the arms of said torturer? I couldn't figure out how Jace was making me so physically ill; but the sicko was doing it. I spent the hour trying to keep my legs from cramping. If it wasn't a Charley horse that made me want cry out in pain, it was my pounding headache. By the time I massaged the knots from my neck, back spasms forced me to arch and twist for no reason whatsoever. At least my breakfast decided it wanted to stick around.

Between all that, the nausea, clammy skin, and a headache that had come out of nowhere, I was exhausted and cocooned in sweat. I'd given up on fighting him, deciding that if he wanted to make me suffer, there wasn't anything I could do. I was surrounded by people who couldn't possibly know Jace was the culprit of my current state of health. Even I wouldn't have believed me, if I didn't live through the torment.

Only when I surrendered to him did I relax enough to breathe normally. A serene tingling sensation trickled through me. Since I wanted nothing more than to knock Jace on his back, I knew the tranquility couldn't possibly be mine, but I was simply too tired to fight anymore and was apparently delusional. When the bell sounded, I turned to Bree and informed her that I needed to make an emergency stop at the bathroom before lunch—by myself.

Bree hesitated. "You sure you want to go alone? You don't look the greatest."

"I fell asleep listening to the teacher drone on and had one of those nightmares that you know isn't real but couldn't wake up from," I lied and prayed that she believed me. My foot cramped suddenly. I winced and pretended that Bree hadn't noticed. Jace stood up and walked away. I breathed a sigh of relief that he was finally going to leave me alone. "I just want to clean up a bit before lunch."

I knew she didn't believe me for one second. I pressed my lips together and held my breath, hoping she wouldn't make a big deal in front of everyone. She hesitated but promised she'd save me a seat at lunch.

Waiting long enough for the room to empty, I closed my eyes. Students shuffled out the door after Miss Conner left. I waited for the room's utter silence before I made any attempt to move. If I was going to fall on my face, I would prefer to do it in private. My legs threatened to buckle so I kept my hand on the desk. As soon as I was sure I wouldn't topple over, a smoky aroma drifted around me.

Jace walked up behind me as close as he could without actually touching me. I swore I heard him leave the room! How did he slip back in without me noticing? He brushed my damp hair away from my neck. Apparently sweat didn't bother him in the least.

"You're right. Sitting so close to each other is torture! What kind of sick game are you're playing?"

"I'm not playing a game. Your tolerance is poor. If it were stronger, being in close proximity to me, while I'm in my true form, would have been so much easier, dearest." He spoke like it truly bothered him that I was utterly exhausted.

"In your true form?" I repeated. "And what is that? A silhouette of fire?"

"Fire?"

I knew I shouldn't say anything but... "It hurts to look at you, but I can't look away."

"You are attracted to me because of what I am, what *we* are."

I recalled the comment about immortality mentioned in one of my visions with the nice man who'd ultimately kill me. "What do you think we are? Immortal?" I asked sarcastically.

He swore in a language I didn't recall but was familiar all the same. Instead of answering my question, he edged closer. His hot breath trickled down my neck and onto my chest. Swallowing hard, I faced him. His white silhouette shimmered brighter than I'd ever seen, making my eyes water. I wasn't sure if my legs would hold me, or if my bones would crack under the pressure, but I didn't back down. He didn't either.

Even though I was sure I'd trip or do something else that was just as graceful, I crossed my arms and stood as defiantly as possible, considering my current state of exhaustion. Clenching my jaw, I tried not to notice how every molecule of spit vanished from my mouth when I took a deep breath, taking in his tantalizing scent.

He deliberately put me through hell for an hour, I reminded myself. I pointed at myself. "I'm not desirable."

"I disagree," he moaned.

After dimming himself significantly, he reached for my hair

again. I slapped his hand away. His light flared, but he quickly regained his composure. Grabbing my wrist, he held it and easily blocked my right hook. Twisting my hand in his, he pulled me against him with such excitement that a moan grew in his chest. He silenced it before it escaped his mouth; the mood between us shifted. My irritation turned like he'd flipped a switched. I wanted nothing more, needed nothing more, craved nothing more, than taking in his sight.

And he knew it.

"Your gasp beckons me," he whispered. "You stand against me, refusing to indulge in your desires and temptation, yet your pulse beats loudly enough to deafen my ears. You bat your ocean-eyes whenever you look my way. You flick your hair whenever you catch me staring. Even now you are leaning into me, trying to pinpoint my scent, yet you can't admit that you're attracted to me."

Even though he called me out, the deepness of his voice lured me closer. I couldn't deny any of it, but that didn't mean I wouldn't try. "Fine, I'm attracted to you, but that doesn't mean I want anything to do with you!"

He released his grip but stood close enough to tower over me. His figure brightened slightly when he dropped my hands.

"Lie," he said coolly.

"Oh that's right, you're like this hunk-a-licious dude that has too many muscles to count," I said, doing my best blond impression. "So you're not used to hearing the word no. I get it, but I'm sorry buckaroo; I'm just not into jocks."

He chuckled, "You have yet to tell me to leave you alone."

I groaned in frustration. He made a similar sound but not because he was frustrated.

"Splitting hairs, aren't we?" I said, and then backed away. After picking my backpack up, I walked towards the door. My legs obeyed. I couldn't have been more grateful.

"Turning your back on the truth is the *Master's* signature move, not yours," Jace called out.

Soft green grass tickled my legs I as kneeled. The wind stole seeds from the cottonwood tree canopy above. A small dagger, frosted with ice, glistened in the sunlight. A young girl, no older than twelve or thirteen, with auburn hair glowered over me and tapped her fingernail against the blade, creating a soft crack. She made no attempt to speak as she grabbed my hand, slicing my palm. The cold blade pierced my skin, chilling me to the bone as it vibrated against my flesh. Deep crimson flowed from my cut.

Another beautiful woman sauntered in a circle around me. Her pure white dress rippled slightly in the breeze. She was a few years older, perhaps sixteen or seventeen, but looked like a fallen angel. Her light blond hair skimmed the top of her waistline as it shimmered in the sunlight just like the frost on the dagger. Her angelic laugh rang out in the meadow as she watched me bleed. Her sun-kissed cheeks glowed as she smiled. It was a political gesture, nothing more. The contempt leaked from her golden-colored eyes as they flashed dark black.

"You seek for humans' immortality to end." My voice hung in the air like her laugh. "Playing with fate has consequences not even my sister can always foresee."

"Do it." Her beautiful voice was laced with hate.

The hatred burning in the fallen angel's eyes ripped at my soul. Yet, I agreed to her request. "Then you condemn the Fates."

98

This vision hurt my very soul, like it had just stolen years from my life. The young woman wanted something horrible from me, and I agreed to it. One day I would make a pact with the devil, who looked like an angel—but why? My chest felt like it was tightening around my heart; yet, I didn't understand why it hurt so badly.

I willed my heartbeat to slow. What kind of a person was I to become? I *hated* these visions! What events led up to this? Ugh! It would help *just a little* if I knew who the people were in these visions. Were they friends or foes? The sight of the angelic woman made me want to pick up homicide as a hobby and start with her.

"Who is the *Master*?" I said through clenched teeth.

Jace sniffed the air around me. "Her scent lingers on your skin. You claim that your memories are gone, but you do remember her, don't you? What just happened? Tell me!"

"No! *You* answer *my* question! I'm sick of being in the dark about everything!" I yelled uncontrollably. I was frustrated beyond belief. Jace was right. I *hated* that name and I didn't know why. He did. That pissed me off even more.

"Analee is the Master."

The Rippler. The Healer. The Master. I started to piece together that these people were associated with each other but apparently weren't on a first name basis.

"Is that a call sign you people give each other?"

"Sort of."

"So what is she that master of?" I demanded.

"She is a collector of sorts," he answered, leaving out much needed details.

"Collector of *what*?"

"Of *who*," Jace corrected. "She has many people who do her bidding."

I thought of the young girl in my vision. Did she belong to the Master? "Do you do her bidding?"

"We have different agendas, but we have a common goal. Thus, our cooperation with each other is pertinent."

"You work with a woman who collects people—*slaves?* How could you?"

"So you do remember?" Jace said with an accusatory tone. His frustration eclipsed my fury.

"I remember nothing! I don't recall a moment with you! I don't know how you know these things about me, but it freaks me out! Stop finding reasons to be near me! I don't want anything to do with you!"

I stood still, wishing my angry tears would stay put and not fall down my cheeks. I wished that I knew what was going on. I wished I knew him! Deep down, I trusted that his intentions were good. I knew he cared for me; he didn't even try to hide it. Yet, I knew almost nothing about him. I wasn't this Deino chick he thought I was and a part of me was crushed by knowing that. I wanted to be his...

Chapter Nine

Max barked cheerfully as I got closer to the Thompsons. Distracted by my thoughts, I nearly tripped over a scared, little girl when I walked up the stairs to the front door. Her soft crying should have been a dead giveaway, but my mind was otherwise preoccupied.

"Elsie, is that you?"

More tears.

I sighed but couldn't convince myself to walk away and let her be. Runaways would flee till they felt safe—I knew from personal experience. Since she'd returned to the Thompsons, I assumed that she used to live too far away to walk.

"Scoot over, sweetie," I spoke softly so as not to startle her. "I've had a bad day too."

She sniffled a few times but moved a few inches. Plopping down next to her, I listened to her cry for a bit. Each one of her sobs stung about as much as the new-found scrapes on my hands. Since I still couldn't even handle a pity-pat from my best friend, I assumed Elsie wouldn't find comfort in it coming from a perfect stranger like me. I didn't think she'd want to talk about what was bothering her either, but the silence was eating at me.

"I remember the first night I stayed here," I said, recalling how my own string of nightmares finally ended. I'd be the only participant in the sad little conversation we were about to have, but what I had needed to be said. "I hated John and Martha, and the few other kids staying here at the time. They tried to win me over with candy when I got here, but I already played that game and knew how it ended. They wanted me to trust them, but a Crunch Bar wasn't going to cut it."

Instead of telling her every personal detail, I hit the highlights about how I cried myself to sleep, refused to go to school, and ran away every moment I could, but would only get lost. Once, a police officer found me five blocks away from the house. I'd walked for hours but only managed to make it five measly blocks away. A tear threatened to slip, remembering how alone I felt those first several years of my life. Statistically speaking, I should have been adopted quickly, since I was only a child when I entered the system, but few parents were prepared to take care of a blind child, especially one associated with an ongoing murder case.

Out of the corner of my eye, I saw Elsie's small hand reach for me, but she hesitated. At least she stopped crying. I continued my story. Martha picked me up at the police station but didn't scold me. The trait continued as months crept by. Soon the police stations became farther away, but Martha always picked me up. My voice cracked when I told her that the last time I ran away she got me, brought me home, and made me my favorite meal—spaghetti and meatballs. She never yelled at me. Instead of thanking her for everything, I trashed my room and prepared to leave that night. That was until I walked past her and John's bedroom.

A tear slipped down my cheek. I quickly rubbed it away.

"John was comforting Martha," I said, shutting my eyes because the guilt was still very much alive in my heart. "Martha was hysterical because she knew I would leave again. She knew I hated them. She knew how I felt about living here, how I plotted against them. It made my heart ache, because I never let myself hear how much she'd already loved me."

We sat in silence, listening to the sounds of the leaves rattle in the wind, while I gained control over myself again. I didn't need to say anything more. I wasn't here to promise Elsie a happy life. I just wanted her to know I knew how it felt never to belong.

I don't know how long we sat on the front step as the day drifted by. Soon my guilty memories gave way to the visions I'd foreseen. Images of the old man holding a bloody knife stole my concentration. The one of the beautiful young man ending my life unraveled, the old man growing young, and finally the latest one where I made a pact with a fallen angel.

Rubbing my eyes, I told Elsie that I was going to scavenge the freezer for some premade cookie dough. If she was interested in a snack, she could join me in the living room. Max greeted me like always when I opened the front door. Elsie stayed on the front steps. I refused to force her into our house.

Waiting for the oven to preheat, I massaged my forehead and tried to figure out the mess my life had recently twisted into when I heard a hushed clamor coming from the living room. The breeze seeping through a cracked window rattled the mini blinds. A white silhouetted figure was running from the open window.

***

I woke unexpectedly in a wheat field at daybreak. My head throbbed. At least my stomach wasn't retching. The hard soil did a number on my knees. My hands smashed into the dried grass around me. No flower petals this time. My hair tickled my nose as the wind pushed it around. Cottonwood seeds floated in the air around me, almost invisible in the light.

A rush of regret washed over my soul, but it wasn't an emotion that had come within my achy soul. It was Jace's.

"I can't stay away from you," he whispered. "No matter how hard I try. I'm drawn to you."

He gently moved my hair away from my neck. He muttered something right before his smooth lips caressed my skin. My hesitation vanished. I leaned against him and began to enjoy myself once more. When the thought surfaced again, he flicked his tongue over my skin. I squirmed, which only encouraged him.

"Let go of reality, dearest."

Reality, I reminded myself. This wasn't it. I needed to wake up for sanity's sake. This wasn't real. Soon, I wouldn't know what my subconscious was creating. It was becoming more difficult to know what was impossible and fake. My visions dragged me to the limits of my sanity. Falling for a heartthrob in my dreams, while in reality he was dangerous, both emotionally and physically, was where I would draw the line. I needed to wake up! For my sanity's sake, I couldn't pretend to be Jace's lover, not even in my dreams.

I elbowed him in the gut out of sheer desperation. He didn't flinch. I spun around and connected a right hook. He didn't fight back, so I aimed lower. He blocked me. Grabbing my wrist, he suppressed a chuckle. I tried not to cry out when he twisted my wrist to the point of breaking. Instead of *saying uncle* like I should have, my elbow got familiar with his eye.

"That was unnecessary," he grunted.

Using my free hand, I pounded his stomach, hoping to knock the wind out of him. No shirt—picture my surprise. His hazy outline focused. The muscles became defined. I could see that he simply wore jeans and nothing else. An image flickered in my mind of water dripping down his hair and onto his hard chest. I bit my lip remembering how it felt to be held as water splashed on us in my last dream.

"Indulge in more thoughts like that," he said, as if he could see the fantasies play out in my mind.

I couldn't get the image of the beads of water drizzling down his chest out of my head even when I attacked him. He fought with skill and was fast enough to block all of my charges.

"What are you, some kind of gladiator?" I asked.

"Not anymore."

He slowly released his grip like he didn't trust me not to hit below the belt. Smart guy! He didn't move, so I stood up and walked away. My body begged me not to. I wanted nothing more than to lose myself in another dream like this, but I couldn't. As precarious as

Jace was, I was losing a grip on what was real. It didn't seem like a good idea. My reality was making less sense, so losing myself in my dreams was dangerous on another level entirely…especially since I was considering that immortality may actually be possible.

A half a second later, Jace was walking through the wheat field beside me. My skin burned as he reached for my hand. I turned hastily. He changed course and followed me.

"Running again, dearest? You left me several lifetimes ago, and I'm still chasing you. There's no point in making this difficult when it doesn't have to be."

I stopped and turned to him. Small colorless flames rippled from his skin. My skin prickled as they grew more intense. My mouth dried. Smoke floated around us. If charisma, raw hunger, and undying lust could be wrapped up into one hot package, it'd be called Jace. A part of me didn't care if I got burned—which was exactly why I didn't let myself indulge in the temptation he was offering.

He was in front of me before I could blink. His hot hands were on my shoulders, holding me still. Even in my sleep I couldn't evade him—and I didn't want to. I fought an internal battle with wanting Jace to steal me from my pathetic life and to run away from him. The closer he was, the more often he touched me, the more my mouth watered for him to kiss me. He was like a drug—addictive. And like drugs, he had to have dangerous repercussions.

The smoke grew, threatening to block out the beginning of dawn. Flames leaped from his skin to mine. Just as quickly as his touch burned me, I wanted more. It hurt, but as painful as it was to get burned from the fire creeping over us; it left no evidence of damaged skin. Either his fire wasn't hazardous, which I doubted, or he healed me faster than his flames hurt me.

I hadn't understood how it was possible. But then again, most dreams never made sense. *A dream. This wasn't reality.* I needed to remember that. Instead of embracing him, I slammed my fist into his gut. He never released his grip on my shoulders. His fire engulfed us. Smoke blocked out everything but his face, which started to define around the edges. Even with the intense heat, I couldn't look away. Tears gathered and trickled down my cheeks. Within their dark color, a flicker grew. His eyes trapped a single colorless flame. It was impossible and beautiful. The more rigid his body became as he pressed himself against me, the hotter I burned for him.

"The chase," he said as his hand slid up my back and behind my head. "The chase has tormented me for the better part of my existence, but it doesn't hold a flame to what you are doing now."

"What am I doing now?" I asked, squirming in his grip even though I didn't want to be anywhere else. I hungered for his touch just as I refused to admit the sinful appetite he brought out in me.

"Fighting—I always wanted, prayed even, for you to find a little bit of fight in you, and now that you do it makes my blood boil." His voice rose the longer he spoke. His anger was evident. "Not because it doesn't please me to see defiance grow in you, but because you insist on *fighting me*! For heaven's sake, stop it. *I'm* not your enemy!"

His words bred frustration when combined with his body language. He slid his trembling hand down my side and then around my back. He abruptly pulled me up against him just as he gently slid his other hand under my jaw. He leaned into me like he was going to give me another taste of his kiss.

107

"Every past experience could've been prevented if you had any fight, any fight at all! But no, you preferred to be passive, which cost us immortals dearly!"

He stepped away from me like he suddenly couldn't stand to be anywhere close to me. Seeing him engulfed in his horrific, beautiful fire did me in. The morning sun couldn't warm my skin the way Jace could. Now I never felt colder or more alone...

"Jace, stop!"

He didn't. I needed to say something, anything to keep him from leaving. I hadn't known why he was so angry. How could he be so adamant about us being together, yet walk away?

"Don't leave me!" I yelled.

"I screamed that very line to the heavens for years, but you never answered my pleas."

Chapter Ten

I knocked on Elsie's door. It was next to mine at the Thompsons. Martha had gotten Elsie to write her name on a piece of paper and tape it to her door. She'd done the same with me years ago.

"May I come in?"

Instead of a reply, she opened it for me. I handed her the beater. After a quick inspection, she shoved it in her mouth. Her window was open.

"Thinking about your escape plan?" I asked. When she didn't reply, I figured I'd give some advice. I leaned on the windowsill. I recalled when this was my room. It was smaller than I remembered. "Honestly, if you need a quick escape, my window is right in front of the tree house. If you're not afraid of heights, you can jump from the ledge and onto the tree branch. It groans, but I haven't broken it yet, and I'm bigger than you."

109

"Why are you telling me this?"

I smiled. "You aren't a prisoner here."

"You don't think I'll do it," Elsie said, like she wanted me to challenge her.

I turned to look out the window. "Running away is a hard life, Elsie. It's not so bad here. John and Martha are lame sometimes, but they're family."

"How about me—do you consider me *family*?" Her voice cracked on the last word.

I glanced back at her. I wasn't sure where we were going to stand in the future. People were born into a family or came together by chance. Not knowing how long Elsie would stay, I knew I shouldn't get attached to the girl, but I couldn't help it. I looked back out her window and then offered my hand. A few moments later, her small hand slipped through mine.

***

The smell of aged paper and worn covers greeted me after I crossed the library's threshold. The first time John took me to check out their blind peeps selection was ages ago. Yet, every time I pushed through the heavy wooden door, the laws of the metaphysical world shifted like I'd wandered into an unguarded room of heaven. Hector was a saver of old books and refused to throw any away—no matter how worn or beaten.

Hector instantly took to me, offering to read any book if he couldn't find in an audio or Braille version. His passions soon became mine. It wasn't long before I acted like his shadow, following him to KnockOuts. He changed my life, showing me how easy living could be if I simply let it be. It wasn't as hard to let go of all my hurt knowing he was there watching over me like a big brother.

Originally a bank, the two-story library only had few windows to let in natural light. However, I could maneuver around without problems from all the time I'd spent between the shelves. I folded Stella and slipped it into my backpack. I listened. Only my footsteps echoed through the old building. Architecture from the early 1900's tended to creep me out, making me feel like I was being watched by ghosts or another supernatural force that was just as farfetched.

"Hey Hector!" I called out.

"You have the wrong guy, sweet cheeks."

I jumped; I hadn't heard anyone moving in the building and hadn't expected a stranger to be wandering around. My sight was acting up and now my hearing was no longer reliable. I should have been able to hear him. Turning toward the direction of the voice, I peered around the oldest shelf in the building. The mammoth dark shadow, who had a nervous twitch, flipped through a book. From the rate at which Marco was tossing the light gray pages across, he couldn't have been reading.

"So as soon as I demanded that Jace leave me the hell alone, he promotes you to Head Stalker?" I said, hoping to come off as confident. Secretly, I was paranoid he'd bust out his *Hulk* moves and pummel me into the floorboards. I don't care what Jace said, I know more happened that night at Strikers than he'd have me believe. "If you had any manners at all, you'd apologize for body slamming me when we first met."

Marco laughed, "The first time we met, there was more remarkable weaponry at hand. Regardless, there has been and will be few apologies between us."

Well, at least he wasn't being confusing at all.

"You kicked Jace to the curb again?" Marco asked casually.

"He didn't tell you we had a fight?" I asked, a little surprised that our fight wasn't common knowledge.

"He doesn't report to me."

"Oh that's right. He's teamed up with the Master," I said, not bothering to hide my hatred for the women I never met.

"Listen, I get that you're making Jace work hard to get back in your good graces, but he is a lady's man. Eye candy. A stud-muffin. I could go on all night, rattling off the many names you women have used to describe the Healer, but repeating them is making me second-guess my masculinity. Eventually, he'll get sick of hearing you tell him no, even if it's from your pretty lips. He will move on, I assure you of that."

"Is he interested in someone else?"

"There's always someone who's been interested in him."

The sun shone through a charred knot hole, no bigger than my slender finger. It was the only light in the enclosed, narrow box holding me captive. My hands were smooth and polished, not gnarled or wrinkled; I had years of life ahead of me so why was I buried alive? Sweat formed beads on my brow. They dripped down my face. A pungent stench choked my lungs as the heat rose inside my coffin.

Death and decay grew stronger as a set of shuffling feet skimmed the top of the wood. A spicy aroma, his fragrance, intertwined with the rot, took over my senses. I heard two feminine screams. One echoed in my mind while the other cursed out loud. I peered out the tiny hole and caught a glimpse of my captor in her white dress—the girl who looked like a fallen angel—the Master. Her unforgettable golden-colored eyes flickered black, as she smiled down at me. Her beautiful voice beckoned, enticing me out of my personal cell if I'd only swear to bow down to her.

"You'll regret this, Chronicler. This is positively unnecessary. You'll give me my wish if I have to kill you for it to be granted, and you know I will," the Master said, and brushed back her silky blond hair.

"My death is insignificant compared to what you're asking." My voice was as innocent as hers.

A massive man with deep red hair appeared behind her, when nothing but empty space was there a second before. He kissed her lightly-tanned cheek before paying any attention to me. His green eyes deepened in color until they were just as black as the woman's eyes. While his eyes shifted colors, his rotting stench grew stronger. He smelled like death.

"If you don't, I'll kill your sisters," the Master said. "Or do you so easily forget their humanity grows when you are separated? You're not just putting your life on the line. You'll sacrifice your sisters as well by denying my request."

"Only when I can't hear their screams will they be far enough away to die a human's death," I said. "It'll take days to accomplish."

She laughed. "Oh, but you haven't met my latest consort, Chronicler. Show her your craft."

The massive man disappeared from behind her. A moment later, the girls' screams were silent. Frantically, I searched out my peep hole to look for them when his face instantly appeared. His blackened eyes sent chills down my spine. His head jerked slightly as his smirk grew.

"Reaper," I stated. "We've met."

"Your Healer will never get here in time. I'll kill them before he can get here to save you all. If you don't give the Master what she wants, I'll see to it that your Scavengers will die with you."

"She only pays attention to you because you have something she wants right now, Reaper."

"Lies," he said, and spat in my face. The putrid acid burned my face. I wanted to cry out but refused to give them the satisfaction. "Do it now, or you'll bathe in their blood."

"Remember what happened last time you played with fate?" I called out to the fallen angel. "My sisters and I foresee humanity's fate as well as deities'. The string of our life is tied to theirs, thus, when they started to age, so will the Fates. When my sisters and I parted ways, our bodies aged. Together we became immortal again and stopped aging. But it had a nasty little side-effect to the rest of the deities, didn't it? It made immortals killable, even if you didn't start to age like my sisters and I."

"Your point?" the Master asked, trying to sound bored.

"My point is, when the hunters found out they could live longer, and grow young, if they killed a deity, it made you not only vulnerable, but your wish gave our half-breed offspring a reason to hunt us down," I said.

"The past is the past. There's nothing I can do to change it. Break the bond completely with the humans or break the bond with the Scavengers," she demanded. "It's up to you."

"You seek humanity's chaos, destruction, and fatality if that bond is broken. Without purpose they will become no better than animals."

"Your choice, Chronicler," she hissed. "Humans or Scavengers."

I chose. A tear trickled down my cheek. She laughed; to weep was a sign of weakness while I saw it as a beautiful truth… no matter how agonizing. A moment later, my soul unraveled. While I beat against the burnt wood, the essence composing my very being separated itself. The coffin's top popped off. I rolled out of the wooden box and onto the ground. I scratched at the soil, needing to apologize for not being strong. A white, transparent hand, clawed at the earth below me, as if it was furiously trying to come to my aid. I gripped his hand, wishing for the strength to hold onto her soul. She embodied the other part of my soul. She clutched my soft hands in her hard, calloused ones. There wasn't enough time—I felt myself tearing in half. The two parts of my soul, the creation of life and death, which were never meant to divide, did. Images of hundreds of mouthless corpses were torn from my heart; they no longer answered to me in a matter of seconds. My Scavengers, howled out with hopelessness.

Not a squeal left my mouth as the dirt engulfed her, locking it away from me. My torn soul silenced me. Tears bled from my eyes as I gave the Master my Scavengers—the world's unspeakable past, or death as humans perceived it. Analee's muffled laugh ripped through my damaged soul when I felt them bow to her.

Tears formed in my eyes when the vision flickered away. Swallowing hard, I willed myself to forget the misery that frayed my soul. My body trembled. My eyes stung like I'd spent years mourning this loss even though I'd not yet lived this moment. I wanted to cry until I realized I was in the library—standing in front of a stranger.

I suppressed my tears and promised to give myself time to grieve in private. Forcing myself back into the conversation with

115

Marco, I took a deep breath. That's when I recalled his scent—it was from the vision. I studied his general shape and size. Considering his unforgettable scent and nervous twitch, he had to be the man in my vision—a mammoth of a man, dark green eyes, and deep red hair.

At least I knew that we weren't destined to be BFF's.

Wiping the sweat glazing my forehead, I leaned against the bookshelf. Its rough surface felt entirely too similar to the scalded coffin I couldn't forget and the hand of the corpse I never wanted to let go of. Standing upright, I bit into my tongue, forcing myself to think clearly.

"Do your green eyes always bleed black?" I asked.

He advanced soundlessly toward me. "I *Muted* myself for you, missy. It's a tactic we use if we don't want to make humans *Addicts*."

The simple, impractical answer confirmed my suspicion that Marco was the man I'd just seen in my vision.

"So you're working for the Master too?" I said more than asked. These people made me sick working with someone so evil.

"I'll do what is necessary to find all three Fates," he said, advancing to me. "And the thing is, Jace is right. It will be easier to find the other two with you in our possession."

His scent became more pronounced when he came closer. Marco's voice calmed me in a similar manner that Jace's had, but I didn't understand a word. When I did not react, his shadow lightened. It was in perfect coloration to the pounding headache. It wasn't nearly as excruciating as what Jace put me through last week but still wasn't pleasant. He stopped a few feet from me. His light shadow became dark once more. My head stopped throbbing immediately.

"I just wanted to make sure Jace's opinion of your tolerance threshold matched mine," Marco muttered like it explained his change in appearance. "It's not my place to build you up. Leave that up to Jace, the *Healer.* With my dumb luck, I'd give you a stroke or an equally fatal injury. You chalk that up to another human Analee can add to her collection of death."

I closed my eyes to test a theory. He didn't have a smoky haze like Jace, but a silver outline wavered in his place. Instead of reflecting light, the silver seemed to absorb light. No wonder I had trouble seeing him from a distance with my eyes closed. Ironic that a giant like Marco would be nearly invisible. At least I'd be able to spot people like Jace and Marco. It was a consolation prize, but they were clearly different from the rest of the human race.

"You don't look like Jace."

"You don't look exactly like the Fate I remember either, but here you are and here I am, both not looking like we should."

That made perfect sense. Not.

"How many of you people are there?" I said, wondering if Jace and Marco were the ones spying on me from my yard.

"Enough."

"Can you answer one question without me wanting to bang my head against the wall?"

"Probably not without being dragged to Hades by dirt

crawlers. Pesky *Oath* and all that," he said and then tossed me the book he'd been flipping through.

Its starved body was bruised and beaten as it crawled out of the dried ground. Every vein, blood vessel, and artery pulsating deep purple, showed on its hairless head. Its translucent skin was pulled tight, especially over the joints. It smelled clean and crisp like the sea even though the few shreds of clothing covering it were stained. The sewn marks over his mouth kept him from whispering of the unspeakable past. Empty hollows were where the eyes should have been.

It walked to me. Instead of running, I opened my arms to embrace it. Its ghostly skin was razor sharp but never cut me. It brought my hand to its mouthless face. When my smallest finger brushed against its coarse lips, I felt at home again. The walking corpse wiped a fleeting tear from my eye. In my mind, I heard it speak in a mysterious language. Even though I didn't understand it, a sense of immense sorrow washed over me when it released my hand and turned its back to me. I trembled as I watched it sink into the dirt.

It'd been stolen from me by the fallen angel.

Rage.Exploded.In.My.Heart. I gritted my teeth and breathed through my nose. The ugly monster was a part of me but I loved it unconditionally. There are awful, horrible, ugly parts in everyone but that doesn't make them a bad person. That horrid creature, that Scavenger, was a part of me. I knew in the depth of my soul that it had been ripped from me. The feeling of pure emptiness residing in my heart was because it was gone.

I unclenched my fists and tried to calm my nerves. I peeled open my eyes and the first thing I saw was the book Marco had thrown. I gently picked it up, but it practically fell apart in my hands. The paper felt like tissue and was definitely not a Braille version. I sniffed it. It's spicy smell made me think of both Marco and death.

Chapter Eleven

The moon's light shone through my open window, illuminating a light silhouette. A young man sat on the edge of my windowsill. Hoping that I'd imaged it, I blinked a couple of times. The two people I'd seen outside the windows earlier couldn't have been by chance. I was constantly being watched, but by friend or foe? My heart skipped a beat as his familiar warmth passed over me, which calmed me, but was accompanied by his anger too. It prickled my skin. I closed my eyes. Jace's clearly defined outline stretched around him as it poured like smoke into my room.

"You cry in your sleep," Jace whispered.

I sat up and nonchalantly covered my pillow. The feathers had absorbed my tears. Times like today, it would have been easier if I were in a coffin next to my family.

Jace whispered my name so softly it felt like he'd caressed my soul with his voice. "You've been screaming to the heavens for years

119

too, haven't you?"

I clenched my teeth, willing my swollen eyes not to flood with more pointless tears. I buried my own suffering deep in my soul. He acted like he had known me when we'd only just met a month ago. He hadn't earned the privilege of seeing me cry about lost loved ones. As often as he picked up on the feelings I'd broadcasted, I hoped he didn't acknowledge the grief still alive in my broken heart. The sense of loss had consumed my life for as long as I could remember.

He moved from the windowsill like he was going to comfort me when the floor creaked by my bedroom door. I tore my gaze away from Jace for a split second to look at the door. After I saw Elsie's dark shadow, I looked back at the windowsill that Jace had been perched on. The window was now closed; Jace was gone.

"Were you talking to someone?" Elsie asked.

"Only in my sleep," I admitted and turned my pillow over to hide my misery from a girl who had no family.

***

The tantalizing smell of taverns made from yesterday's spaghetti sauce was the lunch special. I scanned the assortment of dark shadows until I spotted Bree sitting at our usual table in the far corner. Ryker was nowhere to be seen, so I took it as a hopeful sign he developed malaria or some other disease and had to drop out of school. I'd even settle for mono, because then I'd be rid of him for a couple weeks.

"I got you some grub," Bree said, pushing a tray of steaming food toward me.

120

"Where's your boyfriend?" I asked.

"He went off campus with the team to grab a slice of pepperoni pizza. Apparently, this slop isn't edible for football players. Why do you ask?"

"I have a proposition for you," I said. "It'll involve a double date with you and Ryker. You'll have to find me a date and I swear I'll die if it's Jace."

"I can't invite scar-face as your evening companion?"

"Scar face?"

"Yeah, Mr. Right has this thin scar under his left eye; Jace is totally dark and secretive about it," Bree said, distantly, like she was picturing Jace beating up a gang of ninjas that robbed a bank on Valentine's Day. "And I heard he's rich, like loaded so he could buy you things all the time. Sorry, what part of the deal do I have to uphold?"

"I need you to read something for me." I pulled the worn book Marco tossed me from my back pack. I lied, "I'm getting some extra-credit if I do an essay paper for my history class. But, it's sort of hush-hush."

"Fine," Bree said. "But only if there is a *ten page maximum* clause. I'm not going to spend the entire lunch break with my nose in a textbook."

I handed her the book Marco had tossed me. If the book had a title or a copyright date, it had long been rubbed off.

"*Nephilims.*" She read the title before cracking it open.

121

"There's a disclaimer. It says, and I quote, anyone who reads this cannot utter a word about the immortal truth, or they shall find themselves in the poor company of the Reaper himself... Winnie, what kind of a paper were you planning to write?"

"One he's never read before."

Bree read, "Greek mythology told a tale of an immortal race—a group of gods and goddess. Ireland called them fairies. England thought of them as part of the Nephilim race. Conversely, they prefer to address themselves as *deities* rather than immortals or the undead."

"So a deity is a *god*?" I asked, clarifying what Bree had read. I remembered my vision before I died. I talked about immortality to my would-be killer.

"Gods and goddesses are just folklore," Bree said. "It's not like they are actually living beings. Regardless of heritage, their source of power was thought to flow from Elysia. The Elysian in their blood separates them from humans. They're killable, although it comes with much effort. They're the survivors of history itself. Wars, plagues and treachery repeat; yet, this race had survived it all. Stories have been exaggerated throughout the ages, especially about their supernatural powers and unimaginable riches, but one tale has been repeated for ages and appears to hold some truth. If an offspring of a human and deity spills Elysian blood, the offspring will grow young instead of old. They're notoriously known as *Hunters*."

"So these Hunters are deity hybrids?" I questioned. I remembered Marco wondering if Patrick was a Hunter. If they were sworn enemies it made *a little* sense why Marco wanted him dead.

"Appears so—it says that the most heinous murders in history was the slaughtering of countless souls in hopes to shed Elysian blood. The Hunters gain one human lifetime for every deity they kill."

I clarified, "So they kill these deities to become ageless?"

"Looks like the Hunters are trying to become immortal like the deities but have to keep killing in order to stay young. I bet the deities don't bump uglies with humans anymore because they basically were creating their own worst enemy in doing so. It also says that humans are attracted to deities. The words are almost gone, but it says that if a human spends too much time with an immortal they will become *Addicts*."

"Sex slaves?"

Bree shrugged her shoulders. "I guess so, but I can't read more into it. The words are completely rubbed away."

"What else does it say?"

"Their immortality rested with three Fate sisters. Rumors state that they were the unsung queens of the deity race and human race as well. The sisters' immortality sealed the deities' immortality. However, their destiny would ride on the hinges of the human race. When the Fate sisters were together, they were ageless—immortal. When they were apart, their human mortality aged them. Because of their Fate connection, this once unstoppable race was inevitably hunted down and killed by their offspring. Those who survived eventually faded from existence when the Fate sisters aged and died...*That sucks*," Bree said, pausing from the passage she read.

"So all the Fates died?" I questioned.

"Appears so," Bree said and continued to read. "It was said that the Fate, the *Chronicler*, the sister with the unseeing eye was their true leader and commanded the nameless *Scavengers*—soul binders…or eaters, I can't really make out the word."

I clenched my hand. The mention of them, the Scavengers instantly made me guilt stricken. It was even more so than when I first met Jace. It overcame my ability to think or breath. I wanted to die…maybe then I'd be reunited with the other part of my soul.

I couldn't believe I was even considering this…

"…the Chronicler was able to change the course of a human's or deity's fate by manipulating their thread of life. Chaos and greed would flourish, as predicted by the mute sister—the *Prophet*. She preferred to play with the fate of groups, rather than individuals. She determined the length of life, not only for her people but of all races. The sister who ends life would eventually sacrifice her own—the *Cutter*. She was thought to live on after her two sisters died, hopping from body to body. She confides with guardian angels, if such a thing even exists."

"This is twisted." I leaned back in my chair. Since Jace, Marco and their deity friends thought I was one of the Fates, I was in serious trouble.

"What else does it say about the Chronicler?" I asked, hoping that no one would overhear our dinner conversation about the supernatural.

"That reincarnation is real. She'd come back and be reborn as she once was. She would avenge the Scavengers that were taken from

124

her if she is able to defeat the deity who ripped them from her soul…Winnie, this is some deep stuff."

I lied again, hoping that all these lies wouldn't catch up with me. "It's complex, which is probably why it's extra credit."

"It mentions an *Oath* the deities took but much of the description is water stained."

"Read me what you can," I pleaded.

"That they must seek out the Fates or the Scavengers will eat their souls," Bree said and then shuddered. "There's more. It says that if the Chronicler, the unseeing sister, is captured. She must grant her vanquisher what their heart most desires, but only if they are willing to kill her for it."

Chapter Twelve

My visions had officially reached an unreliable state. Jace quite literally thought he was a deity—a god. And that I didn't consider the entire notion of a Nephilim race completely absurd was a testament to my insane life. Nothing made any sense, especially not my affection to the Scavengers that looked like bringers of death. Whatever the future held, it scared the living daylights out of me. Normal teenagers didn't worry about the uncontrollable future and potential kidnappers. Needing to get away, I figured I could find some comfort at KnockOuts. Hector would know what to do; I just needed to find a way to tell him without sounding like a complete lunatic.

"Hector had an emergency and couldn't make it, Winnie," Charlie said when I pushed through the glass doors.

I left a message on his phone asking why he was MIA lately and hung up. As much as I wanted my "big brother" around, I could still beat away my problems on a punching bag.

I found my way to a full-sized punching bag without much thought. Out of sheer habit, my legs carried me where I needed to go. The worn leather grazed my fingertips when I slipped on my gloves. I grinned. I rolled my neck and loosened my arms and legs. Standing lightly on my toes, I reeled around my bag. Jabs, uppercuts, and hooks, it dissipated the tension in my shoulders. Sweat drizzled down my arms and legs. Punch after kick after jab, I drowned in a boxing haze while my brain did its own thing.

Reoccurring images of a crystal clear blue sea penetrated my consciousness. If I concentrated on the salty fragrance lingering in the wind, I could hold the vision longer and analyze it. I mutilated the punching bag, while losing myself in the sand shifting through my toes. A gentle, warm breeze blew my cream-colored dress while the sun did its best to incinerate me. Kicking into the punching bag, I could almost feel the sun tan my skin. Flying in the deep blue sky, birds sang melody after melody. Their songs reminded me of a language I didn't quite recognize.

After my arms were too tired to lift, I slammed my legs against the leather. I beat the leather until the scent of burnt wood and ash lingered with the stale sweat smells of the gym. My unwanted company decided to join me.

"Jace," I said, acknowledging his presence without turning around to face him. I didn't dare. A lump had already formed in the back of my throat. I wished that I wasn't so damn turned on by him! "I thought we'd decided not to be all up in each other's business."

"Actually you just yelled a lot and said things you didn't mean," Jace retorted. "So, what's it like being a blind freak?"

"Call me that again, I dare you," I warned, whirling around to face his arrogant self.

His silhouette radiated white, illuminating everything around him. His blaze grew like a fire, encouraging my tears to flow. Unable to take him all in, I closed my eyes. His hazy outline filled my vision. He threw his jacket along the wall after shrugging it off. His thin shirt—hopefully he wore a shirt—delineated his lean upper body. He had the kind of a stomach that made me want to give up on working out altogether and just start eating my way into a super-sized grave. Hanging onto the punching bag next to me, he grabbed a chain connecting the bag to the rafters. His jeans looked like they were sewn around his wash-board abs.

"Freak," he whispered.

I charged. He dodged faster than humanly possible and was behind me before my eyes could follow.

He chuckled, "All bark and no bite, dearest? I thought you were a fighter."

Relying on my hearing, I focused on the sound of his shoes squeaking over the gym's rubber floor. Estimating he was about five paces away, I spun around, charged him, and aimed low. My fist grazed his side before he moved around me again.

Laughing, he closed his fists around my gloves that were currently drilling into his stomach as fast as I could throw them.

"Done fighting me yet?" he asked.

I answered soundlessly by kneeing him in the groin. He grunted—or suppressed a laugh—I wasn't exactly sure since his voice distracted me. He dropped and then swung his legs out under me, knocking me on my back. The air fled from my lungs. By the time I was able to suck in a breath, Jace was lying a couple feet from me. I groaned. He'd propped himself up with his elbow and was seductively tracing the mat with his finger. I'd never imagined how an unattainable boy model would look before, but I'd gotten the impression that Jace could pull it off effortlessly. Perhaps in another life he'd been an underwear model.

"You don't want to start this again, Gwyneth," he advised. The scent of scorched wood rolling off his skin guaranteed that I'd get burned but would love each second. "There may come a day when you can hold your own, but today isn't it. Stop fighting *me*."

My heart trembled erratically, yearning for him never to stop speaking. Again the need to lick his words off his lips as he spoke invaded my mind. "Then stop stalking me!"

"Stalking sounds so ominous," Jace said lighthearted. "I prefer to see it as me offering you protection, from a distance, and often from an unknown location."

"Care to tell me why you and the Rippler broke into my home? I found the window opened," I said, passively informing him that I wasn't a complete idiot and knew that two white figures had been conducting surveillance on me.

He said nothing, analyzing my question like it had different meaning. Ever so slyly, he sniffed the air around me. I wanted to tell him that it was called sweat, and it might not be the most lovely body odor in the world but tended to happen in a gym. Before I commented, a thread of made-up curse words echoed in my ears. He slammed his fist into the mat. I trembled as the floor shook for several moments afterward. An electrical charge prickled over my skin like an aftershock—like a warning of sorts.

"Your location's no longer a secret," Jace muttered. "Ashwick is not safe for you."

"Why? Because Hunters are on a killing spree or your friends think I'm the Chronicler?"

"Because the Master assured me no one but Marco and I knew of your location. If he knows, the others know too."

"News flash! Analee sent him."

"She'd do many things but put you in jeopardy is not one of them, unless *she's* the one putting you in harm's way."

"Meaning kill me *she* wants to be the one to kill me in order to get what she most desires."

He cocked his head to the side. "You're remembering."

I wanted to tell him that Marco had damn near sat down and explained everything to me, but I kept my mouth shut. He had his secrets; I could very well have mine.

"Regardless, we need to leave town," he said desperately.

"Fat chance I'm going anywhere with you!" I jeered and pushed away to make a dramatic exit.

"I'm not done with you just yet," Jace said, patting the mat.

The electrical trickle crawling over my skin intensified into a surge. The sensation of my bones gradually being split apart pulsated through my body with each surge he caused. I toppled back down.

"Stop doing that!"

"Then give me the time I deserve, calm down, and stop
fighting me, so I can protect you before you end up six feet under!"
He yelled. "Regardless if you are the Chronicler or not, people are
looking for you, and they will kill you without hesitation. There have
been countless human casualties and your death will be no more life-
changing than the rest of them. So do you want to look over your
shoulder ever second of every day or will you freaking let me do what
I promised and protect you already?"

The ringing in my ears escalated, drowning out everything
except his voice. Everything around me went utterly dark. Panicking
that he'd actually stole my sight; I looked to where I'd last seen him.
His blazing abyss was there, making me nauseous. Flickers of
shimmering colorless flares wiped across his white skin. I gave my
well-practiced *back-off glare* since my voice box had decided to take
five. My threatening scream came out as a pathetic squeak. I felt him
smirking at my pitiful defiance. Jace chuckled softly, confirming his
sick sense of humor. Even when he laughed he still managed to
sound imposing…or maybe his commanding characteristics seemed
so much more threatening because he had basically tasered me
without so much as lifting a few fingers.

"You're making this complicated when it isn't necessary,
Gwyneth," Jace insisted.

Just as quickly as he took away my sight, the usual gray
shadows of objects once again filled my vision. The distant ringing
plummeted, and once again I could hear everything like normal. Jace
weakened himself—Muted himself, just like Marco had. He was no
longer flickering, just shining bright—nauseatingly bright. It only
took me a moment to realize why he returned my senses. Footsteps

squished along the outer edge of the gym's rubber floor and quickly became louder.

"Everything okay over here?" Charlie asked. His dark, burly shadow was a sight for my sore eyes—literally. They itched like they were sun-burnt after Jace returned my senses back. I tucked my hands under my back so I couldn't be tempted to cover them. "Unless it's supervised, guys and gals don't fight."

"My apologies," Jace said smoothly. "But we weren't really fighting. It's more like intense flirting."

Jace had a death wish.

"Flirting?" I scoffed.

"You could do better than this punk, Winnie," Charlie said. "It's almost quitting time. So it's probably best if you grab your things and call it a day."

Gritting my teeth, I maneuvered my lips into a forced smile and tried to convey that everything was all right. As soon as Charlie rounded the corner, I rolled over and buried my face onto the mat. My cheeks flared hot. Counting to ten, I pressed my palms on my eyes in a poor attempt to block out everything. Sweat dripped from my brow. The salty fluid stung as it seeped into my palms. The cuts I had endured from sliding onto the sidewalk had yet to fully heal. If that weren't enough, my stomach twisted into knots. Jace was still prodding me, seeing how much I could handle.

I couldn't figure out what was more infuriating—that his mission in life was to pester me or that I was beginning not to hate it. Overshadowed by the initial disapproval, my infatuation with the title of his *girlfriend* filled me with unexplainable delight.

132

"Intense flirting?" I asked.

Jace shrugged his shoulders and resumed his previous position as the glorified model sprawled out on the mat. Being that my expertise with the male species was unfortunately unpracticed, I treaded carefully. The Unknown Territory of Man-land was Bree's specialty, not mine.

When a deep moan escaped Jace's chest, a clasp closed around my throat. The mat sank under the weight of his body as he slid closer. The burning in my cheeks had returned, and my heart beat like I was in mid-sprint.

"You are not safe here. Too many people with too many different agendas are looking for you here. And if they know anything about our past, they know if they find me, you wouldn't be very far away."

"So you are to blame for making me a target."

He swore under his breath. Granted it was in a language I didn't understand, but he was clearly displeased. "You are making this difficult when it doesn't have to be. Please just trust me when I say I don't want you do die in my arms."

I excelled at being difficult. He was going to learn real fast just how difficult I could be. "And what is your agenda or are you too concerned with pleasing the Master that you've forgotten what is truly important?"

A fiery blaze shot around him. The fine lines, definition of his body that only used to become visible when I closed my eyes now created an entirely different picture in white glory. Intense pressure hit my eyes. The back of my skull felt like it was ripping apart. Flames skimmed his body, blanketing him in a white abyss. His shoulders melted away from the white orb to those of a young man's I'd seen somewhere but couldn't quite place. Muscles grew from his once shapeless arms, chest, and torso. The inferno growing over him blocked out much of the detail of his face.

"You're right. If I hadn't sworn the Oath, I would have returned you to your home the moment I laid eyes on you." He vigilantly wiped the damp hair away from my face. "You deserve to visit a place without suffering. You deserve to see *Elysia*."

Love poured from his words but hinted of remorse too. A warning of what once was, as well as the unknown future, was woven throughout his adoration. My cheeks burned from his touch. He awakened a lost reminiscence hiding within me. Watching his body ignite awakened a passion I couldn't deny.

A red haze clouded my vision. Dark tears, blood, leaked from my eyes. "What's happening?"

"I am returning some of your Elysian so that you may catch your first glimpse of home."

Copper filled my mouth. I wanted to scream that this place tasted like death, but my tongue refused to work. He wiped the tears from my cheek. He inspected the liquid. Something about it pleased him. Rubbing the dark liquid between his thumb and forefinger, he turned his focus on me.

"My body is aged, and my soul is broken," I whispered, like it was a phrase in a song. I frowned, wondering why I'd just said that. I didn't usually speak in riddles, especially ones that didn't make sense to me.

"So give me a taste of your kiss, and let me be reborn into a life of eternal passion." Jace said, speaking in the same melody. He rested his chin on my forehead and rocked me. My skin started to prickle with hope. "You're in there somewhere, hiding from yourself, aren't you, dearest?"

My eardrums crackled. He silenced the ringing after caressing my ear and drew back blood. Placing his palms over my ears, he recited a verse in his strange language. His deep, methodical voice promised that he'd keep me safe even though I was to endure suffering. His words caressed my soul just as they tortured my body. The flickers of colorless fire intensified, consuming us as he embraced me.

"I'm not anybody important, Jace," I whispered. I needed to tell him the truth. He deserved that much. "I'm not Deino."

"I believe your sisters would disagree with you."

My body blistered apart like I was being burned alive, but I couldn't move, couldn't blink, and couldn't inhale. Jace held me. I was his prisoner. I was unable to do anything while gawking at his daunting, yet beautifully unattainable, sight. I looked where his eyes should have been—utter colorlessness beckoned me.

"Forgive me for all the lost years," he said as I let go of consciousness.

Chapter Thirteen

The morning sun greeted me. I sat up. Dew had collected on the grass around me as well as coated my pajamas. My body was cold, and my mind was groggy. I'd awaken in my back yard. For the life of me, I couldn't recall any dream with Jace.

There was only a place, a place I could hardly fathom. It was what I would describe as heaven. Colors undetectable to the human eye bombarded my sight. Fragrances of flowers I'd never smelled flourished. The melody of a song I'd long forgotten echoed in my ears. It was a place of absolute peace. It was difficult to return to wake, squinting at the glaringly bright sun, but it was even worse to hear the sniffles of a child.

Elsie was in front of me sitting cross legged. "Were you running away?"

"No," I promised, wishing she'd stop crying. I wish she'd believe that I wasn't going to leave her. "Sometimes I sleep walk."

I reached for her hand. She led me in the back door. She'd taken to guiding me around the house. I didn't have the heart to tell her that I could rattle off how many steps it was from the garage door to the fridge, how many paces it took to get from my dining table seat to the bathroom and then to the couch. I knew exactly how many steps it took for me to walk from the front door to my bedroom. I knew that the seventeenth step on the stairs groaned when someone walked across it. I had the entire house mapped out, but that wasn't as important as making her feel like she was safe.

***

That night, I paid up my end of the bargain to Bree—a double date. She came over to pick out my clothes—big mistake. She let me veto the heels only because I'd be a walking disaster in them. Opting for ballerina flats, I slipped on a pair of her pants that she swore up and down weren't from the bottom of my dresser drawer, but the musty smell indicated otherwise.

"You look great," she said, after I got a little long-winded about not being twelve and how I shouldn't dress in pants I wore back then. "Besides, you never wear anything that shows off all those long hours at the gym."

"I'm not wearing them!"

"Then how about this?" she tossed me jean skirt.

"It's a little chilly for skirts don't you think?"

"It's either that or sport just your granny-pannys."

"I don't wear old women underwear."

She laughed, "Winnie! I've seen the inside of your underwear drawer. I know exactly what you are sporting."

To prove a point, I reached in said drawer and grabbed a black thong that I wore under my Spring Formal's dress last year. I left out the detail that I had been mortified about string underwear in general. Nevertheless, I was glad to have them now.

"I dare you to wear that black little thing with a skirt."

Not a chance in hell! I opened my mouth to voice my opinion but she stopped me short.

"That's what I thought," she said. "You'd never do something so scandalous as to wear black underwear with a skirt."

She knew how to push my buttons. She knew me better than most... but I swear she was impressed when I changed into the thong and skirt.

"What am I going to wear for a top?"

"Your date is never going to be able to take his eyes off of your legs," she said. "I don't think it matters what you wear for a shirt."

Even so, she handed me a pile of them. It was only after I slipped on three different shirts of different lengths was she satisfied with my appearance.

"I want you to blow him away with your hotness!" she claimed.

"Shall I put nail polish on Stella then too?" I joked. "Who did you find to go on a date with me?"

"It's a mystery."

After pulling out my ponytail that took me all of forty-five seconds to whip up, she took a flat iron to my hair. By the time she was done, I could touch the tips of my hair if I strained my shoulder by reaching around my back. She still sprayed me down with a canister of hairspray. I gagged. I couldn't get the window cracked open fast enough. A vehicle pulled into the driveway. If I wasn't mistake, it was Ryker's *Mustang*.

"He's got perfect timing!" Bree said.

Leading me out of the house, she helped me to the passenger side of the two-door car. The cool air sent chills up my legs. I should never have let Bree bait me into wearing something so damn short. At least she insisted I wear a coat. It was barely shorter than my skirt. Nonetheless, I still felt incredibly naked.

She opened the door and tilted the seat forward. I attempted to enter the back seating area as gracefully as possible, but that was easier said than done. The car was barely big enough for me to crawl around in.

"You don't look utterly hideous," Ryker said when my butt was right in his face. "You do good work Bree."

"And you didn't think I could pull this off."

I pulled the seat back so Bree could sit when I noticed the driver side door opening. I knew who it was from the scent. Jace. He entered the vehicle from that side. A *slight* wave of nausea hit me, but it wasn't anywhere as intense as it was the first time I met Jace

Eatros, the guy who'd snuck off with my heart. After Ryker got out, he pushed the seat forward and sat down next to me. My stomach fluttered. He was exactly who I hoped would be my escort for the evening but shouldn't want. I licked my lips and tried to forget the taste of his dreamy kiss.

If there was a way to forget him completely so I could live a normal life, I'd take it. I didn't want to be falling for a guy who was in love with someone else. He may invade my dreams, but I'd never be the girl of his—not when he found out I wasn't lying. If only I was Deino, then I could give into my feelings and just let myself fall for him completely.

In effort to make sure Jace got the signals he had to from me, I pushed the back of the seat to get out. I couldn't encourage him. He'd hate me when he would find out the truth.

Bree blocked me. "We had a deal."

"I said anyone but *him*."

"I musta forgot that part," she said, obviously lying.

"She's playing hard to get," Jace said. His voice was so deep I forgot to breathe. My resistance was a *turn on?* How was I to discourage him if everything I did only excited him more?

When we arrived, Bree reminded me that I owed her. "You're getting in the way of yourself. Just enjoy tonight, okay? For me?"

"Where are we going?" I asked which was code for: *I give up.*

"The Circus."

She shut the door before I could second-guess myself and escape. Ryker drove fast, which I loved. I rarely got around fast. Once we arrived, Ryker and Bree quickly departed to claim their reservation. I stayed back, not sure if what I was going to do or say was appropriate. Nonetheless, I had to try to get Jace to understand that I just couldn't have a relationship with him.

I bit the inside of my cheek and grabbed his arm before he was able to vacate the vehicle. "We need to talk."

He reached for the driver's door handle and pulled it shut, closing us inside. The atmosphere suddenly became very intense. Behind closed doors, when the rest of the world wasn't watching, the demeanor shifted between us.

"That we do," he said seriously.

Everything else faded away, like it wasn't as important as what he was saying. I caught my breath when he reached for me and gently stroked my cheek just like he had in my dreams. I shivered. When he caressed me I forgot every thought bouncing around in my mind. However, it wasn't just that my thoughts evaded me that left me speechless. His hand reshaped so I could see more than just his fingers; their coarse edges, knuckles, even nails became more defined. He no longer looked liked a blurred, white silhouette, his physical attributes were more pronounced. He had an athletic leanness going on. His shirt was tight enough for me to see the rise and fall of his chest. The longer I stared the more rapidly he breathed. He clenched and then relaxed his fist before reaching for me. For a blissful second I thought he was going to kiss me. I wanted him to—oh heaven help me I wanted Jace in ways I shouldn't. Instead of silencing my gasp with the kiss I'd been envisioning since the first time I dreamed of him, he brushed the hair off my neck.

"The Elysian flowing in your veins is responding well to me now, and your tolerance is better."

"You think I am a deity? An immortal?"

"Do you?" he questioned.

Apparently we were playing a game of *Who is Going to Admit They're Insane First?*

Jace hastily picked up my hand in his and kissed it with a gentle fierceness. "You are divine to me."

My skin erupted in fire where his lips caressed. My hand throbbed where he kissed it. I wanted him to touch more, kiss more. Oh I wished Ryker's windows were tinted.

"And I'll be *your* Healer again, if Fate allows."

"You think I am a Fate?"

"I think you are many different things to many different people," he said, not giving any indication of his true self.

"I am not your Fate, Jace. I am not her."

He paused, calculating his response. "When we first met at Strikers I apologized to you. Remember? I said that you reminded me of a girl I once knew."

"I told you that I am not Deino. I promise I'm not her."

He tucked my hair behind my ear and leaned close to me. He grabbed my skirt, pulling me close using the belt loop. His chest touched mine when he took a deep breath. It hit my skin and warmed me with his fiery passion.

"I'm looking at the goddess I want."

"I want you Jace," I whispered and was rewarded when he tightened his grip on my hips.

His lips were almost touching mine. I only had to lean a fraction of an inch to close the distance. My hands betrayed me, sliding up his shirt. He was as powerful in my dreams as he was in real life.

"If I kiss you, you will hate me," I said and then pressed my lips together. I didn't want to speak the words I had to, but they needed to be said. "But you have to know the truth. I am truly not your girl. I'm not the person you fell in love with… I can't be with you. If I play along and pretend to be her, then you'd just hate me when you finally came to the conclusion that I am right."

Before I could take back anything I'd said, I pushed him off of me and climbed out of the vehicle. Jace was out of the car and in front of me before I'd gotten the chance to look back. He walked me backwards, sandwiching me between him and the cold side of the car. His hips pressed into mine. A sense of eagerness, engulfed in agitation, overpowered my own hostility.

"Don't make this more difficult than it has to be!" I said. Was he going to make me say words I couldn't take back? "You are in love with another person. *You* are lying to *yourself.*"

Jace was silent, calculating my comment. "Give yourself to me completely so that I may heal you. That should have been my first priority, not the Master's agenda, regardless of the Oath I swore. Then I'll show you a world that has just been unveiled to your blind eyes."

My cherubic dream surfaced. I couldn't imagine a place more blissful than that place. Wait. I tried to piece together the nights. I went to the gym and then woke up in the middle of my yard. What happened in the middle? I tried not to think about that, not yet. I needed to focus on one thing at a time. And right now my sight was on the table.

"Don't be cruel, Jace. You can't fix my sight."

"I'm never cruel to someone who can see truth through eyes like yours."

"How am I supposed to believe that you can do something so impossible, like returning my sight," I said, and twisted out of our embrace. I made a bee-line for Circus' front door.

"Ditch these guys and come with me. Or would you prefer to be scrutinized all night," Jace called out.

I stopped in my tracks. That was the last thing I wanted.

"You know they are going to have a discussion about us afterwards too," he said. "Or we can bomb around by ourselves tonight."

"Ryker has the keys."

"You don't think I know how to hot-wire a car?"

Chapter Fourteen

The engine purred; vibrating sensations pulsated through me. I liked it in ways I shouldn't have. Jace's warmth grew. I pressed my legs tightly together, hoping he'd get the impression we weren't practicing anything scandalous today. I pressed the button to unroll the window but nothing happened. Child-lock. I heard the click of the locking system, and he unrolled the window for me. I hung my arm out the window and closed my eyes.

"You like how the wind feels on your skin?" he asked with intense curiosity.

I replied with a lazy nod. Jace clicked a button, and the car's roof unfolded. Wind oscillated around me. My legs were covered in goosebumps. Jace must have noticed as well, because he placed his hand on my thigh. It was higher than I'd ever been touched by a guy. I stiffened. Jace *had* to notice but he didn't utter a word. In fact, he slowly moved his hand up and down my leg as if to warm me…which it did but not in the places he was touching.

A scarlet petal fell from the sky like a feather. It drifted back and forth. Someone behind me blew it lightly, making it twirl in the air. One after another, petals rained around me. I laughed, loving the shower.

"Close your eyes," the young man whispered. His voice was strained like he was having a difficult time controlling himself.

I obeyed and waited eagerly. Using a single petal, he caressed my lips with it.

When Ashwick's horizon was in his rearview mirror, Jace hummed a tune under his breath. It was soft and sweet. The melody was lively yet had an unimaginable calming effect.

"My friend Deino wrote it," Jace whispered, like he wasn't sure if he wanted me to hear. Her name danced off his tongue the way only a lover could utter their partner's name. "She had a way of fumbling words in order to change their meaning."

Trying not to sound too eager to learn more about him, I prodded a bit. "Did you leave her?"

Heat erupted from around him. I half expected to see flames dancing from his skin like they did in my dreams. He spoke carefully but I could tell he was losing his cool demeanor.

"She left me."

I knew I shouldn't pry but… "I'm still waiting for the rest of the story."

"She broke my heart! Can't we keep it at that?" Jace shouted, swerving on the road. Gripping the steering wheel with both hands, he steadied himself.

However, my skin burned and tingled as his anger grew. I braced myself, unsure of what he'd do if his control vanished. I sat up, and started to slide off the car. I hit a nerve; his temper was erupting. I wanted to be on my own two feet when he exploded. His figure reformed, growing bright. The air became hot around him. An image of his dark chocolate brown eyes formed in my mind.

"Reborn as what I once was?" I asked, tracing his thumb since he refused to return my gaze. Smoke rose around us. It seeped over the wheat grass, whilst every building around us went up in flames.

"Playing with your fate is dangerous." His voice burned, apologetically. "But I can feel the life leaving your body. I've never asked for you to grant me anything, dearest. Grant me this."

"…she left me, Gwyneth!" Jace said, continuing with his rant that had been interrupted by my vision. "Not the other way around. I've spent the better part of my life searching for her."

I cleared my throat, trying to regain my place in the conversation before the vision. I wanted to stand on my own two feet, but my nerves were jumping. My adrenaline was pumping; my heart was racing from the vision.

"Why look for someone who doesn't want to be found?" I asked, hoping he didn't notice the waver in my voice.

"She begged me to find her," he admitted.

I rubbed my forehead, trying to figure out the riddle he presented. "What happened, Jace?"

"Analee's *horde* will come for me if I tell you everything, you know that, Gwyneth," he said with growing frustration. "I should have never sworn the Oath."

A horde of ghostly white warriors flickered in my mind. Their eyes were empty holes. Their mouths were sewn shut, but it didn't silence their cries. The forgotten past hacked a part of my soul while I beat on the wooden coffin.

"Forgive me, my Scavengers," I yelled as my soul was torn to pieces.

I may as well have just been divided because my heart hurt like a part of my very being just died. The vision was over in seconds, but I was shaken. It felt like I'd been buried alive in this last vision. In the one just a moment before, I had been dying in the arms of someone I'd love who'd eventually kill me. The blood drained from my face as I tried to figure out what was going on between Jace and me. I didn't understand what he talked about or his logic. I wanted to run; I wanted to hide. I was in the middle of nowhere with a person whose obsession with me had reached unsafe levels.

"…my temper gets the best of me sometimes. I should have shielded it from you," Jace said, as he stroked my leg again while I trembled in the passenger's seat.

"It wasn't that. I just saw…" I said, and immediately wished I wouldn't have said anything regarding my visions.

It piqued his curiosity. As always, he deemed my reactions to him, and everything else, as important. His interest in me had always become profound after I'd witnessed a vision.

"You look like you could use some fresh air," he said.

He pulled over in the middle of nowhere and turned off the lights. Only the soft hum of the radio interrupted the silent night. He got out of the car, walked around to the passenger door, and opened it for me. He offered his hand to help me out.

For the life of me this moment felt more important than a simple gesture. He was literally offering to help me; I just had to accept it. In spite of myself, I finally took it. Warmth flowed from him and twisted around me. However, he merely stood in front of me. I didn't trust my eyes, but I swore flickers of light dancing over his skin like flames. I couldn't take my eyes off him. He was breathtaking in my sight; I couldn't imagine how I'd react if could actually see his every detail.

He walked me around to the front of the car. I started to lean against the door when he suddenly gripped my hips and raised me onto the hood. My legs should have burned from touching the metal, but my skin didn't blister, even though they should have, considering how long the engine had been on. He didn't back away; in fact he edged between my legs so that there was little distance between us. My skirt was pulled up entirely too high, but Jace's focus was higher up; I knew because he lifted my chin with his finger.

"Your eyes captivate me," he said, making me feel a little better about my position.

He was an addiction—my hang-up. The close proximity of his presence absorbed into my skin. My soul warmed. It comforted me, which scared me. I opened my mouth to tell him I needed space, but he pressed his finger over my lips to keep me from arguing. I bit my tongue. My lips parted when he withdrew his hand and wiped an escaped tear with his thumb. His very touch was like a drug. The tortured hours of not being near him, returned the moment his fingers trailed away.

"Do me a favor and shut up," he said and brought my arm

behind me and rolled me onto my back.

I clenched my mouth tight like it'd prevent me from giving into temptation and kiss him. He leaned forward. His arm rested next to mine. Our fingers intertwined. I couldn't bear it if he left me like everyone else in my life. I couldn't stand to lose anyone else that I cared about. I felt gutted as it was; Jace could destroy me if I let him into my heart, and he stomped on it. Even as torn as I felt, I still couldn't breathe when he was this close to me, and I didn't care. I longed to be closer to him; I was at war with myself. Raising our hands, he placed mine on his chest.

"Feel how your pulse makes mine frantic, Gwyneth. I lean in close to you, and your body warms, even though we're barely touching," he whispered. His strained voice made me shiver with excitement. "You haven't breathed since I began speaking."

I couldn't deny any of it. He knew it. He knew me. It terrified me just as much as I wanted to lose myself in him. Sensing my hesitation, he pulled me upright so I was sitting next to him. I heard myself gasp when the warmth emanating from his body enclosed around me. He made a sound from his throat that I didn't know was possible. Tracing his nose against my cheek, he merely breathed; the hot air hit my skin, boiling my blood. I stopped thinking and stopped fighting. His heart pounded against his chest, matching speed with mine. My skin burned like my proximity to him would set me on fire. Everywhere his breath lingered over my skin made it tingle with exhilaration. I bit my tongue to keep from turning my head and kissing him.

"You can feel my adoration burning on your skin, can't you? It warms you, doesn't it?" he said, and traced my skin along my arm with a finger. Everywhere he touched, my skin absorbed his fervor.

"Passion is in our blood, just like humans. The difference lies in how we feel it. Both races feel their own desires, but we can feel each other's. When you lose your breath, my lungs refuse to work. Your sexy little squeal echoes in my ears for hours after, just like you hunger for the sound of my voice. My skin lights on fire when you allow me to touch your smooth, beautiful, porcelain skin."

My voice cracked. "But you still think I'm Deino."

"I believe you are the person you were before everything was taken from you," he recited. "Before you lost a large part of your soul."

"My soul is still broken."

"I know," he whispered. "But I can't change the past so let me do what I can. Let me fix your eyes."

"Jace, nothing's wrong with my eyes, not physically," I said. I looked up at him and hoped he'd see my acceptance of my handicap instead of the lie hiding my eyes. I pushed him away so I could sit up; he could easily overpower me but didn't. Instead he gave me the space I so desperately needed. "The trauma from my family's deaths forbids me to see anything. The doctors say it's some kind of coping mechanism."

"So you'll turn down the only person who can heal you?" You'd rather wallow in your own self pity than take a chance for an actual meaningful life?"

"I do just fine without my eyes. Seeing isn't important," I lied, looking to the horizon which just happened to be the exact opposite direction of his glowing face. I wished I could see the reds,

151

yellows, and oranges, like I had in the vision just moments before.

"If sight isn't enough, then what is?" he asked and forced me to face him. His calloused hand gently stroked my cheek. He refused to speak again until I gave in and looked at him. "I'll do anything if you let me open your eyes to a world bigger than black and white, more than color, more than anything a human can see."

I brought my hand up over his. I skimmed his hand that was cupping my face as I looked back at the horizon.

"If you find the person who murdered my parents and my sister, I'll give myself to you," I said hoping he'd succeed because I was as desperate for his kiss as he was for mine.

Chapter Fifteen

Hidden within an old shoe box, tucked in the back of my bedroom closet, was the only remnant that my family even existed. The cold case file of my family's brutal murders amounted to a few pieces of paper and a forgotten police report. There were only a few papers inside the manila envelope, yet it weighed heavy in my hands. My heritage amounted to a police report. Kneeling on my closet floor, I thumbed through the pages. I knew what was on each one even though I'd never seen it with my eyes. I'd dog eared the pages at different lengths so I knew for certain what information was on each page. Nonetheless, I was surprised when a flower petal slipped through the pages and landed on my lap. The petal was fragile, threatening to crumble if too much pressure was applied.

It was a lily, for my sister. Hector gave it to me on the first anniversary that I had asked him to come to Bakker's Cemetery with me. I cherished the flower about as much as anything else in my life. I held it up to my nose and breathed in it's faint scent. It smelled more like old papers than a lily...

153

A faint whimper echoed in the darkness. I didn't know why the girl was crying, but I recognized her lovely voice. The faint scent of lilies lingered. I walked toward her. A fragment of light began to gather around me. It reflected off the broken glass shattered on the ground. I carefully stepped around each piece, looking for the crying girl. When she clasped her hand around mine, I jumped. A dirty, young girl sat on the ground; scissors in hand. Cuts littered her skin. Her vindictive smile hid her true feelings—she was overjoyed to see me and felt nothing regarding her wounds.

The reflection of another young woman with beautiful, wavy brown hair shone in the shattered glass. The girl lying on the shattered glass screamed into the night and then laughed so viciously it sent shivers down my spine. She stood suddenly and opened her arms to us.

"The unseeing past and unspeakable future are once again surrounded in death's embrace."

The moment the three of us touched, three distinctive sensations had come over me. Rage erupted inside the young woman. Derangement tore at the girl's sanity. Calmness encased my soul; I had to be patient if I was to find my revenge. I closed my eyes and reflected on my life experiences, my memories. The past would repeat itself… it always did, in one form or another. I only hoped to see something in my memories that I'd missed before, so this tragedy would never repeat itself.

I heard a cry escape my throat. It sounded similar to the dirty girl sitting on the shattered glass but more piercing, like the older girl's scream. Their essence tugged at my soul. The vision scared me. Not because of the images I'd seen, but because I hadn't understood them. Who were these girls?

"*Sisters* make the best friends."

The whisper was eerie yet captivating. I looked by the shirts hanging around me. Elsie was peeking her head through the crack in my bedroom door.

"Do you want to be my friend?" I asked, clutching the files to my chest so she wouldn't see the horrible words written on them. I stood and walked over to her, shutting the closet door behind me.

"If you want to be mine," she said happily, slipping her hand through my fingers. "We will be sisters."

I choked up. My biological family may be buried underneath the cold dirt, but when I wasn't paying attention my makeshift family had grown around me. Was it really worth Jace's efforts to dig up the past and uncover all the pain that I tried to keep buried deep within my soul? I had a family who loved me; shouldn't that be enough? I thought about the blood pooling around me in my vision—the one where a man had grown young. *Blood gushed from a young girl next to me. My pink blanket turned red. Colors blurred until everything melted into a shade of gray.* Forgiveness was not one of my strongest virtues, because deep down, I knew I'd never stop searching for that man who stole my family from me

"What's that?" Elsie asked, poking the envelope in my other hand.

"Homework?"

"I hate homework," Elsie admitted.

"I do too," I said gravely. "Luckily for me, this homework is for Jace."

***

I couldn't think of anyone else but Jace. It was like he'd followed me everywhere. He was constantly on my mind, but I couldn't see him, feel his presence, or even fight with him. I'd rather argue with him instead of getting the cold shoulder. Even after the vision where my soul was frayed, I'd wished he was with me. The once physical burden that once overwhelmed me when Jace was near, now presented when he was away.

Luckily for me, he'd snuck into my bedroom while my foster parents were away at a student conference with Elsie's teachers. Jace leaned against the windowsill. My sight had improved to the point that I could see his hair with my eyes open. It fell around his ears and blew gently in the evening breeze from the open window. However, when I tried to focus on the detail of his face, my sight still blurred. His chest rose and fell slowly before he answered my question. It was like he'd been trying to figure me out, piece my reactions and comments together to make sense of what he believed.

"Police reports indicate the man who broke into your parents' house entered through a bedroom window on the main floor, but left via the front door."

"Your point?"

"One report said the window was broken in the far right room, while another states it was the most southern room of the house," Jace said, and then sighed heavily. "There had to be more than one person who slaughtered your family."

"The most southern room was the far right room," I said, pacing the room. He found a dead end. "I walked through the house a few years ago."

He walked to my bed, carefully avoiding the creaky floorboards. I strained my ears, but I couldn't hear a single footstep. I didn't move as I watched him plop down on it, making himself comfortable. He picked up my phone that was on my night stand and began playing with it. I jerked it away from him.

"I'm programming my digits into your phone," he said. "Or would you prefer to call upon me the old fashion way?"

Old fashion way? "Don't guys usually give a girl their number and let her decide if she wants to call him?"

"Isn't that what I am doing?"

True. "I suppose you'll want mine then?"

He laughed, "Don't you think I already have them?"

He can hot wire a car, find a restricted number, and make a girl like me care about the type of underwear I wear around him; what can't he do? I turned away. I haven't even kissed him, not in real life, and here I was wondering if I should shave my legs or go on a lingerie shopping spree. I was getting side tracked. He needed to get off my bed if I had any hope of thinking clearly.

He wiggled deeper onto the comforter.

I took up pacing again. The floor boards cracked under my weight. I wasn't a big girl, but I wondered how Jace got so good at missing all the whiny wood.

"How did you gain permission to walk through the house?" Jace said, picking up where we'd left off.

157

"I broke into it," I coughed over my B&E confession.

"That was dangerous," he said softly and ran his hands through his hair. I wished I could see what he looked like—for real. I wished I could see life like I did in my visions. I wanted to look into his eyes and see if I could uncover the truth in them.

"And stupid, yes I know."

"I should go," he said, sitting up abruptly. He walked over to my bedroom door and almost slammed it in my face.

I grabbed the handle, stopping him. "Why?"

He braced himself again the door like he'd refused himself permission to enter. "Because you've forbid me to kiss you until I figure out what happened that night. But if I stay in this room alone with you one moment longer, I am going to steal what you have forbidden."

***

The next day, I walked up to the only white silhouette leaning against the lockers in the Senior Hall. I couldn't get to Jace fast enough that I should have noticed the differences in the figure whom I tapped on the shoulder. The headache that had diminished long ago, accompanied him once again. A wave of dizziness enveloped me when he turned around, but his shape was smaller, less imposing. He didn't smell like a rich cigar drenched in what I imagined lust smelled like.

It wasn't Jace.

"Well, it's obvious you can sense us. But it's not proof you're one of us." A soft, angelic, female voice echoed in the halls, perfect to be the muse to any musician.

It was beautiful, captivating, and heavenly, yet I hated the very sound of it. Fury I didn't think any one person could possess boiled in my heart. The unearned anger I felt toward her was how I imagined the animosity an insane serial killer must feel before committing a murder. My jaw clenched tight.

"Do I know you?"

I cautiously closed my eyes to see if she looked anything like the hazy figure Jace appeared to be in my sight. Light glistened under her skin, illuminating her like a glow stick.

"Oh come now, you remember *me*. The Master."

She sounded like a fallen angel who'd escaped heaven's doors only to be captured and tortured by hell's demons.

"Listen *lady*—"

"I don't care if you *are* the Chronicler; you'll address me by Analee, or the Master," she hissed. "And until you find your precious sisters, you'll treat me with the respect that any human would."

I bit my tongue; I almost smarted off to her and told her I wasn't human.

"Jace has been keeping you to himself," Analee said. "I don't like to be kept waiting and you've kept me waiting, little girl."

"Good."

"He says your tolerance isn't strong enough. I had to see for myself," she said and flicked my hair back.

The proximity bothered me more than I cared to admit. "Why does that matter?"

"Because there are more of us who want to see you for themselves," Analee said. "They want to see if you are one of the three…and I have been beginning to think that Jace has been purposely making this *tolerance build* take longer than necessary."

"Why?" I asked, genuinely curious too.

"Because he wants more time with you," she said. "Before everyone with a knife comes at you and the real danger starts…"

"Who's your friend?" Bree said, coming up behind me.

I'd been in an intense staring contest with Analee and hadn't heard Bree approaching. "Analee," I muttered. I figured telling Bree that Analee liked to be addressed as *the Master* would bring complications that weren't necessary.

"She's an acquaintance of Jace's."

"Jace and I are anything but acquaintances," Analee said. "He and I have an intricate and dirty past."

I *refused* to believe that Jace ever touched her.

Another white figure moved in closer. I hadn't noticed him approaching either. Either Analee was doing something to block out everything else in the world, or I had a bigger obstacle than Jace.

When the other one got closer, an instant pounding of a headache set in. For a moment, I thought it was Jace, until I closed my eyes to make sure. In the orb's place was a colorless ripple, looking much like a current in clear water. He flicked his finger at me like I was a speck of dirt he was trying to brush off. My ears rang. I opened my eyes as tears gathered.

The young man whispered as he leaned against the locker wall on the opposite side of the hall. He played with a curl in his hair while he watched my reaction to the sound of his voice. I couldn't hear him but felt the air vibrate around me. My eardrums pounded; pressure formed around my skull. It hurt but was nothing to what Jace put me through. I wobbled but didn't have to lean against a locker to brace myself. I was stronger; perhaps my tolerance to these insane people had improved. I straightened my shoulders. I'd be damned to lose control in front of Analee, whoever she was.

"I've been waiting lifetimes to take your life," she whispered just loud enough for me to hear.

With that, she turned away. The farther they walked the less nausea I endured.

When she was out of sight, Bree leaned over to me. "Well, that Barbie was a hoot. I hope she and her manly friend don't enroll in school here... Just FYI, I know you don't care, but she and her curly-haired Ken doll were *both* hot—like, plastic surgery can't even make you this hot-hot. He was unreal gorgeous, Winnie. I bet his baby blue eyes have dropped a few panties before he hooked up with her."

Mondays sucked.

Chapter Sixteen

The Thompson's doorbell rang at ten minutes to seven. I'd been pacing the living room for the better part of an hour, and was closest to the front door. Max howled until I opened it. Jace slid off his sunglasses and stepped into the house before I welcomed him inside. Max sniffed him like he wasn't sure whether or not to allow him inside until Jace kneeled down to give him a good scratch behind the ears. That won Max over.

"You are nervous," Jace said.

"I've never invited a guy to dinner before."

"Good," he said in a low voice that made me shiver.

That one word *screamed* volumes. I was his, no matter how much of a distance I kept him.

"Let's meet the family," he said, acting like it was the first time he'd been inside my house.

162

Jace reached for my hand. It stopped me dead—not because I was having an adverse reaction to touching him, but because it felt completely normal. My cheeks instantly warmed. I looked at my feet and was pleased that I'd worn my hair down. It hid my rosy cheeks.

"I'm Jace, Jace Eatros," he said and extended his hand after Martha introduced herself.

She led us throughout the house and pointed out the different rooms—a mini house tour. John and Elsie busied themselves in the kitchen, following whatever direction Martha dished out. She refused to let Jace or me help, so we sat in the dining room pretending the situation wasn't awkward.

Elsie brought an extra glass and plate. They rattled the entire way from the kitchen to the dining room. She set them on the table by Jace and then hurried around to the table's other side. She nearly knocked over Martha who was carrying in green bean casserole.

"So how did you and Winnie meet?" John asked casually as he carried the lasagna to the table.

"Art class," Jace said without hesitation. "Apparently someone sat in someone else's seat, and she wasn't exactly receptive—but we fell madly in love shortly after."

"Actually, we met at the bowling alley," I said. "And you struck out that night."

"But it didn't stop me from winning you over, dearest," he said, and reached for my hand under the table.

He took my hand in his and brought it to his face. The moment he kissed my hand, my mouth went dry. I bit my tongue to

163

bring myself back to sanity. I barely heard him whisper a phrase in another language. Listening to his captivating voice made it difficult for me to breathe. His touch was so utterly soothing that I actually thought I'd been drugged. I went through the motions of eating, while Jace entertained my foster parents. Elsie and I were two peas in a pod; we barely mumbled a word.

"Do you play football, Jace?" John asked.

"I don't really have time for that between the honors courses I'm taking at school and prepping for college," he said. "But I love to watch the game."

"You trust him?" Elsie whispered to me when Jace and John were deep into their pig skin conversation.

"Why do you ask?"

"The pretty ones are good liars."

"He is pretty, isn't he," I admitted.

"How do you know what people look like?"

"I get a general picture from my hands," I said and touched my face, showing her how I saw. "Would you let me see you?"

"Ummm, can you show me with someone else first—like him?" Elsie asked nervously and pointed to Jace.

The other's dinner conversation paused to listen to ours. I could tell Martha was beaming. Apparently Elsie hadn't been doing well in school or making new friends. The woman barely heard Elsie talk.

"Gwyneth and I haven't really advanced to face-feeling yet. We're still trying to master being in the same room with each other," Jace said quietly.

"Afraid I'll find out how ugly you are?"

Jace chuckled then full out laughed. Finally he agreed to Elsie's request. His laugh sounded like I imagined heaven would to my ears.

"He sounds nice," Elsie whispered.

I couldn't help but smile. I stared, in awe of how his white silhouette fluctuated with his laugh. "That he does."

Martha held off on dessert so I could show Elsie how I see. I guess we were all eager to do anything to make her feel like this wasn't a scary place to live. She and John were so aware of their new foster child. They were amazing parents and chatted casually between themselves so Elsie wouldn't get spooked with so many people watching.

"Sometimes it's easier to feel the way a person looks by standing behind them," I said.

Elsie walked around to Jace's chair. I took her hand and placed it on his forehead. I took a deep breath and started. With my hand, I showed her how to let her hands trickle down until she reached his eye brows. I doubled check—no unibrow. I showed her how to measure the distance between the hairline, which was as soft as silk, and his chin. I then showed her how that measurement should be the same size of a person's hands. She followed my lead, mimicking my actions, on the opposite side of his face.

"Let the tips of your finger go over his eyelids, and pay careful attention to how deep the eye socket is in relationship to the formation of his brow."

I gently slid my fingers to the sides of his eyes. I informed Elsie to feel for any skin abnormalities or bumps, when I felt it. A dimple. It was perfectly buried in his cheek. I swallowed before letting my fingers trail along his jaw line, which was hard and straight. His facial hair was shaved to the skin but started to prickle. He probably needed to shave daily to keep up the smooth skin. My hand trembled as my adrenaline surged. It was ridiculous how much I enjoyed the feeling of his scruffy face. I started to pull away when he reached up. He gently held my hand against his face. He rubbed his thumb over the backside of my hand, encouraging me not to pull away. I heard myself gasp when his thumb rolled over my smallest finger. Immediately, the vision of the perfect lips jarred me from my thoughts. I regained my composure quickly. I wanted to see Jace so badly, instead of showing Elsie how I did it. I bit my tongue to keep from asking her to move over so I could see how to picture him in my mind's eye. Barely controlling myself, I showed her how feel for the contours in his face.

The tip of my finger caught the tail end of a thin scar following nearly the entire length of his left eye. A deep moan grew in Jace's throat as I traced it. The sound hit my ears like some glorious echo had sounded.

We repeated the motion until reaching his nose. I showed her how to follow along the side first so she could get a general picture of the shape of the nose before examining length, depth, and skin health. Jace's nose was slightly wider than I imagined and had a slight crook in it, veering to the left.

"Broken nose. Compliments of your younger sister," Jace muttered.

"What did you say?" Elsie asked.

"Ignore him," I said before Jace had a chance to answer. "He's not supposed to talk—messes up the features of the face."

Jace bounced slightly, while he failed to suppress his chuckle. Just when I wished he'd open his mouth so I could hear its sweet sound, another vision hit me.

My skin was smooth and youthful, just like his, as I cupped his face in my hands. I brushed back the dark brown hair that fell over his chocolate-brown eyes. Flecks of gold shimmered in them even though dirt clung to his hair, like he took a shower in mud. Smoke filled the edges of my sight as dawn broke. I thanked my sister for not cutting his thread when he searched the Master's cave looking for the lost parts of my soul—my Scavengers. I didn't fight his touch as he traced his dirty finger over my hand. I craved it.

"Did you uncover their orders?" I asked.

"Anyone who utters their name will greet death."

"They rise as death's henchmen, disregarding forgotten memories, only to collect the dead."

The same man who'd kill me one day held onto me like I was his lifeline. Jace grabbed my shaking hand. I clenched my teeth, trying to make sense of my visions. I died in the arms of a youthful man, who didn't age as I did. The vision had happened so many times before that it had to be significant, other than giving me insight to my future and inevitable death. I fought back my tears; now was not the time or place to have an epiphany. My lungs burned, but I wasn't the

167

one holding my breath—he was. I tapped him, and the clasp on my throat loosened.

"Gwyneth?" If one word could say so many unasked questions, it was when he spoke my name.

"Lips are a little tricky, just like the nose," I said, ignoring Jace's concern. "Like the nose, outline the lips to get a general picture of the shape. In your mind you can divide them in half, or you can ask Jace to part his lips, slightly."

Jace parted his lips before she asked. My skin tingled when I wondered if his lips felt like silk.

"Are you scared?" Elsie whispered.

"No." I was freaking terrified. I begged for my hands to steady themselves. "Let's take turns like we did with the nose, or our fingers might bump into each other and get a bad read."

Jace placed his hand over mine when it was my turn to see his lips. His hand burned in mine as I traced his mouth. He slowed my hand down, prolonging it. My breathing became irregular. Keeping my hand on his lush, bottom lip, he spoke. "Have a better picture of what I look like now?"

I focused on standing. The way his deep voice sounded made my entire body shiver. I didn't answer him. I didn't trust my hands to stop with simply seeing his face. Instead I asked Elsie if I could see her. She exchanged spots with Jace. He didn't bother letting go of my hand until I positioned my hands on Elsie's face. He backed off, but I could feel him right behind me, watching my movements.

I was able to get a pretty decent picture of Elsie in a short amount of time. Letting my fingers run the motions quickly, I knew she had full cheeks—even after losing her baby fat she would most likely have a round face. Her eyebrows were beginning to fill in, and she had a slight crook on the tip of her nose. It wasn't broken, but rather the cartilage formed slightly to the left. The space between her eyes was slight, so I figured she had some kind of Asian descent.

"So, I assume you have beautiful black hair?" I said, running my hands down her shoulder length hair.

"It's like you have superpowers!" Elsie said.

I chuckled, "No powers, Elsie, just lots of experience using my hands to see."

Jace blew out a hot breath of air, which trickled down my neck. My throat tightened. A moan grew in Jace's chest as I slowly took a deep breath in, testing how my desirability affected him. It was impossible, to feel another's attraction, but just as absurd as it was, I still couldn't get over the warmth Jace brought me whenever he was nearby. My knees weakened when he stepped close behind me. He gripped the chair's back, steadying himself.

"Well, whatever you call it, you're amazing," Elsie said, breaking up the intensity in the room.

"She really is, isn't she?" Jace said, pushing away, but not before tucking my hair behind my ear. In the quietest voice he spoke, "There is so much about our world you have yet to uncover, dearest. So much to feel and experience, I promise, this is only the beginning."

Supper lasted entirely too long. Jace sat next to me and never

169

once let go of my hand. I couldn't even recall taking a bite of my food. The only thing I could focus on was him. After excusing ourselves, I escorted him to the door, so we could get a cup of coffee and discuss my family's untimely death. He surprised me by helping me with my coat. He opened the door for me. And as soon as we walked outside, the cold breeze hit my face.

The image of a man's full, perfect lips bombarded my mind again. I craved him, addicted to his touch. Everywhere his hand caressed me, my body ignited in a fiery passion I didn't want escape. I leaned into him, begging for a kiss that would never come.

The vision quickly slipped away when Jace spoke my name. He grabbed my arm to keep me from losing my balance. "What just happened, Gwyneth?"

Instead of answering, I pushed him up against the side of the house next to the door. He moaned in exhilaration when I reached up for his face. His body warmed me even though the wind insisted on cooling me. I ran my fingers through his hair while he gripped my waist. He pulled me close, encouraging me to do whatever I intended. I never felt someone's hair as soft as his. It was longer than I suspected, three or four inches, but it was styled. Tracing my steps backwards, I followed along his jaw line, up to his lips. His skin was rough from his facial hair but perfectly smooth otherwise. I couldn't find a single flaw. The tips of my fingers tingled as I focused on getting an accurate picture of him. His dimples hid from me, but after relocating the one on his left, I found it on the right. Placing my palm over his eyes, I felt his eye lashes flutter again my skin. With the distance between my hand and his face, I knew his lashes were long and curled.

Pressing myself against him, so he didn't try moving away, I

170

let my hands fall from his face and onto his throat and shoulders. I attempted to quickly get a descent picture of his muscular development, but each bulge in his arm kept slowing me down. He wasn't huge but clocked quite a few hours in the gym. He was exactly how I imagined him to be.

I skimmed his arms until his hands found mine. His pulse jumped with mine as our fingers slid around each other. He leaned into me while pulling me closer. I kept my head down even though I wanted to feel his lips on mine. So badly, I wanted to feel the hot air come from his lungs and breathe life into my body. I bit my lip.

He released one of my hands and tilted my jaw up towards him. He leaned into me. I parted my lips. His body was shaking against mine, barely containing his anticipation. My skin tingled and burned as he started to lose control. He spun me around faster than humanly possible so my back was against the house. He pressed himself against me, holding me exactly how he wanted me. He leaned forward again, but it wasn't to kiss me. He trailed his nose along my forehead and pulled me in closer with the arm he had wrapped around my waist.

He whispered in my ear. "I want you."

He leaned back, like he was memorizing exactly how I looked. With the hand that was on my jaw, he rubbed his thumb over my lips. They burned with desire as his thumb trailed over them. His skin was as hot as I felt. My body tingled and tightened. He leaned in closer and dropped his hand, enough that he didn't block his way to my lips. I gasped, taking in the hot air he breathed. I wanted him, needed him. As I stepped on my tip toes to close the gap, he backed away, just enough to not give me what I craved...

Instead, he lifted my hand and placed the longest, sweetest kiss on my hand, before releasing me. He walked down the steps, to his car. The heat drained from my skin the farther he went. It took me a ridiculous amount of time to get my bearings in order to make it to the car. Jace rested his arms against the top of the car door, watching me carefully walk down the steps to the driveway.

Neither of us spoke a word as I climbed into his car. He opened his door, slid into the driver's seat, backed out of the driveway, and drove to JJ's, without any directions from me. The purr of the engine didn't compare to what Jace had just done to me. Once there, he opened my car door and offered me his hand for assistance. I couldn't take it fast enough. Still not having spoken a word, I let him maneuver us into the coffee shop.

Bells chimed upon our entrance, and the rich brew filled the air. He led me to a booth in the back and left to order. It took a few minutes before the coffee was ready. Apparently the new staff was having a difficult time figuring out how to make two black coffees. By the time Jace returned, I'd come to the conclusion I was being a mute moron. Passive aggressive wasn't usually my style.

"Which sister of mine punched you in the face?" I asked, playing his game. Lily, in my mind was still my only sister, but if I accepted that I had more, I wanted to know about them.

"She switches names like it's a game," he answered. "Most of us prefer to address each other by our duties anyway."

"Which is?"

"The Cutter," he said blandly.

"Where does she live?"

172

"Location unknown."

"And my other sister?"

"The Prophet," Jace said, leaning in closer to me. "Her whereabouts are just as mysterious. You three have been hiding for quite some time and have gotten to be perpetually good escape artists. Every time we think we are getting close to one of you three, you leave town. Finding an orphan with a paper trail shouldn't have been so difficult, but yet you hid for years."

"What did you do to instigate the broken nose?" I said, focusing on what I could understand.

"I told her you were the pretty one," Jace chuckled. "But the Cutter was maturing into a complete psychopath at the time, so I wouldn't put much weight in her actions."

Okay, he insisted on me having two other sisters; I insisted on only having one. Right now the number didn't matter. I needed answers on why Lily and my parents were taken from me—that's the sister that I cared about. I hesitated to ask my next question. I didn't know if I could handle the answer, but I knew I'd regret never asking it. "My family—that night they were killed. Why was I spared when they were killed and mutilated?"

"Most likely your parents posed a threat," Jace said. "You didn't appear to be a risk, a liability, or a target since you were so young. What troubles me is how a Hunter could make the mistake of killing a human and sparing you. Do you remember anything from that day?"

I hesitated. I definitely hesitated too long because Jace was sitting next to me half a second later. He put his arm behind me, resting along the back of the booth. It felt like he was protecting me from the rest of the world while I spoke my confession.

"Not enough." I thought through every detail of my vision. "I can't even remember seeing more than one person."

Jace sat in silence, weighing my words. His knee swayed under the table. He never brushed my leg. If I didn't know better, he was playing with the warmth he/we/I created between us. "You act like this memory recently developed."

"I've been suffering the aftermath that man instigated, but I'm recalling more every day," I said, thinking of the vision of how he bent over Lily with the knife in hand. My eyes began to water as I pictured the knife, shining in the light. It was a surreal view from my vision.

For the briefest moment, I thought it was my eyes that were being threatened with the knife, not my sister's. It was like we suddenly traded places—or he decided to hurt my sister instead of me. It didn't really matter—it felt like I was living my sister's last second of her life but then watching her die from another person's viewpoint. "Take me to the house."

"A *man* did this to your family?" Jace questioned. "You're sure it wasn't a woman?"

"Take me there," I said, coming out of my trance. I opened my eyes and noticed my hands trembling on the table. I immediately rested them on my lap. Jace did exactly what I hoped he wouldn't. He reached for mine, comforting me. Tears threatened to break through my eyes. "I need to see that house again."

Jace vigilantly stroked my hair. A heat wave trickled from his fingers onto my head and down my body, warming me from the inside out. "Kiss me, and I'll take you."

"Kiss me, and I'll take a page from my sister's book and re-break your nose."

He burst out laughing. My ears went soft; it was like I was given a drug every time he laughed.

"I'll take you to the house after you meet the others, I promise," he said seriously after I squealed in a way I'd rather not admit to doing.

Tickling my ear with his finger, he traced designs on my neck and then onto my jaw. He tilted my chin up. His breathing deepened, and mine soon matched. He took my hand and brought it up to his chest. His heart pounded against his chest. Mine matched his pace. His hand trembled against mine as I lowered my hand, feeling just how chiseled his chest actually was. Releasing my chin, he traced his fingertips over my eyelids. They burned like fire, but I didn't care. He whispered that there was nothing more he'd rather give me than my sight…I just had to give him permission. Moving his hand carefully behind my head, he leaned in, so his lips were inches from mine.

Instead of closing the gap, he began to moan words I had no understanding of, but they sounded like every promise I needed to hear. I could feel the deep vibrations trickle from his throat, flowing into mine. Squirming while listening to the melody I didn't understand, I couldn't take it anymore. I had to know, I needed to know what his lips felt like.

I leaned close and then was slammed with a wave of nausea.

My eyes burned like they were being doused with poison. I pulled away and pressed my hands over my face. My body shook. Jace yelled in the language I didn't understand. His anger trickled over my skin and ignited my body with his resentment.

"Mute yourself, Analee!" Jace demanded, pushing himself as far away from me as possible. "You're as likely to kill her as to make her an Addict, especially with so many of us around!"

"Addicts are fun." Zalen's voice rippled through my ears like a sound wave.

"Addict or not, we must know *now* if she is the Chronicler," Analee said, crossing her arms.

Jace bolted out of the seat. He stood face-to-face with Analee, brooding that she was intruding. "She has to be *willing* before I can lay a hand on her! There isn't much of a chance for me to heal her sight or return her Elysian if she doesn't trust me!"

"If you turn her to an Addict, she'll do anything you want," Analee spat.

"Except she won't have free-will!" Jace fired back.

"That doesn't really matter if she is a slave via her addiction," Zalen laughed vindictively.

With each high pitch of his laugh, another wave of vibrations slammed my ears. Tears flowed from my eyes, distorting my gray world into a red haze. I closed my eyes and kept my hands shoved over them, so I wouldn't have to see their shapes, even with my eyes closed. My ears were burning. I would have stood and walked away, but my legs were cramping. I touched my ear and drew back blood.

176

"Mute yourselves!" I demanded, thinking of how Marco had kept me from getting sick at the library.

Eventually, I started to relax. I opened my eyes just long enough to see four dark shadows in my vision instead of their usual white figures. Marco and Jace had Muted themselves. And for the first time, their essences drew away from me, like the very fibers of their beings that called to me shied away. Their souls weren't as apparent.

"If I somehow get addicted because you didn't Mute yourselves, I'll never let Jace restore me to my full power," I swore. Since they fully believed I was the Chronicler, I might as well use it to my advantage. "And then none of you will ever get what your heart most desires."

"Marco, do it," Analee said in a low voice.

Without warning, Marco grabbed my wrist and pulled me toward him. Instincts took over me, and I tried struggling against him. He laughed at my attempt. I had to give him this one—it would have been like fighting Goliath.

The moment of connection, the world around me began to melt. The shades of gray twirled around each other. The white silhouetted figures blazed. In a blink of an eye their figures were blended together. Analee screamed but it was in the language I didn't understand. Jace cursed. But the voice that got to me the most was Zalen's inane laugh.

Then there was silence.

And pain.

Chapter Seventeen

Marco's spicy scent bombarded my sense of smell. It wasn't so much his aroma as the rotten stench that lingered. Even so, my focus wasn't so much on the smells as it was the sensation that my head was being pummeled and that my body was being ripped apart. It was the exact horrible feeling that started out every blissful dream with Jace. However, instead of the happy ending with Jace, there was Marco and a knife pressed up against my neck.

Marco grunted, "Enough of this. We must know if you are the Chronicler."

I pressed my lips together. I knew Marco was *off* and wasn't sure if he wanted to harm me, but the cold blade told me everything I needed to know. Nonetheless, I wanted to stay cool and in control but my insides weren't happy with being inside my body a moment longer.

"Just answer and the Master will be satisfied one way or

another," Marco said, pressing the blade more tightly against my skin. A trickle of blood seeped from a small cut he'd made.

"I'm not afraid of death," I gasped.

"Of course you're not," he said, pushing me away from him. "You've survived death countless times."

I collapsed onto the floor. Digging my nails into the cement floor, I dry heaved. Where was I? Where was everyone else? *Where was Jace!* I needed my Healer!

"What are you afraid of?" he pondered, walking around me. He grabbed me by the neck and held me up in the air. His head twitched. His nerve tick revealed a secret. He was afraid of me; not my current state, but he feared the Chronicler. "You've never been a fan of injustice, so if you don't answer me I'll kill your beloved. So I'll ask one more time. Are you the Chronicler?"

A tear slipped from my eye. The thought of losing him wasn't something I could bear. In the pit of my heart, in the cracks of my broken soul, I knew the answer. It'd been staring me in the face since Jace laid eyes on me.

"Yes," I gasped.

He let go of me—not by the release of his hand and lowering me to the ground, but rather by shifting out of the room entirely. He vanished. I collided onto the floor. My head was going to explode. Copper filled my mouth and blood dripped from my ears.

I screamed out in pain. My cries stifled Jace's entrance. I hadn't heard him appear, but there he was nonetheless. Marco was standing over him.

"She confessed. She is the first of three," Marco said and then disappeared.

Jace rubbed my back, soothing me, like he'd done before in my dreams. His touch never felt so good. My broken body no longer felt torn apart. The pain wasn't so unbearable that I could think. Granted, I was covered in sweat, but I was alive.

"The dreams were real, weren't they?" I asked, looking up at my Healer.

I so ferociously wanted to see how he truly looked; to see the shell of the body that made me come alive. Heat seeped from him. A colorless fire started to ripple around his body. Yet I couldn't see any defining lines. I couldn't gaze into his eyes; I couldn't lose myself in the colors of his hair; I couldn't make out any feature of his shape any better than I could using my touch.

"I never told you that you were sleeping."

"You just let me believe it."

"You were looking for any excuse to believe it wasn't real, but you always knew the truth."

I closed my eyes and concentrated on breathing. I didn't hear Marco shift. No one made a sound as they gathered around me. But if I concentrated, I could feel their spirits, their souls, their consciousness, their *threads of life*—whatever you wanted to call the essence that makes up a person—materialize in the room. They tugged at my soul like it was a lifeline. I rubbed my hand where I first felt their presence before it went deep inside my very being. It was faint, like they were weak or dying; they weren't at full strength. I looked up and saw six dark, Muted figures stood in a room.

Analee's glow indicated that her arm was draped over a ripple that I'd labeled Zalen. A small frost-covered one huddled next to one who seemed to be made of ice. From their small willowy figures, they couldn't be very old—twelve or thirteen. Marco's silver figure flickered in my sight; he was moving closer to Jace's hazy outline. Jace was standing next to a flickering orb. I glanced behind me. Leaning against a wall, stood a tall, dark silhouette.

Bree's warning resonated in my mind. It was when she was reading the Nephilim Book. *The Chronicler was able to change the course of a human's or deity's fate by manipulating their thread of life.*

"The Chronicler is your creator?" I whispered.

"You can stop speaking in third person anytime now," Analee hissed.

"The Chronicler has the ability to weave Elysian into the very threads of life, cupcake. Thus, we're doomed to extinction without her. That is why she must be found and Elysian returned to her," Marco said a little more gently like I could trust him.

Hell, I didn't trust him; he just threatened to kill me and...I looked up at Jace. I wondered if he knew how expendable he was to Marco.

And she grants the heart's deepest desire to anyone who's willing to kill her for it. No wonder everyone was desperately searching for her. I may be her, but I didn't remember how to do either. I wonder why I had forgotten so much. Did it happen in death? Was it part of the deal I made in order to be reborn? What good were these abilities if I had no idea how to use them? For that matter, what was the extent of my abilities? Did it start and end with those two?

"Can the Chronicler give Elysian to a human? Can she make someone immortal?" I asked.

They were silent. It was unnerving, standing in a room while everyone watched, studied, and formed opinions of me. No one jumped to answer, which either meant they didn't know or that it was just another question they refused to answer.

"How can one person save an entire race?" I asked.

"Mankind can give you that answer, dearest," Jace said. "There are powerful rulers amongst their kind. We're no different."

"Dazzling us with the melodramatics again?" Zalen said, sending prickling sound waves over my ears. My skin crawled at his voice. The vibrations hit the back of my throat. It hurt to swallow. I bit down hard on my cheek. If he would choose never to speak again, that would be fine with me. "The Chronicler always was theatrical, but this is a bit much. Stop pretending you don't know what is going on one minute but then do the next."

"Let the Healer return *all* of your Elysian, and we'll see what she can do," Marco said cautiously.

"Wait," Analee said, barely above a whisper. Nonetheless, all the deities looked to her, even Jace, but his anger seeped from his skin in heat waves. She may not have their affection, but she has their obedience. "I like her weak. Her tolerance needs improvement. But she will be easier to handle as a human."

Jace's silhouette brightened, losing his temper. My chest clamped tight. I couldn't breathe. I subtly tapped my chest and hoped

Jace would catch on. He must have because I suddenly could breathe again.

"You're afraid of me," I stated, realizing one of the benefits I reaped. The corner of my mouth tugged. That thought pleased me more than it should have.

"I'm a strategist." Analee's voice echoed in my mind. Like always, she sounded heavenly, but it wasn't difficult to hear the contempt lingering in her voice.

"She is vulnerable!"

"Your point?" Analee hissed. "As long as she's in my possession and we still have the two others to find, why does she need her powers restored?"

"She can die as easily as any human!" Jace yelled, standing up beside me. He positioned himself in front of me, blocking Analee's view of me.

"There's an easy solution for that, Healer. Don't let her die. And if you fail, you'll have to waste more centuries looking for her."

Jace's figure blazed. The room instantly became hot. Jace yelled back at Analee. Within seconds, they were in a screaming match. Zalen laughed, making my skin itch. The two ice girls stayed in the corner, watching everything play out, while the others argued in their own language.

"There are plus sides to keeping her in this form..." The figure who had spoken looked like a dark shadow, like a normal person in my sight. He sounded rough, but if I wasn't mistaken, his voice held a hint of humor.

Jace relaxed, and the temperature in the room dropped. His white silhouette no longer challenged the glory of the sun's blaze. Analee's shimmering outline never faltered; she wasn't backing down. Jace made a comment, masked in disdain and anger. I didn't have to know their language to know he and Analee were still at each other's throats.

"She is not a lab rat! Have you no compassion?" Jace yelled. "Or are you just a heartless bitc—

"Do you forget who you are addressing, *Healer*?" Analee spit out his name like it was a swear word. Even at her worse, her voice still hung in the air as she spoke in their secret language. Jace fell on his knees, like it pained him to stand as she spoke. I wiped sweat from my brow; it felt like someone was forcing me to my knees as well. It wasn't completely overbearing, but my legs somehow became utterly weak. I got dizzy. I wished I had Stella to hold onto, since there wasn't a shadow of furniture in the room.

I held a knife to Marco's throat. He was larger and stronger than me. His eyes were bright green, unnaturally beautiful. His face was unshaven. His hair was in distress, but somehow incredibly attractive. I never fought my own battles before, but I refused to let him bring me to the Master again. He gripped the knife that I held to his throat. He hadn't even flinched when the blade sliced through his skin. A thick scar trailed across his knuckles—moving like it wasn't attached to his skin. It slithered under his wrist, hiding itself from view.

I was on my hands and knees when the vision cut out. Jace was there; his hand on my back for comfort. "I tried to keep you from experiencing the Master's wrath, but she has vast powers."

If he wanted to believe I passed out because of something Analee caused, I was fine with it. The excuse prevented me from having to discuss my visions. He brushed my hair out of my face. His fingertips grazed my temple; it tingled blissfully; my anxiety eased.

He sniffed the air around me then muttered that my scent had changed slightly. He helped me back onto my feet. I hoped I hadn't peed myself. The vision startled me, but it wasn't complete nonsense anymore. Pieces of my visions were starting to form together. It was like I was living parts of them, but they were out of order.

"What did Analee do?" I asked.

"The Master relies on her abilities to get answers instead of simply asking like the rest of us," Jace said.

"I get results. Besides, I've been fooled one too many times," Analee said, glaring at Jace.

For being on the "same side," Jace and Analee sure hated each other. I wasn't going to lie. It made me like Jace even more. I wonder what he'd do if he hadn't sworn the Oath to find the Fates. I wonder how long it would take before they fought to the death. The corner of my mouth twitched. I'd love to see a Scavenger come for her rotten soul. I'd love to see her scream, terrified of the unknowing death.

"She smells like the Prophet," the flickering orb said, before Analee and Jace had at it again. Her voice echoed in several different languages once she was done speaking.

"And death," Marco said, sniffing the air around me.

I glanced around the room. Everyone else was utterly still as they smelled me. I decided that I didn't have to explain myself to them if they refused to return the favor.

His shadow erupted into a hot blaze. He flung himself away from me. A searing, colorless fire burst from his feet. His shoulders smoldered, like they were being burned. His hatred erupted onto my skin. It was surreal. I had to be hallucinating, but I swore my skin blistered before it immediately healed. My jaw clenched. If Jace continued to let Analee get under his skin, I was likely going to go into shock. Unable to stand the scalding pangs that melted my insides, I collapsed to my knees and curled into the fetal position.

"Jace!" I begged. "Control yourself!"

Jace's fiery outline flickered, dimming and brightening. I got the impression he and Analee had a long, drawn out history. He dimmed himself a little more, but wouldn't control himself well enough to be close to me. He backed into the furthest corner, but refused to leave the room without me by his side.

Analee snickered, like the evening was unraveling better than she could have planned. Looking at her beautiful reflection, I stood up and marched toward her.

A blurred, dainty thin scar that trailed along her hairline formed in my sight. With much restraint to not brush up on my fighting skills, I placed my hand on her shoulder. I expected her to move. I expected her to slap my hand away. I expected her to make a snide comment. What I didn't expect was for her to stand perfectly still. She acted like she was waiting for me to strike.

"You don't scare me," I said, staring at her captivating scar that looked like a thread...

"I should," Analee hissed. "Because I am quite curious to see how much wrath your human body can take."

She made a comment I couldn't understand because it was in their cryptic language. As soon as she stopped speaking, the ice girl crawled over to me. Frost caked my skin where I'd sweated. The young girl reached for me and wrapped her dainty hands around my wrist. My skin froze over my chilled flesh, and my hand tingled for a few seconds, before becoming numb. I clenched my mouth shut to keep my teeth from chattering. A migraine formed. My entire body trembled like I was stranded in the middle of a blizzard. Ice coated my eyes. I couldn't move my hands without fear that my finger would snap off if I moved it.

"Enough of this!" Jace yelled. His temper pulsated through me. He wanted to protect me, tear Analee's head off, and tear the slaves off of me simultaneously, but he could only do one—and that was to be by my side.

"You will pay for this, Analee," I hissed, through clenched teeth.

Analee made another comment to the ice girl. The girl clamped her hand down on my shoulder, freezing my upper body before Jace could react. I wanted to cry but refused to give the Master the satisfaction of hearing me scream for mercy. Jace rattled off a series of curse words. Analee mocked him; her heavenly voice filled my mind.

"If you're going to insult me, do it in English!" I yelled.

Dead silence. No one moved, except the girl released her hand from my shoulder and wrist. The air around me fluctuated from freezing cold to blistering hot. My skin started to warm slightly, filling me with newfound energy. It wasn't long before Jace's heat blanketed every inch of my body. I opened my mouth to ask what was going on, but I couldn't exhale. The fiery warmth grew until it burned around me. The warmth was a heavenly sensation, which made the utter quietness around me so confusing.

"What?" I said, not understanding what was so significant.

"Well, she definitely has some lingering Elysian in her blood if she figured out we're a bunch of talented, super-natural ventriloquists," Marco said.

"You'll want to grant this one. Think of it as a gift."

"A gift for whom exactly?" I asked.

"Give your sister's voice to us, and you'll give all of us deities a way to speak up against the Master. Give us a voice to speak our mind without retribution from her horde."

Jace grabbed my hand like he was pulling me to a safety net of his embrace. His lips felt like the smoothest silk as he kissed my hand. His figure brightened, flickering like hot coals on a fire. Whispering my name, his lips lingered on my hand. Warmth wrapped up and down my body, following the movement of his hands. Jace finally took a breath, releasing the clasp around my throat.

"Something else you can't tell me?" I guessed.

He whispered my name. In my mind, I heard *Gwyneth* again. This time it sounded more like a whispered echo. He repeated it over and over. I heard my name and then the echoed version. His lips skimmed my skin while he spoke. Their texture was silky smooth on an otherworldly level. I wanted to look around the room to see what

188

everyone else was doing, but I couldn't tear my gaze away. He stopped kissing my hand only to turn it over.

Guiding my hand to his mouth, he kissed me and said my name once more. But his lips didn't move. I gasped. He repeated my name over and over, yet his lips didn't move.

"Jace?" I gasped.

I refused to believe what was happening—he couldn't speak without moving this mouth! With my fingers pressed up against his lips, he said my name—it echoed in my mind like it had whenever they spoke in their foreign language. Again, his lips, throat, chest didn't move, yet I heard him speak my name.

"Impossible," I whispered.

"The night you fell down Strikers' steps, I swore that I heard your screams beforehand. They were nonsensical, but it was coming from *you*," Marco said. "That's how I found you."

"I screamed as loud as I could *in my mind*, but it wasn't like I was telepathically reaching out for someone to hear me."

"But you did cry out for help," Jace said. "It's possible that you just didn't know what you were capable of, dearest."

"She's in her human form, without a sufficient amount of Elysian," said the shadowed figure. "It shouldn't be possible for her to speak in our dialect."

"We were always under the assumption the Fate's abilities didn't work unless they were within close proximity to each other, when their immortality flourished. Perhaps they were lying. Perhaps

189

they had powers even when they were apart, as mortals," Analee said.

"Or, perhaps, they were merely stronger when they were together," Marco uttered as he watched me with impossible intensity. "Apparently, the Fates were the best secret-keepers of our kind, as well as the most powerful."

"I beg to differ," Analee said.

"Yet, she can only grant what the heart most desires when she is captured," Zalen added. "Maybe their proximity to each other, only influenced their human aging, not their power. Perhaps, she can actually communicate soundlessly."

"Well, let's just find out how much Gwyneth can do without her sisters nearby, shall we, girls?" Analee signaled her other slave girl to me. "I swear on my life, Jace, if you let a squeak escape her lips, I'll kill her."

Jace's frustration and vehemence crept over me. It burned my flesh until it reached my heart. As much as I'd been through tonight, it couldn't compare to Jace's misery. The frost-covered girl whispered the echoed name Jace called me. It sounded like an angel had spoken. Dragging her legs, she crawled to me, using only her hands.

"Please believe that I don't want to allow this. I'd rather not bow to the Master anymore, Gwyneth. But she is a powerful goddess and a great warrior. She's better to have as a friend than foe," Jace said, holding me tight. The tone of his voice changed, when he spoke again, it was with adoration. "I'd follow you to the end of world again, if you'd have me, Gwyneth."

The way he said my name made my heart flutter. I swallowed and tried to take in a breath. Jace shook his head; he refused to give me my right to breathe. The girl grabbed my ankle and sunk her boney fingers into my flesh. Her grip felt like daggers, piercing my bone. I opened my mouth to cry out.

"Scream soundlessly for me, Chronicler," Analee demanded.

I wanted to tell them I couldn't breathe, therefore I couldn't speak. I fought Jace, squirming in his grip. He didn't budge. I beat him, as the girl climbed up my leg. My bones felt like they were shattering under her grip. Blood seeped from my flesh. It pooled around my body. I turned my attention to the girl digging her nails and her fingers into my thigh. I grabbed her hair and tried to rip her off of me. She hardly reacted to my pitiful attempt to keep her away. I started losing consciousness as I pulled her hair until the frost girl grabbed one of my wrists and jerked it out of the other girl's hair. Prying my hand open, I caught a flash of light as it bounced off a dagger. It cut my skin. As the blood pooled in my hand, the vision flooded my mind—me in a meadow, when the young girl cut me with the icy dagger. While the vision played over in my mind, the frost girl shoved her fingers into my palm. My blood chilled. She was freezing my blood. My fast heart beat started to slow.

I opened my mouth to scream, but not a sound came out. Jace prevented me from taking the breath needed to expel my pain. The two girls crushed my body, freezing me. I prayed for the heavens to save me. My cries echoed in my mind, as I expressed the long-standing pain that I'd enclosed in my soul as well as the immediate pain the ice girls brought my body.

The girl released my hand to cover her ears. The one that had crawled up my leg pushed away. Analee fell to her knees. Marco and Zalen disappeared. A thread of screams in several different languages rang in my ears as the shadowy dark figure held onto the flickering

191

one. Black liquid dripped from Jace's ears. I felt his lips gently brush my cheek.

My world became dark as he rocked me in his arms. I embraced unconsciousness...

Chapter Eighteen

I woke in my bed, without a clue as to how I got there. The last thing I remembered was passing out in Jace's embrace while young girls froze my body… and the dream. Elsie was curled up by my side underneath the sheets. She was like a little heater, snuggled up next to me. Not wanting to wake her, I lay still. I felt like I was living a lie—living with a family who could only claim me on their tax forms, a sister who'd never be blood, and a future that was as unexplainable and unreliable as the next high school kid's. And then there was Jace.

And the life I'd forgotten…

I looked out of my window. The beginning of a sunrise formed along the horizon. My eyes hurt more than normal. I badly wanted to see the colors of the sun. A nagging headache persisted, but I tried to ignore it as I lay in bed playing with Elsie's hair. My other hand was asleep from Elsie's weight, but I couldn't bring myself to move, even though it felt like it was being crushed. My body ached. Only when I was convinced my arm had to be amputated to move, did Elsie make a squeak.

"Did you kiss him?" she asked.

I smiled and closed my eyes. Out of everything she could have possibly said, that was the most perfect question. It made me feel almost normal. It made me feel like I truly had a sister.

"Only in my dreams."

***

I went through the motions in my classes, trying not to get called on for failing pop quizzes. My algebra teacher threatened to give me in-school suspension if I didn't change my attitude and answer his questions without chiming in with a snide remark. My third-period teacher excused me a minute early, so I didn't have to wander the halls, but I highly suspected she was sick of putting up with me. I was sick of myself too.

I sank into my fourth-period seat, despising my headache that began to ease the moment I got into the room. It smelled like Jace. I glanced around the room. No one, not even the teacher, was here yet. Could I have been so in tune to his scent that I smelled him because he usually sat behind me?

Students trickled in, distracting my thoughts. Jace walked in with Bree moments before the bell rang. She giggled at his joke, but I wasn't paying attention to their conversation. I didn't care if she flirted with him, because for the first time all day, I didn't feel like crawling out of my own skin. My body warmed, and my head cleared. His proximity was incredibly soothing.

"Good morning, dearest. How did you sleep?"

I rubbed my temples. If I was a drinker, I'd swear I had a hangover. He studied me for a half a second before cursing obscenities in whatever language he preferred to speak when he was aggravated. Immediately dimming himself so he looked like a shadow, he slammed his books down on the desk behind me and took a seat.

"I apologize for how last night ended," he whispered once the teacher started lecturing. "I have no wish for you to feel the obsessive lust an Addict craves, which is what you are experiencing now—the *Craves*. They aren't permanent and will pass if I don't string you along."

Bree coughed, as if to ask what he was referring to. I pretended not to notice her blatant inquiry. Her irksome eaves-dropping habit was making me weary.

After the bell rang, signaling the end of class, Jace rested his hand on my shoulder. He said that there was something important I needed to know. After packing up her backpack, Bree said that she was meeting Ryker for lunch and that we four should meet up later. Ryker had been missing school to visit a few colleges about scholarships, which was why he hadn't been around. It was a pity that my own problems were getting too out of hand. Otherwise I'd enjoy my Ryker-free moments. Jace removed his hand from my shoulder only to pick up my backpack.

I took the bag from him and was careful not to touch any part of him. It wasn't that I didn't want to. I did. But, I was scared. It was becoming all too real. He said nothing as we walked through the noisy hallway. Locker doors slammed shut, while students hurried to get to lunch.

"I understand why you and the others want to find all three Fates, but why do you obey the Master?"

"We do her bidding because we swore an Oath to find you and your sisters before all else. Those who did not swear allegiance were dragged to Hades by her horde. I can't go into further detail without attracting unwanted attention."

"Unwanted attention from the horde?" I clarified.

"The Oath binds me to her," Jace said and rubbed the back of his neck. "Not really her in particular but rather *her* horde will come for me."

"And what?"

"Carry my soul to hell."

"You will be reunited in death. The beginning will always have an end," I said as if reciting a script. I frowned. That did not sound like me. It was as if there was a ghost living within my soul. I thought of the Scavenger who came for me after it was torn from my soul. "Death is not meant as a punishment. It is a natural end to the beginning. Creation and destruction are reliant on each other as much as it pains them to be forever bound."

I swear Jace's lips turned to a smile. "You have a way of twisting words."

I clenched my jaw. If he dared call me Deino again or make another comparison of how I was her, I would kick him in his man bits. I didn't care if *she* was me; I didn't have her memories. I wasn't the same person.

How's this for jacking up words? "People fear death because the Master has abused the Scavengers' purpose!"

He clamped his hand over my mouth and waited. Only the sound of the clock ticking interrupted the otherwise quiet hall. After a full minute, the tension in Jace's shoulders eased. "It would be wise never to utter their name, not even you. They may not recognize you, and if they do they're as likely to come for you out of revenge."

"Revenge?"

"For siding with the humans and sacrificing them to the Master," Jace said, leaving out much needed detail. "Because they answer to her now, not you. It's time you accept that."

My eye twitched. It would be a dark day in hell that I ever forgot about my Scavengers. They.Were.Mine.

Chapter Nineteen

The comforting smell of a fresh brewed cup of Joe lingered in the library, even well into the night. Hector must have been working late. I didn't know what would cause a librarian to stay late, but I was grateful. I needed a little time to collect my thoughts and this place, the sanctuary of old books was that for me. There was something about the smell of an old book that just did it for me. Fiction or otherwise, to feel the worn pages on my fingertips, to know that so many different souls read the same thing was pretty touching.

"What could you possibly be doing to justify a late night?" I asked and slid into a wooden chair next to Hector's desk.

"I'm just finishing up a few projects," Hector said.

The light caught several pages on his desk. He certainly was busy orchestrating something. He tapped a pen on his table. That and the sound of the coffee pot gurgling were the only sounds interrupting the silence.

"I can wait here all night, Winnie. What's troubling you?" he said, taking a drink.

"Have you ever felt like you were living a lie?"

He took a deep breath. "I am living the life I was meant to. We only get one, Winnie."

"Lately, I've just felt like I'm meant for bigger purpose in life but I haven't a freaking clue how I'm supposed to be this person people want me to be."

"Oh Winnie, we are who we are. There is no changing that. You are going to do great things in life, and there is going to be times that you feel utterly lost. Both are okay."

I let those words sink in. Hector stood to get another cup of coffee. His limp was more pronounced on the whinny, old wooden floor. He stopped midway through to rub his knee.

"I swear my knee cracks more than the floor," he said.

"You're getting to be an old man."

"Don't remind me."

He poured another cup and hobbled over to the desk, he sat on the edge. After taking a careful sip, he asked if I was still seeing that guy from school.

"Jace?" I bit my lip. "Still too early to tell."

He chuckled, "You're a terrible liar."

"Like you're any better?"

"I've had a few more years of practice. Don't tell the ladies, but I've been finding more and more grays hair." He took another sip. "Honestly, what's your hold up with this fellow? You know if he breaks your heart I'll be there to beat him up."

Like a good big brother.

"Give him the beating of his life if he hurts me," I said. "Bree thinks I'm insane for *playing hard to get*. She treats him like he's the hottest thing that walked the Earth—like a god even, but no, she swore she didn't tell him anything about that night."

"Is he a god? I mean, do you find him attractive?"

I nearly choked. It was the furthest question I expected him to ask. "I like him. I'm drawn to him, even when I don't want to be. He's brilliant, romantic, strong as hell, sexy—"

"That's enough!" Hector said. "I don't need all the details. But if you're so into him what's the hold up? Do you fear him?"

He was dangerous and I didn't trust myself around him. I didn't trust anyone else around me. And I was constantly looking over my shoulder.

"It's not him I fear; it's his friends I am not a fan of. They are truly obsessed with me."

"That will suck the life right out of you."

"You say that like you know from personal experience."

"Let's just say I've had my fair share of stalkers."

Chapter Twenty

Bliss found me at night, while I slept. Stars hung in the sky like fireflies, while the moon lit the land around me. Larkspur petals cushioned my feet. A sublime mood encompassed me. To escape the complications in my life was a gift. Lightning bugs danced in the sky. A meadow stretched out endlessly. The horizon was uninterrupted—no buildings or street lights to alter the glory of the night. My body hadn't fought itself at the beginning of the dream like the others. I felt stronger. I glanced over my shoulder just in time to see Marco vanish. And then I was alone…but, I could have sworn I'd felt Jace's warmth pass over me. I spun in a circle. There was no glaring white silhouette; no Jace.

Confused that I'd be brought here only to be left alone, I closed my eyes. Unless, it was Analee trying to cage me like some animal in a place that could be anywhere. However, when I reached out with my mind, I searched for Jace…and then, I felt it; the slightest tug on my finger. I welcomed his presence into my soul.

My hair moved slowly away to one side of my neck; it was *his* doing. Jace had Muted himself completely so that I would not see him in the darkest of nights. He was careful not to touch my skin as he brushed my hair aside. A smile grew on my face when the smooth touch of his kiss was placed on my neck. I leaned back into his embrace and allowed myself to melt into him. Jace's body warmed after I whispered his name. A tidal wave of zest flooded my heart. I couldn't sort my anger from the enthusiasm we had for each other. I turned to take in his beautiful body and immediately lost my breath. Colorless flames crawled from his skin onto me. It tingled instead of burned; rather it felt like my body was awakening for the first time in my life. The rapture was surreal. I hadn't cared if it was his aura over shadowing mine. I'd always hoped that one day I'd be happy; perhaps I was looking for joy during the wrong time of day.

He turned me in his arms and then hummed a tune I couldn't quite place. I rested my arms around his neck. He pulled me close against his bare chest. One hand was low on my hip while the other crept high on my back. His dazzling, deep voice echoed in the night while he mesmerized me with his melody. The song promised suffering, but the outcome was worth it. When I realized he was repeating a verse over and over, he'd engulfed me in his fire.

Jace leaned in close like he was going to let me lick the song right from his lips. "Close your eyes, dearest."

I obeyed. Instead of his hazy outline, his fiery essence captivated me. His entire body rippled with flames, fueling each other. His fingertips ticked my skin just behind my ear, while his thumb traced my jaw line.

"You see the world by the touch of your hands; I want you to know what I see when I look at you."

I had spent my entire life hiding from what I looked like. I didn't care about appearances, especially not mine. Jace changed all that. I tried to look away. His rough hands were gentle on my face, but he wouldn't let me hide from him—or the truth.

"You use that gorgeous blond hair of yours to cover your porcelain face. You tried to hide in your own skin, but no matter what you do, your sheer beauty radiates from every laugh line." He slipped a hand behind my neck and muttered something about my captivating scent. "For centuries, men have been awestruck at the wonders hiding just below the ocean's surface. I'm no different from them, Gwyneth. For years, I've wondered what's buried deep inside your soul, as I look through your ocean eyes. I'm desperate to see the wonders you hide from the rest of the world."

I swallowed. It felt like a dream, but didn't, at the same time. I opened my mouth to protest, to tell him he was living in a fairy-tale, but the words fell short because I couldn't breathe. Either he was holding his breath, or I was—I couldn't tell. I looked away; the way he saw me wasn't the way I really was. It was all a lie.

"You have this way of walking that draws me in. Only with much effort can I look away, especially when you're ready to give me a piece of your mind," Jace said, and then gently tugged on my chin so I'd look at him. "You have hypnotic lips. Even when you're screaming at me, I want nothing more than to silence all your worries with my kiss. The pink pigments in them match the way you blush. It makes me lose my mind when you forget to breathe when I speak."

I begged him to stop. I was none of these things, looked nothing like the girl he was describing. He refused to listen. His hand drifted to the small of my back. I forgot how to speak when he said that I deserved more credit than what I gave myself.

"You may look young and naïve, but then you smile. Your wicked grin reveals your intelligence. Your life blurs into a mess of black and white, and yet, you see things that most people miss."

He spoke of my flaws like they were perfection. I was an orphan child, the result of a horrible crime. I was nothing—meant little to anyone. I wasn't this deep person who knew things all along. I hardly had control of my life. I was lost, so lost and all alone.

"You see things I can't imagine with those striking eyes of yours. There are times I swear you gaze into my soul," he said, and rested his forehead against mine. "Sea blue, with a touch of hazel trying to conquer your right eye. I'd willingly drown in your eyes, gazing into them until the end of time. In all my years searching for you, I've never forgotten the beauty of your soul."

***

John already had the pregame on when I came down for breakfast. It had to be pushing eleven thirty in the morning. Elsie sat next to me on the couch with a small pile of books scattered around her. She wasn't making much progress. Martha tried every trick in the book to entice Elsie to get her homework done. Apparently her grades weren't the best.

"What about a girl's date, Elsie?" Martha said. "If you keep your grades up, I'll treat you and Winnie."

"Anywhere?" Elsie asked. When Martha agreed, Elsie quickly picked up one of her textbooks and began reading.

I spent the afternoon answering a few of her random questions about math and science. It was interrupted by the protests of my faux father, screaming at the referees on the television. Elsie started mimicking John's comments instead of working on her questions. I couldn't blame her; my homework wasn't getting done either. I was distracted, trying to make sense of what happened last night. I dug the cell out of my back pocket. For half a second I wanted to call Jace and sort out what happened last night. My dreams felt like reality, and my reality was getting a heavy dose of craziness.

Right before I tucked it back inside my pocket, it rang. Jace's deep tantalizing voice came over the speaker. He wanted to meet tonight, and promised that it'd be worth it, if I could sneak out. I refused to ask my foster parents for permission until he told me what he had planned.

"With everything else that has happened, do you still want to go to your family's old house?"

"Do you still want that kiss?"

"I'll be at your place tonight."

Nightfall couldn't come fast enough.

The moonless sky made it difficult for me to distinguish between the people and buildings. Smaller objects camouflaged themselves in the shadows. I took a deep breath and concentrated on settling my nerves. Years had come and gone since I'd last visited my old home—my stolen life. Jace sat on the hood of the car, waiting for me to gather the nerve to get out. I rubbed my clammy hands on my jeans and then opened the door handle. The cool air hit me, chilling me to the bone. I imagined the trees' leaves floating to the cool ground. Winter was trying to steal weeks from autumn's reign.

"You don't need Stella," Jace said, when I walked up to him.

"If we get separated, I'll need a way to get out of Dodge," I said defensively.

"The only way we'd get separated again is if you take a trip to Hades," he said as he took Stella. "And this time, I'll follow you there too."

The thought wasn't comforting, but I let him toss my walking stick back into the car. I was fine for the first few steps, but since there was almost no light, I stumbled. He offered his hand to guide me. I adamantly refused any help, until I nearly skinned my knees after missing the curb. Since we hadn't even gotten to the hard part of sneaking around the backyards of the houses leading up to my old home, I was going to announce our presence to the neighbors.

"Fine," I said defeated. I couldn't manage without his help.

"Say please," Jace insisted, crossing his arms over his chest.

I groaned. Of course I could see *his* general shape in the darkest night. I started to walk away. "I'm not begging for your help."

The dismissal would've been more impressive if I hadn't tripped a half a second later. I stumbled onto someone's grassy yard. We were traveling at mock-zero—if we were to get to the house before sunrise; I needed to swallow my pride. I muttered 'please' under my breath. He pulled me back onto my feet; instead of offering his elbow, he gave me the choice of holding his hand or walking alone. I voted for the latter because it would be safer—emotionally speaking—but I slipped my fingers through his anyway.

"What do you call the Healer in your language?" I asked, trying to take my mind off the fact that my hands felt like icebergs in his.

He paused. When I faced him, he brought my hand up to his chest. In my mind, I heard him say a word that sounded like *shaman* as he said "Healer" out loud. Then he kissed my hand, and placed it just below my left shoulder. The word *raconteur* echoed in my mind as he whispered "Chronicler." Bringing his hands between both of us, he said out loud, "We are—" In my mind I heard him say *deity*. It echoed, just like when he spoke my name soundlessly.

"Who taught you the language, and how is it even possible for you to speak telepathically?"

"This gift?" Jace asked. "Not all of us could speak telepathically like the Prophet, until a generous person granted us the ability."

He squeezed my hand like it'd come from me. Half a dozen questions spewed from my mouth—how had the gift come from me?

"Someone threatened me with my life simply to be able to speak?"

I held a knife to Marco's throat. He was larger and stronger than me. His eyes were bright green, unnaturally beautiful. His face was unshaven. His hair was in distress, but somehow incredibly attractive. I never fought my own battles before, but I refused to let him bring me to the Master again. He gripped the knife that I held to his throat. He hadn't even flinched when the blade sliced through his skin. A thick scar trailed across his knuckles—moving like it wasn't attached to his skin. It slithered under his wrist, hiding itself from view.

My reflection shone off the blade. Wrinkles creased themselves around my eyes. Even as he kneeled before me, the red -haired man was still at chest height. I pressed my lips together and breathed through my mouth as the stench of rot and decay filled the air.

His skin peeled away from his face as if it couldn't stand it. Yellow puss and orange infected blood seeped from his tissue. It slopped to the ground. The liquid flesh sprayed my legs. The rotting man vanished and stood behind me a second later. His decaying hand held the knife in my hand. It was now pressed up against my throat.

"I won't allow you take me to her, at least not alive," I said.

"It's not for her, ocean eyes," he said. He pronounced my nickname like it was a joke. "You'll want to grant this one. Think of it as a gift."

"A gift for whom exactly?" I asked.

"Give your sister's voice to us, and you'll give all of us deities a way to speak up against the Master."

"Are you thinking of Marco?" Jace said. "Because you suddenly smell like him."

"He infiltrated my thoughts." I nodded, not wanting to tell him about my visions—not yet at least.

He let go of my hand only to slowly and quietly fiddle with the gate's latch. I slipped through; he followed and just as quietly closed it. He reached for my hand, and then we continued through another back yard. I didn't know if it was an unconscious movement or if he enjoyed tracing his thumb over mine, but it was extremely soothing. It was probably just a coincidence, but it was the exact place where I would initially feel another's *thread of life.*

He stopped me just as a light flared to our side—illuminating the surroundings. A light sensor had detected our movement. A dog started barking insanely; a bedroom light turned on a second later. Yelling about a *damn raccoon* resonated from the house. I knew I should have run. However, my flight or fight reaction button must have been broken, because I simply froze. Before I could protest, Jace swept me into his arms and took off running. He leaped over the fence on the other side of the yard and didn't stop until two yards later. Both were light sensor and dog free.

I draped my arm around his neck. My body warmed, and I watched his reaction when it hit him. I don't know how– I just knew that he noticed I was enjoying his touch. Clutching him, I almost let my hands explore. I'd be damned if his chest wasn't chiseled from stone. That he had to concentrate on breathing normally made me grin until it he replied verbally with his own urges.

"I'm not going to need much convincing to abort tonight's fiasco if you keep nuzzling into me, Gwyneth."

"You're still forbidden to touch my lips until I figure out what happened to my family."

"Fair enough. I've only waited a few centuries to feel your lips against mine, what's another day or hour or second."

"You're the one stalking now, not me."

He turned me in his arms so I faced a house—like any other house, except this one used to be mine. The lights were off; the house was empty. He analyzed the situation before he approached a window.

"The windows were not altered during the remodel. Is this the window they entered?" he asked.

"How am I supposed to know?"

He refused to comment and moved on to the next window. I couldn't help to notice that he held me tighter. A night light shone through the next window. I shook my head before he asked if this was the window used. I didn't know how I knew—I just did. Jace said nothing, but carried me to the next. He kept a solid grip on me. When he got close to the window, my stomach began to tighten.

"Which one of these windows offers the most concealment?"

"The first one," Jace answered and lowered me to the ground. "This window led to your parents' bedroom. It's a bathroom now."

"You trust me to pick the window, even though I can't see?"

"You see what others can't."

"Like what?"

"The past," Jace said. "You used to have the ability to see other's memories, their past, when you touched their thread of life. We all leave parts of ourselves everywhere we touch, like DNA, but on a metaphysical level. I always suspected that you could sense that."

Without giving me time to absorb what he'd just said, Jace pulled himself through the window first, positioned himself, and then reached down for me. His handhold was tight, pulling me upward through the window. Keeping his voice just above a whisper, he gave me a quick tour of the house. I instructed him to make sure I didn't walk into anything, which would inevitably cause a ruckus. He agreed without making any snide remarks about my asking for assistance. He watched me with such intensity; it made it difficult to concentrate on my surroundings.

He'd been here at least once to investigate the place himself. So, either he noticed something and wanted to see if I picked up on it, or he couldn't find anything and figured that I had a *Hail Mary's* chance at picking up on some clue that he'd missed. Walking slowly down the hall, the carpet kept my unsteady steps from being too noticeable. I walked around the house—hoping, waiting, for a sense of anything to pass over me. Nothing. Even when I stood in the bedroom where Lily died, I felt nothing other than guilt for living when she hadn't.

"Can you lead me to the bathroom, please?"

He took my hand and pulled me close behind him. I walked in his footsteps. It kept me from walking into anything, since he wasn't behind me to catch random things from falling to the floor. Once inside the bathroom, I splashed water on my face. Clearing my head, I focused on the water as it dripped down my face.

"Will you Mute yourself," I asked. "Please?"

With my eyes closed, I splashed more water on my face and tuned Jace out. It cooled my face as it trickled down. I thought about the fall night; the police reports stated the area was well lit. It was raining, I thought as the water ran off my face. I'd never been successful at triggering my own vision, but wind and water seemed to be key elements. Retracing my steps back into the room where Lily died, I thought of the fall night nearly two decades ago.

"Fan?" I asked as I stood on the spot my sister had died.

Jace turned on the ceiling fan. Kneeling on the place Lily took

212

her final breath, I tried everything to induce a vision, a feeling, anything. My suppressed memories of my derailed life and old vision bubbled to the surface. They exploded through my tears. I beat the floor, commanding myself to see something. *Any* vision!

Collapsing to his knees, the old man grinned vindictively as an impossible gift was bestowed upon him. Smoothing out like his skin was being ironed, the old man grew young. His gray hair deepened in a dark brown, curling at the ends. His insane laugh echoed in my mind.

Warm, brilliant red liquid seeped into my pink blanket. I was a young child, an infant. Lightning flashed across the night sky while rain pelted the roof only to stream down the window beside me. My screams competed with the thunder. But no one listened to me, not even the now young man, who held a bloody knife in one hand and a cane in the other. Blood gushed from my sister. My pink blanket turned red. Colors blurred, until everything melted into a shade of gray.

I felt nothing; what I saw was unfeasible. I traded bodies with my sister. She died. I lived. I didn't know how I was able to do such a thing, but it didn't matter. I was a horrible person. I sacrificed her life to save my own. She died because of me. Not a single thing mattered; no soul could make me *feel* anything again.

"Gwyneth?"

I had no need to open my eyes to see Jace kneeling by me. His smoky figure was blatant in my sight. Concern emitted as he said my name over and over. When I didn't react, he told me I was in shock. He reached for my cheek. I distantly felt his anxiety climb.

"You're crying blood."

I opened my eyes. He looked like a dark shadow, Muted like I'd asked. A crimson haze clouded my vision. I wiped my eyes and looked at my hands in disbelief. I didn't care enough about anything to shed a tear, so why had I cried?

"Red," I said absentmindedly.

He asked me if I trusted him. I nodded. Taking my hand in his, he blew hot air on them. "Would you permit me to show myself as I am—unmuted?"

I nodded. What did I care? He could do as he pleased. I did. I traded places with my sister. I dodged death by sacrificing Lily. Jace slowly brightened. His shape became more defined the brighter he became. A tear trickled down my cheek.

Pity crept into my soul the brighter he became. Guilt accompanied it. Another tear dropped. Regret. More tears dripped from my eyes. Confusion. Heartache. Anger. Sorrow.

"Hold me," I said. He pulled me into his arms before I finished speaking.

Standing above me as I clutched my blanket was the old man, holding a bloody knife in one hand. He was scarred and wrinkled. His hands were wrinkled, weathered. Time hadn't been good to him. He grabbed my arm and cut it. My blood seeped from my skin. The old man leaned in close, smelling me. The smell of fresh rain filled the air. But what scared me was the look in his eye when he smiled at me. It was pure evil.

I looked from a child wrapped in a blanket, to an old man kneeling over me. I looked back to the child, begging me for help. And within a blink of an eye, my view changed. I was the child looking at my sister in the old man's grip instead of me being in his grasp. His hand held onto my sister's throat, choking her. The knife in his hand rose to his face. The reflection of a woman in the knife glistened before blood spattered on the blade.

Collapsing to his knees, the old man grinned vindictively as an impossible gift was bestowed upon him. Smoothing out like his skin was being ironed, the old man grew young. His gray hair deepened in a dark brown, curling at the ends. His insane laugh echoed in my mind.

Warm, brilliant red liquid seeped into my pink blanket. I was a young child, an infant. Lightning flashed across the night sky while rain pelted the roof only to stream down the window beside me. My screams competed with the thunder. But no one listened to me, not even the now young man, who held a bloody knife in one hand and a cane in the other. Blood gushed from my sister. My pink blanket turned red. Colors blurred, until everything melted into a shade of gray.

"I killed her!"

My confession echoed in the noiseless night. Even though I felt his confusion wash over me, he said nothing. Instead, he picked me up and carried me out of the house. We were next to his car seconds later. He lowered me into the back seat of his car. He said that I was freezing and that his healing power wasn't going to help since I was physically fine.

He tried to comfort me, but I didn't want it. I didn't deserve it, so I pushed him away. I don't know how I changed bodies with my sister, but I did. Jace slipped into the driver seat and sped away. She died, when it should have been me. I was no better than the murderer in my vision. It wasn't long before his arms were wrapped around me again. Jace was Muted as he carried me. He knocked on a door. Marco answered. I didn't care enough to be bothered by his company. His spicy scent triggered another vision.

I held a knife to a man's throat. He was larger and stronger than me. His eyes were bright green, unnaturally beautiful. His face was unshaven. His hair was in distress but somehow incredibly attractive. I'd never fought my own battles before, but I refused to let him bring me to the Master again. The past would be forever repeating itself; but today there could be change. He gripped the knife that I held to his throat. He hadn't even flinched when the blade sliced through his skin. A thick scar trailed across his knuckles—moving like it wasn't attached to his skin. It slithered under his wrist, hiding itself from view.

"What's going on?" Marco asked, jarring me from my vision.

"She's in shock. Tell the others to vacate," Jace said. "And I swear to all that's holy, if Analee *or her slaves* disturb Gwyneth, I'll find a way to kill her."

Glancing around the room, I saw a fireplace in the corner of the massive room. I felt the presences of other deities but hadn't heard them. Jace sat down on a couch with me still in his arms, watching me.

"Tell me about what happened," Jace said.

"Lily was defenseless," I said. My eyes filled with tears.

"Defenseless, how?"

"She died by the knife of an old man, but it was me who killed her. I watched her bleed out and did nothing. I changed her destiny by trading places with her," I said, fumbling for the right wording. "I stole her life."

We sat in silence as time ticked away. He stroked my hair. After what seemed like hours, he began singing in the foreign language. It was music to my ears, calming my soul. I closed my eyes and wished my life away. I wished time would cease to continue. I'd never been afraid of death; now I wanted it—deserved it.

"You want to tell me why I just put Analee into a frenzy?" Marco asked as he walked into the room. "She's not one to take orders kindly."

"What happened when you traded places with your sister, Gwyneth?" Jace asked evenly—too calmly.

"My soul lived in her body. I looked at my sister, wrapped in the baby's blanket, begging her for help. Then a second before that horrible man cut her eyes out, I was looking at the scene from her perspective. I stole her body—traded my fate with hers, because he was going kill me. I destroyed her soul. I don't know how I did it, but I did. I know I did."

"Impossible," Marco whispered. "Even if all the sisters are together, they couldn't be powerful enough to—"

"Change another's destiny?" Jace said quietly. "It's their power—their essence—to change the course of fate, for each one of us, as well as the humans. She gave me her Elysian when she died years ago. Her sisters weren't near then; yet, she changed their fate."

Marco grunted like he didn't believe it. However, he didn't argue either.

"The police reports stated it was a rainy night when it happened—the night a man grew young," I said idly. I wasn't following their conversation anyway.

"The night a man grew young?" Jace repeated. "If he grew young, Lily had to have Elysian in her blood… or Gwyneth

217

interfered with the girl's fate, by weaving it into her Elysian into the human's thread of life."

"Or it was the Cutter," Marco offered. "She likes to hop around from body to body. What did she tell me once…it was like wearing a new suit?"

It was Jace's turn to groan. "Mythical rumor. We've gone around in circles about the subject, I'm not about to debate it again."

"Fine, if the man grew young, he was a Hunter. If it was one of them filthy half-breeds, then they have been watching Gwyneth since she was a child," Marco said, and then cursed. "The police officer died shortly after the investigation began. Coincidence or cover-up?"

"Cover-up for what?" I asked.

"People just don't get younger all the time, sugar," Marco said. "Faking a death would be a perfect cover-up. The Hunters are notorious for faking previous lives."

"See if you can find any death certificate or burial information," Jace ordered.

Marco's head twitched nervously. "Head's up, Analee's on her way over here."

"He smelled like fresh rain," I said, thinking of the vision.

"Fresh rain?" Marco questioned.

I nodded. Jace cursed, and Marco spat. A putrid smell filled the air. Blasts of cold air froze the air around me as Jace's body warmed me.

"Rain can smell a lot like the ocean—the Butcher's scent," Marco muttered and then sniffed me. "We wouldn't have necessarily picked up on it right away. It looks like your old friend found Gwyneth before you could."

"You should have killed the Butcher when you had the chance, Jace," Analee said. I didn't hear her enter the room. It didn't surprise me. Her figure blazed bright like always; Jace's went utterly still, like he was getting ready to strike. Before Jace could comment, Marco appeared in front of Analee, and the two of them vanished.

That alone was impossible, vanishing in thin air. But at this point I didn't care.

"I can't do this anymore," I said. I was about to tell him to heal me, but he pressed his finger against my lips, begging me not to say it—not yet.

"Just a little longer, dearest, and I'll find the person who murdered your family. It's always been important to you, even if we didn't understand why," Jace muttered. "Even though you didn't remember why, your instincts guide you to the truth. If the murderer is the Butcher, one of the most noxious Hunters, you'll want him dead, as badly as I do."

"Why would I possibly care?"

"Because he's the reason you died in the first place."

Chapter Twenty-One

Sleep avoided me. Lily was dead; it was my fault. The guilt boiled in my soul. I hadn't even bothered to open my eyes when the floor creaked by my dresser. I was being watched—monitored. His smoky figure came into view. I simply waited for Jace to rescue me away from reality. He didn't utter a word as he brushed my hair away from my face. My body warmed as he hummed the tune he had in my dreams. Captivated by his beauty, I almost didn't see the shimmer of silver behind him. Marco rested his hand on Jace's shoulder.

"You've come to liberate me in my dreams but I don't want to dream tonight," I said, reaching for Jace's face. His coarse facial stubble scratched my palm. Neither he nor Marco moved—it was like they hadn't expected me to still be awake. Jace tentatively intertwined his fingers around mine.

I wanted him in ways I wasn't worthy of asking for. I needed him in ways I couldn't imagine.

Jace shrugged Marco off his shoulder. He spoke soundlessly and then out loud I heard him say I was finally ready to listen. Marco lifted his hand from Jace's shoulder and then vanished.

"I traded places with her so I'd live and she'd die!"

"Gwyneth, look at me." His body went rigid. "You need to stop running from the past and from who you are. Embrace it."

I wanted to scream that we had no past, but the words refused to jump from my tongue. Tears streamed down my face. I was so utterly defeated. He let go of my face and walked away. I shoved my head into the pillow. I begged not to cry out until I could no longer hear his footsteps. My soul erupted; I deserved loneliness and a life of torment. My voice was raw from wailing into the pillow. The bed shifted. I stifled my tears only long enough to realize my foster parents could hear me screaming, but it wasn't Martha or John in the bed beside me.

Jace slid his legs next to mine and then pulled me close next to him. Holding the covers tightly around me, he rocked me. He hummed the melody I'd grown to love—the one from my dreams. Just as quickly as the tune relaxed me, it enraged me. He shouldn't be singing this song for me. His ethereal voice echoed in the room and in my heart. I wasn't worthy of anyone's love. I squirmed, trying to put distance between us. It didn't work. I kicked him, wishing it would distract him. I beat my fists into his chest. I refused to stop until my arms ached.

"Leave! Leave me, Jace. I don't want you in my life. You deserve someone who's better than me."

"Liar," Jace said, wrapping his arms around me so I couldn't

221

slam my fists against him. "You want me in your life, and I want you in mine. You've already made me scream your name to the heavens, begging for forgiveness and another chance to avenge your death. Don't make me do it again."

"What name would you scream this time? Deino or Gwyneth? What about the Chronic—"

"My beloved," he whispered, silencing my insults.

Adoration radiated from his voice as he spoke those two small, yet powerful words.

"I screamed for my beloved to join me again when her body was no longer frail. I'd begged her to heal my broken soul along with hers. I've longed for the taste of her heart-stopping kiss after she was reborn. I crave the eternal passion of the goddess I fell in love with years ago—the very same goddess who now screams into the night, longing for an alternate ending to her tragic life; the night she died, I screamed one request to the heavens." He paused before he whispered the plea. "I prayed that she'd never forget my love...I prayed that if she forgot all else, she wouldn't forget my love."

Chapter Twenty-Two

Waking up for school couldn't have been any more mundane. Monday. School. Kill me now. After everything I'd just found out, spending eight hours at McKesson High was a catastrophic waste of time. If Martha's to-do list wasn't so long, I might have faked an illness. Compared to cleaning all day long or attending school, the latter seemed like the lesser of two evils. After throwing on my school uniform, I trudged to the brick building. Students poured around me. Stella kept them from getting too close, giving me a wide berth. I reached my locker just in time to hear Ryker tell Bree that "the train-wreck is approaching."

The energy to put up with him wasn't something I could reasonably do today, so I kept quiet. Besides, he and Bree were getting inappropriately reacquainted, so even if I had an amazing come-back, it'd fall on deaf ears. I rubbed the sleep from my eyes and dumped my backpack in front of my locker. I clasped the cold metal lock keeping all my valuables safe inside. I needed a break. Monday had come too fast. I rested my head against the door and took a deep breath. I could do this. I could live normally. I could pretend I wasn't a murderer—pretend I wasn't clairvoyant. I'd become an actress in my own life. My life was the stage—my sight, my happiness, my entire existence could be faked.

Bree picked up my backpack and then grabbed my arm. "BFF duties—I need you in the bathroom stat."

I groaned. Another problem? I followed her down the hall. Students piled into the classrooms. I was going to be late for history and Bree decided this was the opportune time to have an emergency? She led me into the handicap stall and locked the door behind us.

"Spill," she demanded.

I stood silent. What was she talking about? She was the one who called the impromptu meeting—she was the one with the emergency that couldn't wait till lunch.

"You're strung out," she stated, and crossed her arms over her chest. "I've played the part of the good friend and decided that you'd tell me whatever was bothering in good time, but you've gone to epic lengths to keep me in the dark."

"I'm fine."

"You couldn't look more like those pictures of drug junkies the health nurse showed us," she said defensively. "I might not know the difference between crack and coke, but I know you, Winnie. You're strung out. What are you taking?"

"You've been watching too many episodes of *Intervention*," I said, and reached for the door.

She slapped my hand away. The flood of sadness I'd buried deep in order to even come to school threatened to trickle out from my eyes; but, I wasn't going to back down. I reached for the door again. She pushed me. My back hit the bathroom wall. The bell sounded. We were officially late for class.

"I'm not on drugs!" My frustration poured out. I barely managed on auto-pilot. Going to get a tardy slip from the principal was like having to scale a mountain, and I lost my climbing gear.

"Then, what is it? You're all secretive. You've been ill a lot, or are you faking all these sick leaves? You say you're fine but your temper is snapping more than usual. You bail on hanging out with me, and then when I call your house, Elsie answers and says that you told your fosters you'd gone to my place. So unless you've grown a 'Bree Clone' you've got some exp—"

"They're all dead, Bree! My entire family is dead. My parents! My sister! I'm the only survivor!"

I couldn't finish. I couldn't say that it was my fault. In my heart I knew it was the truth. Their lives were cut short because a horde of mentally deranged people were after me. I slid down the wall and crumbled into a sobbing mess on the dirty, cold floor.

"Oh, girlie," Bree whispered, and then sat down beside me. She hugged me; I held on with sheer desperation. She didn't know the whole truth—not even close. "The guy who broke into your house that night was a complete psycho. You were just a kid."

"Everything okay in here?" A hall-monitor asked.

I wiped my eyes and prepared for the infamous tardy slip to

225

slide under the door. Bree shifted and dug a thin piece of paper out of her pocket. She pushed it under the door. The hall-monitor picked it up.

"You've got ten minutes," she said, and started to walk out of the bathroom.

"Ten? We both know a twenty buys double that," Bree said.

"There are two of you—ten minutes each."

"Two?" Bree gasped as if she couldn't believe the accusation. "I'm hanging out with my mannequin in here."

"Whatever, you two better be gone when I finish rounds."

The bathroom door shut, cutting us off from the rest of the school. Bree shifted beside me. "Pinky-swear you're not on anything, and I'll believe you one-hundred percent."

My little finger slipped through hers. And as silly as it sounded, I felt better. "Cross my heart and hope to die."

"Okay, then let's get you cleaned up because you look like someone sneezed on your face and you didn't bother to wipe it off," Bree said, and then reached for her backpack. Her supply of make-up, bobby-pins, and perfume would always take priority over school books. She wasn't going to make valedictorian. I wasn't either, but it'd be over her dead body when I walked around looking like a fool. She cared about me, even when I knew I was being difficult. But we were friends—through thick and thin. And that's what mattered.

"I swear to all that is holy, if you make a big deal about mascara today you'll be sporting a black-eye. A little bit of *Maybelline* isn't going to kill you," she said, opening up her make-up kit. She dabbed the foundation on my skin. And then blew on my cheeks. "Dry those pretty eyes."

My reflection shone off the blade's reflection. Wrinkles creased themselves around my eyes. Even as he kneeled before me, the red -haired man was still at chest height. I pressed my lips together and breathed through my mouth as the stench of rot and decay filled the air.

His skin peeled away from his face as if it couldn't stand it. Yellow puss and orange infected blood seeped from his tissue. It slopped to the ground. The liquid flesh sprayed my legs. The rotting man vanished and stood behind me a second later. His decaying hand held the knife in my hand. It was now pressed up against my throat.

***

Martha set the phone on the table stand by the television. She informed me that a boy had called. I frowned. If any guy called, wouldn't he try my cell first? I walked down the stairs.

Elsie's voice came through the phone's speaker loud and clear. "—kiss was like?"

Jace's beautiful, deep laugh echoed through the phones speaker, causing my stomach to flutter. "She won't let me kiss her."

"Elsie!" I yelled. "Get off the phone!"

She gasped and slammed her phone down onto whatever receiver she used. It rattled but hadn't disconnected. Jace chuckled when John's voice came over the receiver to scold her for listening in on somebody else's conversation—privacy violation. He was well into the lecture before noticing the phone wasn't on the receiver.

"You know you could have just called me on my cell phone, right?" I said, taking the phone upstairs with me.

"I tried, but you didn't pick up."

Rummaging through my pants, backpack, Max's doggy bag, I thought of every possible place I could have lost it. "Looks like I'm disconnected until I can save up some dough. Guess I'll be cleaning at KnockOuts again."

"Take mine," Jace said.

"Jace, I'm not going to take—"

"You're a priority for all of us," he insisted. "Therefore, we need to be able to get a hold of you. Besides, I'll just buy another."

"So you'll give me your cell just because you're afraid you won't be able to get a hold of me?"

Dial tone. I punched the redial button, but there was no answer. Within a half an hour, a tap came from my bedroom window. Jace's silhouette hung in the tree—nothing like having a guy hanging outside a window to draw unwanted parental attention. I unlatched the window to let him in.

"I'm not going to wear an electronic leash," I said, blocking the window with my body. He wasn't going to make a habit of swinging through my window to check up on me.

"Glad we aren't going to let our nighttime activities affect our affiliation with each other because this love/hate relationship hasn't been difficult to keep up with or anything." He nudged me out of the way and then sat on the windowsill. He extended his hand, offering me his phone. "It's not a choice. I've already programmed my new number into it."

He just went out and bought a new cell? How much money did he have to his name?

"Not a choice, my butt," I said, and paced around the room to keep myself from wanting to trace my finger down his chest or do something regrettable with his lips.

He walked over and set the phone on my dresser. The wood groaned under his weight. "Lily was murdered because the Butcher thought she was the Chronicler before you traded places. I'm not going to take chances with your life; you're going to take the phone. I can't stay with you every night or monitor you every second. The sheer amount of time we would spend together would most likely end with you becoming an Addict; I promise you the Craves can be much more unpleasant than what you felt earlier."

"Why is everyone so *sure* I'll become an Addict?"

"Mankind is extremely susceptible to the Elysian flowing in our blood. It's like a drug and will affect every human on a subconscious level. It flows through us—attracting others by our beauty, how we sound, and even our very touch."

"That is the reason why you needed to build my tolerance?" I said, thinking out loud. "But I wasn't attracted to you right away; I was sick."

Jace intercepted me while I made my third pass by the night stand. He held me from behind. His hands rested firmly on my arms, using just enough pressure to keep me from moving. "You didn't act like you were a human who'd been exposed. You acted like you'd been around the Elysian your entire life and were immediately going through withdrawals. Marco's theory is that your Elysian reacted so strongly to ours, that it physically overwhelmed you."

"My tolerance has improved, so why the concern that I'll become an Addict?" I said, standing utterly still in his arms. *What I'd give to snuggle in closer.*

Jace nuzzled his face in the nook between my neck and shoulder blade. He said my name like I was his saving grace. "Dearest, do you truly believe you wouldn't begin to crave me, or that you haven't started to already?"

Point taken. "So, you're saying you could *make* me want you, essentially stealing my freewill?"

"I don't want a mindless drone, Gwyneth, which is why you're taking my cell," he said, and then put some distance between us. "The Butcher nearly captured you—again. He smells like rain and is of mixed offspring between us and mankind. He grows young if pure blood—Elysian—is shed."

"Why is he searching for the Chronicler? Can't he just keep killing deities and stay young forever?"

"There are many theories of why he wants you. He almost killed you before…" Jace said, walking toward the window. I could hardly hear his footsteps. "If you could live forever by only by killing someone else, could you do it? Could you keep killing?"

I didn't know. "I'd hope not." I didn't like the idea of putting murderer on my resume.

"Even if someone begged you to? To end their suffering?"

"Suffering is a part of life, not death."

He looked away. His misery crept over my skin. There was a secret burning in his heart. "I kill. I've killed. I don't plan on stopping."

"Are you trying to scare me?"

"I'm trying to show you the truth. I've been trying to get you to see me, who I really am. And now you're finally willing to listen. I am a bad person, Gwyneth."

"We're all a little shady," I said, thinking of the monster, the creature that is all the bad parts of me. I don't love it any less. My Scavenger is evocatively beautiful as is it ugly.

"He wants something only you can grant," he said and sat on the windowsill. "If you allow me to heal you, we *have* to immediately look for the other sisters. If we break the Oath, we'll find a fate amongst the dead. But since we've made an agreement about the investigation, I have no choice but to hunt the Butcher down, before I can heal your sight."

"And then what?"

His vengeance wrapped around me like an uncontrollable fire "And then I'll kill him."

Chapter Twenty-Three

Bree orchestrated a double date; by the end of the week, I found myself in a tea-length dress, lacy sleeved gloves, and heels that Bree insisted were too short but allowed me to wear. Steam punk gone classic chic, she called it. She'd vetoed nine other outfits before this one. When one didn't make me look chubby, it made me look plain. If one actually made me look curvy, no shoes looked good. Since I couldn't say I wasn't interested in Jace, I was at her mercy. However, when she reached for my hairspray, I threw a fit any two-year-old would've been proud of.

"I don't want it to look like I tried too hard," I insisted.

Bree saw right through me; I was nervous and felt out of place, but mainly she knew I hated wearing lots of make-up and having my hair off my shoulders. We settled on flat-ironing, so it lay flat over of my shoulders, hiding the low cut back of the dress, but Bree went crazy with the eye-liner. She said she wanted to make my eyes look electric.

Primping for my first official date was bad enough. However, I truly wanted to die as Martha grabbed the camera to take my picture when Jace and Ryker showed up at the front door. The four of us smiled for the camera; Elsie even got enough courage to peek around Martha's leg to see what all the fuss was about.

"Is this like the girl's date you told me about?" Elsie asked.

"You'll have to see for yourself but *only* if you get your grades up one letter grade before midterm," Martha replied.

Elsie bolted. Distantly I heard her ask John if he could check her math homework before school on Monday.

"Is that still okay with you, Winnie?" Martha asked when Elsie was out of earshot.

"Just as long as you're paying," I said with a smile.

She agreed and insisted on one more "good picture" before freeing us. When she was finally satisfied with a good shot, she reminded us to buckle-up; to have a good time, but not to stay out too late. Curfew was midnight. She handed me Stella and shut the door.

I began to unfold my walking stick; Jace promptly took it from me, re-opened the front door, and then stuck it in the coat closet for safe keeping.

"At least you have proof now that someone willingly dated you, Winnie. Martha holds the evidence," Ryker whispered before Jace returned.

Ryker left for Jace's car, with Bree at his side, while I tried to think of some witty remark. I had nothing.

"Don't waste your breath, Gwyneth. He's interested in you, but doesn't know how to show it," he said, offering his hand. A sliver of protectiveness mixed with spite flowed through his comment.

I burst out laughing. "In what world, would Ryker be—"

"In what world wouldn't he? You look like a goddess standing in that midnight blue dress. Your skin shimmers, even though you hide it under those white gloves. Stars twinkle in the sky, like the heavens are trying to capture your radiance," Jace said, brushing my hair back behind my ear. "Your hair shines like golden strands were woven throughout it. Your eyes light up when you smile, threatening to stop my beating heart."

I.Couldn't.Utter.A.Single.Syllable. I couldn't form one comprehensive word after a poetic speech like that. My non-response must have been the reaction he was seeking because a tingling sensation enwrapped me—his adoration trickling onto my soul.

"And for the life of me, I can't take my eyes off your lips."

I licked them without thinking. The tingling sensation amplified to the point where it was painfully pleasurable. When I finally found my words, all that would come out was that he was laying it on a little thick.

"I've been trained to assess my competition years before we met," he said, leading me to the car. "I'd have to be blind not to see Ryker's true intentions. Or the effect he has on you. But if you'd wish I call you an ugly old hag, using Ryker's method, let me know."

Effect on me? I couldn't stand Ryker!

I bit my tongue instead of debating my relationship with
Ryker to Jace. It was entirely too unbelievable. It'd be like saying that
a booger was actually a delicacy. I dismissed the thought and slipped
into the front seat. Jace shut the door behind me.

Backing down the driveway, he rolled the windows down.
The cool air hit my cheeks. I couldn't bother to stifle my smile,
knowing that he remembered I liked the feel of wind on my face. The
engine roared as we sped away. I stuck my hand out the window and
closed my eyes, enjoying the sensation.

*Waves crashed into the shore. The man engulfed in flames refused to
look at me. I could feel his desire tickle my skin while it burned his flesh.*

"I fought for you, Chronicler."

*"I need a healer, not a gladiator. I need someone who can heal my mortal
wounds now that I am no longer ageless." I wished he'd forgive himself of whatever
past he refused to see. I was tempted to reach for the scar on his thumb and see his
past memories for myself.*

"So you simply need my service?" he asked.

*He was a stunning mess of muscle, but there was more than mere good
looks to his soul. He was honorable and loyal. Above all else, he was persistent,
which is why he was perfect for me. The Prophet said that if chosen, he'd cause my
demise but would serve as a loyal guardian until death bestowed me.*

*"I'll do your bidding, but I must know the truth, Chronicler. After all
these years, do you simply seek my service?"*

*I'd fallen in love with the sound of his voice years ago, even though I
restrained myself from meddling in his life. I could make him fall for me; change
his destiny forever—but I couldn't bear to steal his freedom.*

"I need a healer" I confessed. My desire hung on my words. "Which is why I sought out the best, but I want you."

He towered over me. He could force me to my knees, demand anything in the world if he wanted; he was stronger than I, but he bowed his head as if I were more powerful than he. I stopped him; I'd never wanted a servant—I yearned for companionship. I took his hand in mine and laced my fingers around his. I closed my eyes and bathed in his hazy sight. His blue fiery blaze crawled onto my skin.

"Consequences will be paid if we continue this path, Healer. My sister has seen it," I said.

I expected hesitation; however, I wasn't given any. He immediately pulled me against him and led me into the ocean. He acted like I was the breathtaking one, not him. He muttered that even the ocean couldn't compare to the beauty in my eyes. I didn't believe him, but I didn't care.

"Your adoration is worth centuries of torment," he promised.

"They're using you as bait?" Bree said in disbelief, jarring me from my fantastic vision with the man-on-fire.

"I'm sorry. What did you ask?" I muttered, rubbing my arms. Jace noticed something was different about me; I felt it roll over my skin as a pin-prick. It wasn't anger and definitely not lust; it felt like, curiosity.

"To get Elsie's grades up," Bree said. "Your fosters are using you as bait, bribing her with an outing—a girl's date?"

"I guess so, but I'm totally cool with it. Elsie's really taken to me, follows me around like your puppy-dog-boyfriend here does," I said, hoping to get the point to Ryker that his comment about me having proof I was loveable hadn't gone unnoticed and that I wasn't particularly pleased. "It's crazy that I'm the prize, though."

Jace took my hand that had been resting on the middle counsel. He stroked his thumb over mine. "Not really, dearest."

"So, where are you guys going on this fake-sister-date?" Ryker asked like the subject was irritating him on a personal level.

"Maybe to that spa on the flyer you found, Bree," I said, and then glanced over my shoulder. She was practically in Ryker's lap.

"She's been talking about a make-over ever since you brought over the flyer. Manicure, pedicure, hair, make-up—the works," I said.

"It's risky, but effective," Jace muttered.

"What is?" I asked, unsure what he was referring to.

"Using you as bait," he whispered, as he contemplated his plan. "Get some sleep tonight; tomorrow night you'll need it."

***

I'd never seen the soft, glowing light of the sun reflect off the Earth's atmosphere, but witnessing twilight had to be unforgettable. I imagined the sunset's colors painted across the sky, shimmering in the evening's light. I closed my eyes and hugged the pillow. My bed sheets were chilled from the autumn's breeze trickling in through the open window. Time slowed as I relaxed enough for sleep to take me. My thoughts ran rampant, the deeper I neared sleep. Visions of my sister's death plagued my mind; my imagination played with those images and my memories. Elderly men growing young and pictures of half-starved people—Scavengers—crawling out of the ground faded away when I felt *his* presence. My lucid imagination gave way to reality.

Jace's smoky figure was shaped perfectly in my sight even though my eyes were closed. I opened them. He sat on the windowsill, watching me. My skin immediately warmed when our gaze met. I loved it, and it scared me all the same. I wanted to ask him so many questions; I wanted to believe his answers, but I didn't know if I was ready to hear the truth. Lies weren't always easy to live, but they were tempting to hide in.

"Tonight, we go fishing for Hunters. The others agree that using you as bait is worth the risk, as long as you're willing," he said solemnly. "It's dangerous, but I promise I'll keep you safe."

I sat up in my bed and walked over to my closet. I wasn't going to hang around in my cotton shorts and t-shirt. I grabbed the first thing my fingers brushed across in my closet—a sweatshirt. I slipped it on and took a deep breath before turning around.

Jace pushed off the windowsill and walked toward me. The floor boards groaned under his weight as he passed my dresser. I couldn't move as he walked up to me. I so ferociously wanted to see how he truly looked; to see the shell of the body that made me come alive. Heat seeped from him. A colorless fire started to ripple around his body. Yet I couldn't see any defining lines. I couldn't gaze into his eyes; I couldn't lose myself in the colors of his hair; I couldn't make out any feature of his shape any better than I could using my touch.

My skin prickled. My pulse jumped from my wrist. I caught my breath as he wrapped his hand around the jacket, pulling it from my grasp. I let him. His affection jumped from his skin onto mine when his hand brushed mine. He took my hand in both of his and blew warm air into them. Not only did my fingers warm, my entire body sweltered from his decalescent touch.

I skimmed my finger across his bottom lip. It was as soft as a flower's petal. His hand slid behind my neck. He held me with his lips skimming mine.

"It's seriously taking you too long to close the deal." Marco's voice registered from my tree house. I looked up just as he appeared on my bed, lying on his side and propped on his elbow.

"You have horrible timing," Jace groaned and rested his forehead on mine.

"Oh, don't mind me," Marco said, picking his nails. "I just have this sort-of-big deal on the brink of falling apart if we don't get there on schedule, but you're right, *my* timing sucks. Our plan falls into an insignificant category because my buddy Jace here can't get his royal mojo working."

"Royal? I thought Analee stole that title."

"She pretends, but everyone knows who side they'd be on if you pick up your sword again."

"I used to be a fighter?" I asked.

"You antagonized many, especially when you baited them that you'd grant their deepest desire if they could kill you. Get with the program, Chronicler, or haven't you been reading my book?" Marco said as he continued picking his nails, like he was bored.

"It said that all the deities died after the Fate sisters passed away," I stated.

"Documenting history and adding a twist—you know, to keep it interesting," Marco said. When I pressed further, he groaned. "Fine, you want to know why I scribbled that lie? It was because I knew the Hunters would eventually get their grubby hands on it. I only recently got it back...well, a few decades ago."

"You wanted them to believe you were dead?" I asked.

"Many stopped hunting us after word got out," Jace explained. "They lived their lives and eventually died."

"Why didn't you all die when the sisters did?" I asked, trying to make sense of everything Bree read from the book. Neither Marco nor Jace seemed particularly eager to answer. "Tell me."

"Because the Chronicler gave away the Elysian in her blood before she died," Jace answered, very *very* quietly.

Marco picked up where he left off. "Her Elysian kept us immortal. If she would have kept it when she first died, we would have followed suit."

"She once manipulated the fate of many, by changing the Elysian in us," Jace said. The way he spoke made me think there was something more to it than just playing with blood. "She could meddle with other people's emotions, modify how anyone saw the past—ergo, changing the way they react to certain situations. Alter the Elysian in our blood. Steal free will. It changed their fate over the course of time. Same goes for humans; the chemicals are just different in their bodies."

"How did she do this?" I asked.

"How did *you* do this, you mean," Marco said. "And who
240

knows, you never told a soul."

"Regardless, we shouldn't keep Analee waiting," Jace said, hastily. "It'd be a shame to get her panties in a twist because we're a few minutes late."

"Oh, come now—it was just starting to get good watching you two. What's a few hours when you've waited centuries?"

"Centuries?" I clarified. I wasn't shocked or in disbelief anymore; I just needed to get the facts straight.

"Immortal, remember? Or did you choose not to believe the part that I spelled out before you?" Marco asked, as he got up off my bed and walked over to us.

I wanted to point out that he had written down that all the deities had died, so I didn't know what to believe. "If you are immortal, how can you die? Isn't it an oxymoron? And how are the Hunters successful in killing you?"

Jace held his breath just long enough for me to notice. "We can kill each other; thus, we can die, but not by disease or age."

"The Hunters can kill us with immortal weapons that they steal from us," Marco said, drawing my attention to him. His tone shifted more serious as he laid a hand on Jace's shoulder. "Zalen shifted Analee there. I came here to get you two. This is why I'm here, by the way, missy moo."

Jace sighed, and then filled in the gaps Marco left out. "Mortals can't withstand a shift to Elysia—the place we call home. It's why I'm here—to protect you from the shift. We're going to a place the Chronicler used to cherish, before everything turned south.

241

It's a Hunter haven now. It shouldn't take too long before someone notices you're there."

"Wouldn't that be a little obvious?" I asked.

"We've been shifting to many of your old Elysia hid-e-holes lately. Oh, I mean dreamland," Marco answered cynically. "If the Butcher, or other Hunters, has been tracking you, they'll know this. The Butcher will know; he's a weasel, and I'm sure he's found means of getting there quickly."

"Other means?" I questioned. "As in, teaming up with other's like you—your ability in particular?"

"We're no strangers to traitors," Marco said. The tone made me think there was more to his response than simply knowing a back-stabber or two.

Jace's hand found mine. The moment his hand touched my skin, I stood on a beach. I recalled the first few shifts I thought were introductions to my dreams. I was sick immediately after, now I was simply dizzy. My knees hit sand.

A moonless night was illuminated by the fire crawling across a young man's bare back. He kneeled in the sand and faced the ocean. Blue hues danced from his skin, transforming into brilliant orange and yellow flames. Waves crashed against the shore, echoing in the night. He made no effort to run into the cool water; instead he picked up a stone half buried in the sand and threw it into the ocean. The longer it rippled in the water, the more clenched his fist became. His muscular arms glistened with blood and sweat, as if he'd just finished fighting even though he bore no combat injuries.

Waves crashed into the shore. The man engulfed in flames refused to look at me. I could feel his desire tickle my skin while it burned his flesh.

"I fought for you, Chronicler."

"I need a healer, not a gladiator. I need someone who can heal my mortal wounds, now that I am no longer ageless." I wished he'd forgive himself of whatever past he refused to see. I was tempted to reach for the scar on his thumb and see his past memories for myself.

"So you simply need my service?" he asked.

He was a stunning mess of muscle, but there was more than mere good looks to his soul. He was honorable and loyal. Above all else, he was persistent, which is why he was perfect for me. The Prophet said that if chosen, he'd cause my demise but would serve as a loyal guardian until death bestowed me.

"I'll do your bidding, but I must know the truth, Chronicler. After all these years, do you simply seek my service?"

I'd fallen in love with the sound of his voice years ago even though I restrained myself from meddling in his life. I could make him fall for me; change his destiny forever—but I couldn't bear to steal his freedom.

"I need a healer," I confessed. My desire hung on my words. "Which is why I sought out the best, but I want you."

He towered over me. He could force me to my knees, demand anything in the world if he wanted; he was stronger than I, but he bowed his head as if I were more powerful than he. I stopped him; I'd never wanted a servant—I yearned for companionship. I took his hand in mine and laced my fingers around his. I closed my eyes and bathed in his hazy sight. His blue fiery blaze crawled onto my skin.

"Consequences must be paid if we continue this path, Healer. My sister has seen it," I said.

I expected hesitation; however, I wasn't given any. He immediately pulled me against him and led me into the ocean. He acted like I was the breathtaking one, not him. He muttered that even the ocean couldn't compare to the beauty in my eyes. I didn't believe him, but I didn't care.

"Your adoration is worth centuries of torment," he promised.

The black water hid everything under its surface. Nothing showed through, except for the faint outline of a calloused hand. Just when I was about to look away, a single blue flame sparked just below a ripple of water. The flame danced and flickered in the water, like it would have in the wind.

I had watched the vision play out in pieces, so it felt familiar, more like a memory than the future. Jace's hands were on my face, studying me as if I'd just done something truly remarkable. I knew he wanted to know what was going on, but I felt his hesitation in asking. I shook my head and muttered that I was okay. I looked around.

My world of gray sharpened significantly. I could see defined shapes of Marco and Analee towered over us on a bed of sand. Salt-water scents hung in the air. An endless sea encased one side of the beach. A cliff barricaded the beach on the opposite side. I knew of this place; Jace had brought me here before. Was it not safe then?

Reading my thoughts, Jace whispered. "Marco was keeping watch-out the entire time. I brought you here before, hoping you'd recall the first time we kissed."

I swallowed the lump in my throat; the dreams were real—but that's not the first time we kissed... unless it was Deino he kissed here first. Jealousy dominated my focus. I knew we were the same being, but I didn't hold those memories of her. It wasn't me...I closed my eyes and pressed my palms into my eyes and tried not to worry about my visions at this moment. Now was not the time or place to have a revelation.

"Welcome home, *Chronicler*," Analee said, sarcastically.

"Where's Zalen?" Jace asked, annoyed that she had interrupted the moment between us.

"He's scouting, and what did I say about giving me with the respect I deserve?" Analee said playfully. Her grip closed around Jace's neck; she was hell-bent on torturing him and strangling me while she was at it; I felt her grip caress my neck with ghost fingers. Jace was keeping me from succumbing to her wrath; he fell to his knees beside me. He screamed obscenities after Analee said she liked the way it looked when we knelt down before her.

"How do you know the Butcher will even show?" I asked, trying to prevent Jace and Analee from having another fight.

"Is she really this dumb?" Analee scoffed. She released Jace, only to walk around me in a circle. She snapped her fingers, and Marco disappeared like he'd been trained to shift at that command. He brought back with him the two frozen sisters. "Perhaps we should leave you here alone to wander the beaches while we wait. Jace can keep me company."

"Are you kidding me?" I demanded, furious about a mere suggestion of Jace not being with me and with Analee instead. "I'm sure they have eyes and will notice Jace isn't with me. Isn't that the plan, baiting them close, because they'll think Jace and I are alone?"

My skin hissed. It was no secret my mere existence bothered Analee on a personal level. But it was too late to back down now, especially since the Master's insane angelic laugh echoed in my mind.

"Analee enjoys making empty threats just to see how we would react," Jace said.

Well, that would have been nice to know two seconds ago!

"Excuse me?" Analee laughed. "My threats are not empty."

It felt like she was piercing my eardrums with her fingernails. She circled around me, mocking me. I leaped for her and grabbed her wrist. Her knife-like touch stopped, but she hadn't backed away from me. The sound of the waves drummed the shoreline as we waited for one another to react. I had a suspicion she was used to waiting. She had mastered the art of waiting for the perfect moment to strike.

"You're lonely," I finally said, breaking the silence.

"You speak vaguely," she hissed. "Bow to me, human girl."

At her demand, I fell to my knees, but not because I willed it. My body no longer responded to my orders; I was her puppet. She laughed and requested that I stand. I stood. I was at her disposal—no wonder she was calling the shots. Jace crashed into Analee. I watched, unable to move. Marco yelled in frustration and disappeared. A second later he reappeared next to them only to tear Jace off of Analee.

"We'd make more progress if you two weren't at each other's throats all the time," Marco said, jerking Jace away from *the Master*.

Their curses and soundless screams echoed in my mind as they argued with one another. Analee's angelic laugh rippled through my body when she said something about needing another slave girl. I was the perfect candidate.

I fought for my body to obey my wishes; it refused. My destiny might have already been determined. But I was damned if I didn't put up a fight. Irate that she thought I'd simply bow down to her, I pressed my lips together and screamed in my mind. I didn't know what their words meant so I poured every part of my anger into my voice. I didn't know if what I said was important, but it was my voice—the only one I had. I tried to move, but I couldn't. I closed my eyes as I embraced every horrible experience I'd ever felt.

I stole my sister's life; I ran away from everyone who'd ever tried to love me; I'd failed so many times; I'd refused to live the life I wanted to, I was a scared little girl that ran away from her problems because I might not succeed or worse, positive I'd fail everyone who'd relied on me. I lived with so many regrets; now was not the time to make another.

Dread seeped from my soul, and into my soundless cries. Despair sank its cold fingers into my heart. Depression squandered my happiness.

Tears slid down my cheeks. My voice was raw even though I hadn't opened my mouth. My soul ached. Sand clung to the sweat gathering on my clammy skin. My eyes stung when I looked around.

Five dark shadows knelt on the ground before me. Dark liquid seeped from their ears and eyes. Marco and Zalen disappeared the moment I stopped screaming telepathically. The icy girls hugged onto each other. Jace panted. He was on his hands and knees, looking up at me. His delight glowed as his white silhouette returned.

"You're remembering how to fight," Jace said, proudly.

Analee charged me. I braced for impact when she suddenly fell to her knees. A thin, gray object, stuck out of her back, as well as her chest. Her white shape faded immediately; a dark liquid grew around the gray object sticking through her chest.

"Get the Healer!" Analee ordered, as she collapsed.

Jace's voice echoed in my mind as he raced toward me. He searched the beach, looking for whomever it was that had attacked.

"Analee is dying!" I said, looking back at the spear sticking out of her chest.

He acted like he couldn't hear me or was dismissing my pleas; I hated Analee, but to watch her die without trying to help was another thing entirely. I grabbed Jace's hand and screamed that the Master was dying. He said nothing. Hoping to convey my message, I told him she was power in a dainty, maddening bottle. Yes, we needed her and her ability, but no matter how much we despised her, we couldn't let her die. She was powerful; we needed her. He swore, but agreed with me. The moment he touched the thin, gray object, it disappeared.

"The Rippler's spear," Jace said, and then cursed that he'd forgotten about Zalen since he was preoccupied with the Butcher. "I swear I'll kill him if he hurts you, Gwyneth."

Shoving his hands onto the shadow growing on Analee's chest wound, he spoke telepathically. Within seconds, her chest had begun to rise and fall. Without warning, Jace jerked his hands away from Analee's chest and tackled me. Another spear drove into the ground inches from my head. Jace's hand grazed it, causing it to disappear.

"Don't move," he said, and took off running toward the direction it came from.

Something was wrong. This attack was planned. They baited us, not the other way around. I looked in the opposite direction and saw two figures in the distance. We were surrounded!

Pushing off the sand, I ran for cover. The ground shook under my feet. Sand erupted as a sound wave rippled through the air. It lifted me off the ground only to body-slam me back onto it. Sand gathered in my mouth, scraped my skin, and burrowed into my eyes. Zalen's laugh ripped through the air.

He was enjoying this? Was he a traitor? Who was on my side?

I looked around me. Analee's body was tossed beside me. I couldn't tell if she was breathing. I crawled over to her, reaching her as another sound wave followed Zalen's laugh. It demolished the beach, flipping mounds of sand over. The air darkened, clouded by the sand storm he'd created.

Sand flew through the air. I pulled my shirt up over my nose, hoping to keep too much of it from getting into my lungs. I didn't dare to open my eyes. My skin burned as if it were on fire; it wasn't just from the sand scratching me. Jace was furious. I raised my head, trying to see his hazy outline, but in the sand storm, he was hidden. Another blast sounded; my ears instantly started to ring. I shielded my eyes and looked up.

A mass of blackness that I hoped was Marco rushed my way as countless pieces of sand and stone ricocheted around me. He gained speed and then pinned me on my back, just as the sound wave started to throw me through the air.

My head pounded when I slammed into the ground. Shooting pain spread through me as rock collided into my flesh. My breathing was labored as the weight above me buried me deeper into the sand. Darkness encased me. I couldn't push Marco off. A putrid scent grew around me as I sunk deeper. Everything reeked of rot and death. Sand slipped into every crease, up my nose, into my mouth as I screamed for someone to hear me. I took a deep breath when the slop filled my mouth; I gagged, taking in sickly flesh and sand. I was being buried alive under dead weight!

Chapter Twenty-Four

Sand coated me. My eyes stung from the debris wiping around me. My clothes were soaked. I tried not to think about how the blood-stained mark must've looked. Blood crusted the cuts over my arms and legs, which restricted my movements. Marco's voice trickled into my mind—calming me, even though the world exploded around us. He held on tighter, blocking the particles. Sand pelted my flesh. I cried out when a large rock hit my leg. Marco cursed and then leaned in closer to protect me.

"You scared me there, sweet cheeks," Marco said cheerfully, like we were having a casual conversation at a diner instead of having to shout to hear each other while blasted in a sand storm. "I thought I'd lost you there. I forget how vulnerable you are compared to the rest of us."

"Get me out of here," I demanded.

"I can't shift you out of here unless Jace is nearby because, well, you know. And he'd have my head on a platter if I shifted him when he's so close to getting his revenge."

The beach jolted when another sound wave blasted. Water rose up from the sea and rained down on us. Each drop felt just as hard as the sand, drenching us in a mixture of sand and salt-water. When the shower slowed, Marco slid off of me.

"Jace is taking entirely too long, and I'm getting bored. Try not to die while I'm gone," he mumbled, and then vanished.

Thanks for the advice.

Brown curls twisted over his pale blue eyes as he laughed. My aging skin crawled as he wrapped his hand around my wrist. He was taller than me but only by a few inches. Another woman with tanned skin and coffee brown hair watched as he lifted me from my seat on the grassy field. The sweet scent of lilies filled the air.

Three spears shone in the light. Their tips were thrown into the ground. The woman with wavy coffee-colored hair walked over and touched the spear. It disappeared instantly.

"You won't be threatening my sister with these, not yet Rippler," she said.

The athletic man danced me around the meadow. "You recall everyone's past, even the darkest parts?" the Rippler said softly.

My throat rattled like I'd just spoken. I stared at the scar trickling down his neck. "Especially the darkest parts, Rippler," I answered, gazing at his scar. "Why? Is there something you're trying to keep hidden?"

I breathed a sigh of relief when he pulled away. His touch unnerved me.

"Many of us keep things buried deep. The Master would say you ask vague questions."

"Analee has vague answers, as do you," I said, reaching for his scar. He disappeared just as my pinky finger brushed against the end of his scar on his neck.

The vision of the Rippler cut out as an excruciating scream echoed in my mind. Jace knelt on the ground; a thin, dark object intercepted his usual glowing silhouette—another spear. I gasped. The general shape looked like a spear I'd seen in my vision of the Rippler and like the one sticking out of Analee. A broken-off spear stuck through his shoulder. Following the angle of the spear, I looked up to find the Rippler standing on the cliff's ridgeline. Zalen plucked another spear from the air behind his back, like he'd been hiding a stash of them—from nothingness, he formed a weapon! He created something out of nothing, defying the laws of nature.

I forced myself to breathe slowly through my nose; my heart raced. I hadn't known a lot about fighting tactics, but I knew height was an advantage. Jace needed help. Where had Marco run off to?

An excruciating scream echoed in my mind as Jace jerked out the broken-off spear. The wood ground against his bones as he twisted out the spear. I wanted to throw up. Why hadn't the spear disappeared the moment he touched it like the others? Zalen laughed; it haunted my soul and tore at my eardrums. I covered my ears and buried my face in the sand, waiting for the vindictive amusement to end. When I looked up again, Jace was in mid-run and tearing off his shirt. He bunched it together. Flames crawled over it until it became a fireball. He chucked it at the Rippler, traveling at a speed that my gaze couldn't follow. Zalen flung himself along the ridge like his life depended on it. Before he hit the jagged edge, he threw the spear.

Jace easily dodged it, slowing his pace. I pushed off the ground and raced towards him, hoping he wasn't losing too much blood from the wound.

"Don't die," I repeated in my mind over and over again. The sand shifted under my feet, preventing me from covering ground quickly. I looked back up at the ridgeline. I was sprinting directly into Zalen's firing range, but I couldn't just leave Jace.

While Zalen was distracted, Marco appeared on the ridge next to him. He charged the Rippler, as Zalen tried plucking another spear from the air behind his back. They plummeted off the cliff. I heard myself scream. It echoed in my mind. They soared toward the ground, gaining speed—courtesy of the Earth's gravity. They vanished and reappeared several times, as they neared the sandy beach. Since they both could shift, it was like they were fighting each other to reposition themselves on the planes of this dimension. I'd almost reached Jace when they collided into the ground.

The impact threw me off my feet and onto my back, knocking the wind from my lungs. I rolled to my side and looked up, frantic to find the others. My mouth dropped. Marco held Zalen in place while Jace used him as a human punching bag. Jace might have been wounded, but adrenaline surged through him, empowering him through any weakness he should have had. The injury he sustained should have immobilized him, yet, he wasn't acting like any wound was slowing him down.

Zalen laughed. "Time has not been good to you, Healer. You're not the gladiator I remember."

Jace paused. The fire jumping off his skin grew so hot that the grainy shape of the beach melted away in a smooth pool of glass.

The smell of burnt flesh accompanied the beating of Jace's fists. Zalen screamed out in pain. I clenched my teeth, covered my ears, and prayed Zalen would stop. My ears bled. My sight, that had been getting more defined the longer I was around the deities, started to blur into shapeless mixes of blacks and whites. I wanted to black out from the rippling effect Zalen held over sound waves.

"Mercy, Jace!" I yelled. I couldn't stand the torture any longer. My mind refused to pass out, but my body was bleeding. I couldn't breathe in deeply without smelling the sickly scent of burnt flesh and rotten tissue.

I gasped for air the second Zalen's torture ended. Consumed in his fire, Jace rushed over to me and helped me up from the ground. I lost my balance upon standing upright. His grip around me tightened until I regained my composure. His hands skimmed as much of my skin as he could touch, searching for injuries and healing my cuts and bruises immediately. He covered my ears with his hands. The ringing ceased immediately. He gently traced his bloody thumbs over my eyes. The sharp sting vanished into nothing. My sight returned to what it once was—the shapes of people and objects became more defined. With a soft touch, he healed all my injuries.

"I'm to be *your* healer for Fate has allowed it," Jace said, explaining that the impossible truly had just happened.

He'd promised to be my healer if Fate allowed. I'd always assumed fate was a play on word for destiny. He believed blindly that I was a Fate sister, so was he asking permission from me back then? He tenderly stroked my cheek; it was like I'd just given him back his reason for living. I touched the darkened shadow on his shoulder. He cursed when my fingertips grazed over his wound. My fingertips slid over the mess of blood and torn skin.

255

"Why do you not heal yourself?"

"In time," he said. "I have plans for this bloody wound that Zalen has so graciously bestowed upon me."

"You've always had a flare for how you get your revenge," Marco said. "Sometimes I swear you plan it in advance. You could have dodged that spear he threw, but you let him hit you, didn't you?"

"Why didn't it disappear the moment you touched it?" I asked, trying to figure out what had happened.

"The spear was aimed for me, not anyone else," Jace said. "If another would have touched it, it would have disappeared. Since I was the target, it stuck."

Unsure of what they were talking about, I changed subjects. I told them that there had been others along the horizon watching the events unfold.

Marco muttered, "I can't see a stinking thing."

Zalen laughed. The vibrations passed through me in an increasingly unnerving manner. It was beyond me how anyone could laugh as his skin was charred. Marco released Zalen after Jace confirmed that no one could find the two people I had seen. He vanished and then reappeared on the cliff beside us. He scanned the area and then returned.

"Not a soul in sight," Marco said.

"Whose orders were you following, if not Analee's?"

Zalen laughed so loudly it brought me to my knees again. My ears rang. I could hardly understand what the others had said. Jace pounced onto Zalen, knocking them to the ground. He gripped the Rippler's throat and pressed down, stopping his ability to torture me with his voice. Zalen sucked in air and writhed on the sand. Jace refused to back down.

"Jace!" I screamed. "Stop strangling the man. He's not going to be able tell us anything if you keep him from speaking."

"He's no *man*, Chronicler," Jace spit. "And if he wants to confess, then he can speak in our dialect."

Frustration poured out of Jace's soul when I denied my call sign. He'd been tormented by those who attacked his beloved. I clenched my teeth tight together and tried not to think about *her*. Deino died centuries ago, yet, I competed with her now. I'd never live up to her. In Jace's eyes, I'd fail to meet his expectations. I wasn't so sure he and the others didn't actually believe I was telling the truth in not knowing what they were talking about. Marco informed me, like it humored him; Analee could crush me, like—*where was Analee?*

I scanned the beach and almost stumbled. Analee stood inches behind me, yet, I hadn't heard her approach me. Her usual blazing white shape was still dimmed, especially over her chest where she was wounded. She wheezed with every intake of air. The spear must have been close to her lungs. She should have been dead.

Jace must have saved her life when he pressed his hand over her wound. Her slave girls curled around her feet. Analee clenched her fist. Zalen coughed like someone was strangling him. I didn't have to know that her golden-eyes had turned black to know what she was doing. She didn't want answers; she sought revenge for his treachery. I screamed for her to stop.

"Fine, we'll play by your rules." Analee released her death grip. "The Chronicler is giving you a chance at redemption when I'd rather watch you die; so humor her, or we'll end your pathetic life."

"I thought you were immortal, only to die by an immortal weapon?" I said.

"That's how Hunters kill us," Marco said.

"But we can kill each other," Zalen corrected. A dark liquid seeped from his lips. "Can't we, Jace? Does the Chronicler not recall your final betrayal?"

Jace didn't bother with a reply. He merely placed his hands over his shoulder where the spear had been; the wound's shadow on Jace's otherwise bright silhouette brightened. It shrank until there was no evidence of damage. I touched his shoulder in the same spot where his wound had been. Nothing. His skin was smooth.

"Cookie, you may want to step away," Marco said. "Jace is patient, but he enjoys this part of the fight the best."

"What part?" I asked, stepping away as Jace's excitement mixed with my feelings.

"His revenge," Marco stated, plainly.

Jace placed his hand on Zalen's chest, directly over his heart. The wound that was on Jace's shoulder grew on Zalen's chest. Zalen's white orb started to fade. Dark liquid began to bubble up through his clothing. It wasn't long before it spewed from his chest. Fire grew up into an inferno around Jace; pure hatred flickered with each flame.

"You'll die by the damage your spear caused me," Jace said.

The pleasure he took in ending the traitor's life shook me. How could revenge rule someone's life like Jace had allowed it to rule his? Sensing my objection, Jace raised his chin and looked at me. I couldn't see the color of his eyes or his facial expression. However, I felt his raw power creep over me. My legs barely held me as I welcomed his fiery wrath.

"Love. Hate. Forgiveness. Vengeance. To truly live in every moment is divine," Jace said like no one around us existed. His passion would devour me if I gave into his demand, just as his hate could consume him as well; he wanted me, but he'd wait for me to admit the same. I knew in that moment, if he couldn't have me, hate would eat at his soul.

"Which is why you've spent the last countless centuries wallowing in grief, Jace," Analee said. "Was that *divine*?"

"Sorrow amplifies bliss," he responded to Analee but never looked away from me. "You can't truly experience one to its fullest potential without surviving the other. You can't experience love without understanding hate."

Looking down at Zalen, Analee asked, "Why would you betray me?"

"The Butcher is a visionary. I welcome death in serving him," Zalen muttered. "Whether I sacrifice my own life to extend his or the Scavengers take it from me today—either way, my master wins. He wanted to know if Gwyneth was truly the Chronicler and if she still possessed enough power to grant what he most desires. You all played right into his plan."

"Gwyneth is pathetic and weak," Analee said.

"You said the Chronicler was pathetic and weak centuries ago." Zalen started to laugh, but the blood pooling in his throat stifled his laugh. "There are times when she smells like us; we've all caught our scent on her. But more importantly, there are times when she smells like her sisters; it's undeniable."

I felt everyone's eyes on me, seeking an explanation. "My visions," I said, thinking out loud. "You sense them?"

"Visions?" Jace questioned.

"Of the future," I said, and then immediately knew I'd said too much. Marco pointed out the Prophet saw the future; it wasn't a craft of mine. It didn't make sense. They said the Chronicler saw the past.

"She's weak without the Cutter and Prophet, but Gwyneth truly is the unseeing Fate," Zalen said. "No deity has been born in centuries. She finally fulfilled the Healer's request to be reborn."

I wanted to ask about Lily—how the Butcher grew young after killing her, if I'd been the only deity to be born in years, but the ground began to tremble.

It shook more ferociously with each weakening breath Zalen took. It opened up upon the Rippler's last breath, as if the Earth itself meant to swallow the deity. Marco shifted behind Analee and mumbled that he didn't want the dirt crawler to take the wrong shifter.

260

A starved, mouthless corpse crawled from the ground. Even though my world was still blurred, I could see every detail of the Scavenger. Bruises and cut marks littered its body as it crawled on top of the soil. The Scavenger screamed soundlessly at Analee when it finally surfaced.

Smoke filled the room. I coughed. I was the only one who made a noise even though I could feel vibrations roll across the floor. I felt it ripple through the air but only saw the shimmer of the blade before I was pushed aside. A young man with dark brown hair grunted as if he was startled. A silver spear stuck out of the charred leg. Smoke blocked out everything else in sight.

The man gripped the spear to pull it out, when it disappeared. He applied pressure over the wound on his leg with his hand. A scar on his thumb danced like a thread the moment my pinky brushed against it.

"Next time, I go alone," he groaned. "The Rippler is guarding them, making sure you don't find them."

"They're still a part of me," I said. "I need to know her plan for them. The Prophet said our younger sister is going to be busy cutting as soon as Analee figures out how to command the Scavengers."

My skin was smooth and youthful, just like his, as I cupped his face in my hands. I brushed back his dark brown hair that fell over his chocolate-brown eyes. Flecks of gold shimmered in them even though dirt clung to his hair, like he took a shower in mud. Smoke filled the edges of my sight as dawn broke. I thanked my sister for not cutting his thread when he searched the Master's cave looking for the lost parts of my soul—my Scavengers. I didn't fight his touch as he traced his dirty finger over my hand. I craved it.

"Did you uncover their orders?" I asked.

"Anyone who utters their name will greet death."

"They rise as death's henchmen, disregarding forgotten memories only to collect the dead," I recited as it faded away.

Chapter Twenty-Five

The Scavenger glanced at the dying man before turning its attention back to me. It took my hand and brought it up to where its mouth would be and spoke in my mind. It recited a phrase over and over in my mind, begging me to remember it. I nodded, hoping one day I could not only understand but fulfill its request, whatever it was. Once my pinky finger rubbed against its coarse skin, a part of the Scavenger's soul connected to mine.

Its starved body was bruised and beaten as it crawled out of the dried ground. Every vein, blood vessel, and artery pulsating deep purple, showed on its hairless head. Its translucent skin was pulled tight, especially over the joints. It smelled clean and crisp like the sea, even though the few shreds of clothing covering it were stained. The sewn marks kept him from whispering of the unspeakable past. Empty hollowed holes were where the eyes should have been.

It walked to me. Instead of running, I opened my arms to embrace it. Its ghostly skin was razor sharp but never cut me. It brought my hand to its mouthless face. When my smallest finger brushed against its coarse lips, I felt at home again. The walking corpse wiped a fleeting tear from my eye. In my mind, I heard it speak in a mysterious language. Even though I didn't understand it, a sense of immense sorrow washed over me when it released my hand and turned its back to me. I trembled as I watched it sink into the dirt.

It'd been stolen from me, by the fallen angel.

The Scavenger covered my eyes with its fingers. When it removed its hand, my world was no longer a blur of gray. I couldn't speak, move, or even blink as I marveled at the splendor around me. Dimension. Depth. Color. I could see every line, wrinkle, nail, and every strand of hair. I saw absolutely everything.

Standing next to two beautiful, icy young girls, was a gorgeous woman, a fallen angel. She was the same beautiful blond woman with the golden eyes, who held me captive in a coffin, stood next to her young slaves. Analee.

The giant red-headed man stood behind her. The intelligence shining through his green eyes contradicted the stereotype that he was just another hunk of muscle and no brains. Marco.

Standing alone was a guilt-ridden man on fire. Taking a deep breath, I blinked and suddenly found myself gazing into the chocolate-brown eyes that held a sense of exquisiteness I couldn't describe. His jaw was as I pictured, ridged from not recently shaving. His eyelashes extended long and full, framing his perfect dark eyes. Gold was woven through his dark hair. It flung haphazardly over his face, hiding the markings of a jagged scar trailing across his cheek bone. I saw every vein, every muscle in the arms that I'd let myself melt into. I saw the lips that had made mine swollen. Blue flames whirled from his shoulders, like they had when he promised to heal my mortal wounds since I was no longer ageless.

"Consequences will be paid if we continue this path, Healer. My sister has seen it," I said.

I expected hesitation; however, I wasn't given any. Jace immediately pulled me against him and led me into the ocean. He acted like I was the breathtaking one, not him. He muttered that even the ocean couldn't compare to the beauty in my eyes. I didn't believe him, but I didn't care.

"Your adoration is worth centuries of torment," he promised.

"It's not the future I see when I get visions, is it? It's of the past?" I asked.

I couldn't tear my gaze away from Jace. His eyes widened in realizing that I recognized him. He stepped forward like he'd give anything to hold me. The Scavenger tightened its grip around me. Jace stopped.

"Forgive me of my past," Jace begged. "I saw no other choice than to drive the blade into your chest."

"These visions are of a life I've forgotten," I said, turning back to the Scavenger. "They're memories of a life that's no longer mine to claim."

I wanted to give up—so much was lost. So many years I'd never know again, so much awaited me. The Scavenger brought my hand up to where its lips should have been. It pressed my pinky finger on its temples, triggering another vision.

The sun shone through a charred knothole, no bigger than my slender finger. It was the only light in the enclosed, narrow box holding me captive. My hands were smooth and polished, not gnarled or wrinkled; I had years of life ahead of me, so why was I buried alive in a coffin? Sweat formed beads on my brow. They dripped down my face. A pungent stench choked my lungs as the heat rise inside my coffin.

Death and decay grew stronger as a set of shuffling feet skimmed the top of the wood. A spicy aroma, his fragrance, intertwined with the rot, took over my senses. I heard two feminine screams. One echoed in my mind while the other cursed out loud. I peered out the tiny hole and caught a glimpse of my captor in her white dress—the girl who looked like a fallen angel. Her unforgettable golden eyes flickered black as she smiled down at me. Her beautiful voice beckoned, enticing me out of my personal cell if I'd only swear to bow down to her.

"You'll regret this, Chronicler. This is positively unnecessary. You'll give me my wish if I have to kill you for it to be granted, and you know I will." Analee said, and brushed back her silky blond hair.

"My death is insignificant compared to what you're asking." My voice was innocent as hers.

A massive man with deep red hair appeared behind her when nothing but empty space was there a second before. He kissed her lightly-tanned cheek before paying any attention to me. His green eyes deepened in color until they were just as black as the woman's eyes. While his eyes shifted colors, his rotting stench grew stronger. He smelled like death.

"If you don't, I'll kill your sisters," Analee said. "Or do you so easily forget their humanity grows when you are separated? You're not just putting your life on the line. You'll sacrifice your sisters as well by denying my request."

"Only when I can't hear their screams, will they be far enough away to die a human's death," I said. "It'll take days to accomplish."

She laughed. "Oh, but you haven't met my latest consort, Chronicler. Show her your craft."

The massive man disappeared from behind her. A moment later the girls' screams were silent. Frantically, I searched out my peep hole to look for them when his face instantly appeared. His blackened eyes sent chills down my spine. His head jerked slightly as his smirk grew.

"Reaper," I stated. "We've met."

"Your Healer will never get here in time. I'll kill them before he can get here to save you all. If you don't give the Master what she wants, I'll see to it that your Scavengers will die with you."

"She only pays attention to you because you have something she wants right now, Reaper."

"Lies," Marco said, and spat in my face. The putrid acid burned my face. I wanted to cry out but refused to give them the satisfaction. "Do it now, or you'll bathe in their blood."

"Remember what happened last time you played with fate?" I called out to the fallen angel. "My sisters and I foresee humanity's fate as well as deities'. The string of our life is tied to theirs, thus, when they started to age, so did the Fates. When my sisters and I parted ways, our bodies aged. Together we became immortal again and stopped aging. But it had a nasty little side-effect to the rest of the deities, didn't it? It made immortals killable, even if you didn't start to age like my sisters and I."

"Your point?" she asked, trying to sound bored.

"My point is, when the Hunters found out they could live longer if they killed a deity, they would grow young. Thus, it made you not only killable, but your wish gave our half-breed offspring a reason to hunt us down," I said.

"The past is the past. There's nothing I can do to change it. Break the bond completely with the humans or break the bond with the Scavengers," she

267

demanded. "It's up to you."

"You seek humanity's chaos, destruction, and fatality if that bond is broken. Without purpose they will become no better than animals."

"Your choice, Chronicler," Analee hissed. "Humans or Scavengers."

I chose. A tear trickled down my cheek. She laughed; to weep was a sign of weakness, while I saw it as a beautiful truth… no matter how agonizing. A moment later, my soul unraveled. While I beat against the burnt wood, the essence composing my very being separated itself. The coffin's top popped off. I rolled out of the wooden box and onto the ground. I scratched at the soil, needing to apologize for not being strong. A white, transparent hand scratched at the earth below me as if it was furiously trying to come to my aid. I gripped her hand, wishing for the strength to hold onto her soul. She embodied the other part of my soul. She gripped my soft hands in her hard, calloused ones. There wasn't enough time—I felt myself tearing in half. The two parts of my soul, the creation of life and death, which were never meant to divide, did. Images of hundreds of mouthless corpses were torn from my heart; they no longer answered to me, in a matter of seconds. My Scavengers, howled out with hopelessness.

Not a squeal left my mouth as the dirt engulfed her, locking it away from me. My torn soul silenced me. Tears bled from my eyes as I gave the Master my Scavengers—the world's unspeakable past, or death as humans perceived it. Analee's muffled laugh ripped through my damaged soul when I felt them bow to her.

After the vision faded into nothingness, the Scavenger repeated the same phrase it had spoken before. I couldn't make sense of what it wanted, but I heard its agony loud and clear. I had to listen closely to hear what else reverberated in its cries—hope. It let go of my hand. Once again my world became shades of gray. After walking up to Zalen, the Scavenger took the deity in its arms. They sank into the ground. I fell to my knees. My heart ached.

"It was a part of me," I said in disbelief, clutching my chest. "A part of my soul."

"You weren't very fond of giving them up," Analee said stiffly. "But you know the rules, if one is willing to kill you for the heart's uttermost desires, it will be granted. And I've been waiting years for another wish."

She wanted another wish from me, which meant she was prepared to kill me, and I wasn't strong or knowledgeable enough to grant what anyone wanted yet. That's why she swore the Oath to find my sisters! Who else had intentions of threatening my life! If I'd ever been sure of anything, it was that I needed a protector—I needed Jace.

"You took the Scavengers from me! You stole years from the humans, didn't you? That's what the vision in the meadow meant— when your slave girl sliced the palm of my hand using a knife. You wished for human's immortality to end," I screamed. "I warned you that playing with fate has consequences not even my sister can always foresee."

"How was I to know your connection to every human's fate would eat away at your immortality?" Analee yelled. "Besides, you never uttered a word about *us* dying too! You could have warned me that we would become killable!"

"The Hunters rose to power because of your request," Jace said, stepping in. "You wanted supremacy over humans, but you got what you most feared—vulnerability. Our offspring had reason to hunt us down when you stole humanity's immortality, making us killable because the Fate's connection was weakened. Hunters have murdered countless deities because they seek the Elysian in our blood. There would be no reason for the Hunters to murder us all if you would have simply accepted the Chronicler as sovereign!"

Enmity eclipsed every other feeling I'd ever had. The Scavengers were once a part of my soul, and Analee took them and used them as death's bellmen. She used that part of my essence to do her bidding; thus, making her stronger. To be embraced by death was not to be feared; it was to be welcomed. Analee manipulated their purpose. She forced me to expunge mankind's immortality, and to give up my horde of Scavengers. She deserved a fate worse than death, and I wanted to be the one to give it to her.

Concentrating on the phrase the Scavenger had spoken, I repeated it over and over in my mind. Jace, Marco, Analee and her slaves shied away from me, as if the phrase stung their souls. I twirled around, repeating the phrase and demanding that they listen, no matter how much it hurt. Along the cliff's edge, I saw two figures hiding from the others. If I didn't see the world in black and white, I wouldn't have seen them. They were camouflaged exceptionally well, but I didn't care who was spying on me. The reason my soul was cut in half was more important than anything else in my life.

"Stop!" Marco yelled. "Your emotion connects when you speak soundlessly, not just your words. We feel your misery, too!"

"What does the phrase mean?" I screamed, demanding someone answer me. "What was the Scavenger trying to tell me?"

"The phrase was a plea for you to save them," Jace said. "Remember us. Save us."

The moment the words left his tongue, I sprang from the ground and grabbed Analee. She laughed as I attacked her until I clamped down on the small dainty scar I saw trailing down her neck. I couldn't feel it but knew it was there. Analee screamed like I was ripping her soul from her body. I felt her try to command my body. I fought for control of my body so it wouldn't do whatever she commanded. Instead of backing away like she wanted, I sank my fingers into her neck. An invisible grip clasped around my throat, cutting off my airway. A copper taste filled my mouth.

"You'll steal her revenge if you save her now," Marco said, stopping Jace from rescuing me. "For centuries you wished she'd find some fight. Don't take it when she's finally flexing her muscles."

Her slaves were on me, ripping me off their master. They dug their cold fingers into my side. I felt my heart slow as they froze my blood. My fingers numbed. Yet I fought to find the end of Analee's scar. My knees slammed into the sand the moment Analee demanded I bow to her, but I'd brought her down with me. She fell to her side. I scratched at her back, pulling away her shirt so I could claw at the scar that extended down her back. Her slave girls climbed over me. Analee's howls echoed off the barren cliffs.

I saw Analee's past when my smallest finger trickled over her tiny scar that lingered down her back from her neck. The unseeing past—the memories buried deep—were woven in her thread of life. The scar. I just needed time to sort through the memories woven within it, to view them, to change and manipulate them so she'd obey me; I hated the wretched goddess. I could modify her mind-set, alter her memories, and redirect her fate once I was stronger. I needed to become stronger, so I could destroy her and take back what was mine.

I scratched at her scar, digging my nails into it. The thread of her life should look as damaged as her soul. Analee's grip was on my throat, but I didn't care. I found the end of her life's thread; I don't know how I knew where to search—I just did. A flash welcomed the start of a vision.

Whiteness transcended everything as far as I could see. Winter's chill stole my warmth. I heard no warning of the little witch who stalked me; I just felt her signature weapon prick my neck. I slapped my hand over the wound, thankful she missed my thread of life. I spun around, ready to strike back. She was nowhere to be seen. But she left a memento—a pair of jagged scissors. Crimson liquid drizzled off the cold, metal weapon and onto the flakes of snow. As soon as my blood trickled onto the snow, it turned black.

"They seek revenge, not death," I acknowledged the Cutter's warning.

One slave girl jerked my hair backwards. The other dug her ice cold fingernails into my eyes, keeping Analee's memory at bay.

I welcomed unconsciousness.

I woke to the sound of Jace's voice as he sung a melody I barely remembered. The intense pressure and icy pang from the fight subsided when Jace kissed my eyelids, awaking me wholly. His kiss was the softest, smoothest feeling I dared to imagine. I rubbed my arms; no wounds. My eyes didn't sting, and I could see like my usual self—but I wasn't. I felt different—not all powerful, but lost and scared. Just how many people would kill me without a second thought?

Jace continued to rock me in a rhythm that synced with the waves as they beat against the shoreline. I could lie in his arms forever listening to his deep, alluring voice.

"You remember," Jace said, brushing my hair back. "When you touched the dirt-crawler, as Marco would phrase it, you saw me—you recognized me. You remembered what I did to you. You know that I drove a knife through your –"

"The song you sing reminds me of a life I don't remember," I interrupted, refusing to think about the two different groups—enemies—hunting me for centuries, but that Jace had given me my final blow. Jace killed me—Deino—because of his love.

"But you remember me," he insisted. "You are thinking too hard about it, Gwyneth. Just accept it as the truth."

I looked anywhere but his brilliant white silhouette. There wasn't a soul in sight. A tear escaped my eye. "I don't remember the life you do. I only have snapshots of who I was. I'm not *her* anymore. I'm not the person you fell in love with."

I clenched my eyes shut, hoping to gain control over myself again. I pressed my palms into my eyes, not wanting to see him even with my eyes closed. Jace told me that I had no reason to be ashamed of any tear I shed. Holding me, he encouraged me to embrace the hurt of being separated from a lost love and all that I'd forgotten. He never tried to rescue me. The pain was mine to experience—I needed to feel it, instead of hiding from it.

"Sorrow amplifies bliss," he whispered, and gently placed his hands over mine. When my tears slowed, he spoke. "You may not recall every moment we shared, but you remember my voice."

"I'm obsessed with your voice. That doesn't mean I remember, Jace," I said, trying to hold my ground.

He said nothing for so long, the world around us came back into my reality. The sound of the waves crashing on the beach, the smell of salt, the warm breeze on my skin comforted me. I imagined the burst of orange, red, and yellow as they lit the sky the night I died so many years ago. The sound of birds sang to us as he held me. Slowly he started rocking me to the rhythm of the bird's song, of his song. I turned his hand over in mine. I couldn't feel it, but knew it had to be there—the scar that started at his thumb and wrapped up his arm. When I traced over his wrist where it should have been, I felt his spirits rise.

"You sense the thread of my life, don't you?" Jace said. "You sensed Analee's, too, which is why you tried to rip it from her neck. You wanted her to die by severing it like the Cutter would."

"I don't want her to die. I want her to suffer," I muttered, as I traced his skin. The Chronicler used their threads of life to manipulate their fate, but I couldn't recall how. "What happened to her?"

"Suffering…but recovering," Jace said, and left it at that.

Instead of pressing the issue, I focused on us. He needed to live in the present, not the past. I didn't like that he was encouraged. I needed him to forget about the person he once loved, not try to save her. I didn't remember being here—not really. Glimpses didn't mean I remembered our past; we needed a fresh start.

"You used to say that I hide golden slivers in my hair," he said, and brought my hand up to his hair. "You said that it flickered in the sunlight when you looked at me."

I ran my fingers through his hair. It was like silk in my hands.

I loved it, but didn't remember it. I told him so. I told him over and over I didn't remember her as I ran my hands through his locks. His pulse jumped with mine when I tugged gently on his hair. He liked it—so did I—but not because I remembered it. I enjoyed his reaction.

"My eyes," he said just above a moan. "Even in this life, you remember what they look like."

"Only because of a few quick glimpses I get with my visions."

"They're *memories*, dearest."

I let my hand fall so I could trace the scar under his eye. I wondered why he never healed it, why he allowed his perfect body to be damaged. His hot breath hit my skin, and I forgot how to breathe. His hand slid behind my neck.

"You remember the way I feel next to you," he said, as he slid one hand down my side. His fingers touched the small of my back while his thumb gripped my hip. Not trusting my voice, I shook my head. He grasped my side. "Liar."

I gasped and grabbed his hand. He used my own fingers against me. Tracing them down my side, he brought my hand down until I touched his leg. He guided my hand up his leg. Suddenly, I couldn't breathe, but it wasn't because I was holding my breath. He led my hands up his side, onto his stomach. As soon as my fingers drifted over his skin, he let go of my hand, encouraging me to explore. As my hand passed over his hard stomach, he cupped my face. Tracing my fingers lightly up the side of his torso, I got him to groan so deeply, that it shook every particle in my body.

"You find the only place I'm ticklish. You used to spend hours trying to get a reaction out of me, only because I adamantly insisted that I didn't have a funny bone."

"But I don't remember doing it," I said.

"Your fingers do."

He repositioned himself and lowered me onto the sand. He gazed down at me, and my skin prickled. A breathtaking, colorless fire that started from his knees sent flames off his shoulders. I wanted to see it in color, but watching the air reacting to his heat was enticing all in itself.

"Breathe, Gwyneth," he moaned, struggling to take a breath.

I took a quick breath as he let himself fall down onto me. His hands gripped the sand on both sides of my face. Heat radiated from his body. It promised that I'd get burned but would love it. I reached back and grabbed each one of his wrists, and I found the beginning of his scar with my pinky finger.

A scarlet petal fell from the sky like a feather. It drifted back and forth. Jace stood behind me. He blew it lightly, making it twirl in the air. One after another, petals rained around me. I laughed, loving the shower.

"Close your eyes," Jace whispered.

I obeyed and waited eagerly. Using a single petal, he caressed my lips. It felt as smooth as Jace's lips on my hand.

His lips replaced the rose petal. He didn't so much kiss me as tease me with the possibility of it. He spun me around in his arms. I opened my eyes to him releasing more petals over my head.

276

His hands were calloused, showing the signs of a rough life. A faint silver scar trailed up the thumb and up his lean, muscular arm until hiding underneath his short sleeved olive shirt.

"Forget about *her*," I said as I fought his grip on me. "I don't remember being her!"

"Quit lying to yourself. I know you're dying to remember," Jace said, and pressed his forehead against mine. My rapid breath forced my chest into his. I wanted him—needed him. I was scared. I wiggled my hand from his; he tightened his grip, and the fire crawled over his skin.

I reached up and took his hand in mine. My smallest finger brushed over the scar, and it began to move like it was being blown off his skin. After separating itself, the scar danced in the wind as if it were a piece of thread. Jace sang softly in our dialect, as he spun me in his arms. He pressed his chin gently against my head. The scar wrapped around us as we danced. I closed my eyes as he lifted my chin. His silk lips found mine.

"Forget her," I whispered, but my resistance was depleting.

The image of a man's full, perfect lips bombarded my mind. I craved him, addicted to his touch. Everywhere his hand caressed me, my body ignited in a fiery passion I didn't want to escape. I leaned into him, begging for a kiss that would never come.

"Only you," he promised.

He was gorgeous, authoritative, and devoted. A moan grew in his chest when I thought about what I cherished about him. He clutched my hand like it was a lifeline. His hot breath hit my lips. My lungs scorched with his adoration. His other hand slid behind my neck and then his lips brushed mine. He held me there, only a moment, with our lips skimming the other.

"Death will come for me," I said more seriously. "You must carry the Elysian in my blood so both races survive my death. Without it, I fear chaos will destroy their fate. Besides, the others will need someone to follow in my absence."

"I'm a gladiator and a Healer," he said. "I'm not a ruler."

"Let your heart rule. If you can't find your way, trust your instincts," I said, and then smirked. "It's better than any compass. It brought me to you."

"Our destinies have always been intertwined," he said, pulling slightly away from me. He released his grip on my hand. "I promised to heal you—return the very essence of your soul. Centuries have come and gone while I searched for you. I want nothing more than to fulfill that promise, when the time is right."

I reached up to him. He turned his face into my hand. A tear trickled down my finger; it wasn't mine. His warm lips pressed into mine; his tongue tickled mine; his lips tasted like an angel's kiss. His hands sifted through my hair, and his lips were on mine again. His pulse rose. His breathing became erratic as he tried to hold me gently but never let go of me. His fingertips numbed me as they caressed my skin.

That I knew exactly what he was physically experiencing only made me want him more. That I could affect someone like him this way, that someone would want me this much, was an impossibility that came true. I pulled at his hair, keeping him close as his tongue rolled over mine.

I needed to stop hiding from him. He had suffered, too. Our past had meant enough for him to spend centuries searching for me.

I couldn't imagine killing anyone in the name of love. My voice rose just above a whisper, "Help me remember, Jace."

"I'll do everything in my power, my beloved." Jace said it like it meant more than just a promise; it was a vow.

We missed the sunrise as our passion consumed us. I never wanted to forget the taste of his kiss. Flashes of his memories flooded my mind whenever our scars brushed each other. I wasn't Deino anymore, but her memories would serve me; I needed them to survive. I needed Jace, not only because he lit my heart on fire, but because without him, I'd be lost.

"Kiss her much longer, and she'll become an Addict," Marco said. "She's still human."

Jace broke our kiss. Groaning, he pulled away. I didn't want to stop either. He pushed off the sand and held himself in a push-up position above me.

"So back to the original plan—heal her, find her sisters, and save us from an eternal visit to Hades?" Marco asked.

Jace pushed himself up but hesitated to look away from me. His devotion burned, not just for me, but to find the one who was hell bent on killing me for a wish. Jace wanted the Butcher's death, and he wanted to be the one to kill him. I felt it burning in my soul just like it was evident as the fire dancing over his skin. "Gwyneth has to give me permission to heal her," Jace said.

Marco scoffed, "You really believe Analee will buy that?"

"Analee can shove it," I said, and smiled vindictively as Jace helped me up. We walked up to Marco and braced myself for the shift. "Why do you plot against Analee if you used to be together?"

"*Used to be,*" Marco clarified. "She kicked me to the curb, just like you predicted."

"Does Analee know that you were the one who asked for the ability to speak soundlessly?" I asked.

His head twitched. "Do you think I'd still be alive if she did?"

Chapter Twenty-Six

I woke to Elsie's screams. A woman slammed her hand over my mouth before I could call out for help. Her shadowy figure wasn't as bright as the other deities but more so than humans.

"You can use your pretty, soundless craft to warn the others, and we'll leave. But we promise to hunt down every person you've ever loved and kill them if you do," the woman threatened.

She dragged me off my bed. Jace's phone slipped through my fingers. She snatched it up and pocketed it. She pushed me into the hallway. Gripping the railing, I swung my weight to the side and shoved my knee into her side. Cursing, she grabbed my wrist and twisted until my elbow snapped. I dropped to my knees. Shooting pangs radiated down my arm. I screamed. I grabbed my arm and kicked myself away from her.

Laughing, she grabbed my hair and dragged me down the few remaining stairs. The bones in my arm grounded into each other, but

I couldn't do anything but squirm. Tears streamed down my cheeks. My vision blurred. My stomach flipped.

She dug her heel into my back. My entire body straightened the moment her heel met my spine. When she got bored creating a collage of black and blue marks on my back, she yanked my hair and forced me upright onto my knees. I sobbed. My stomach turned. I thought I might vomit. She jerked my head toward the kitchen. John and Martha were either dead or knocked out cold on the floor.

Elsie was kicking and screaming upstairs. Her feet were pressed against the stairwell, refusing to be brought down by the rest of us. She managed to bite her captor. A man swore and let go. Elsie bolted down the stairs. He hobbled down after her. His limp reminded me of someone, but I couldn't recall who—my consciousness had already started to fade. The man tackled her, knocking a flower vase in the process. The vase smashed onto the living room floor, thus shattering the container.

"I caught this spirited little thing trying to leap from the Chronicler's window," he said. His voice sounded familiar, like I'd heard it from somewhere, but the pounding in my head refused to let me concentrate enough to figure it out.

"You've evaded the Butcher for years, Chronicler," a different man in the living room said. Either he was the one in charge or acting as the spokesman. "But now you'll bow to him."

"The hell I will," I mumbled.

The woman slammed my head forward into the floor. My nose snapped, causing me to tear up instantly. I cried out but was quickly silenced by the blood pooling my mouth. I inhaled some and fell into a coughing fit.

"We've learned something about you, Chronicler," the spokesman said. "You're no more powerful than humans without your sisters. So, you are worthless to the Butcher until then."

"Then…let…me go," I managed to get out.

"We will…for now," the man holding Elsie said. I knew I'd heard his voice before.

But where?

"Convince the Healer to return *all* of your Elysian. The Butcher will give you further directions then," the spokesman said.

"I'd rather die." Blood seeped from my lips.

"Thought so, which is why we aren't offering to spare your life," the man holding Elsie said. "This girl will be the bargaining chip."

Elsie's muffled screams brought tears to my eyes. They couldn't take her! She was just a kid.

"Take me instead!" I begged.

The spokesman responded with a laugh. With that they walked away. Screams of the little girl who just walked into my life became faint until the sound of my front door quieted them. They took Elsie because of me. They took a little girl because they wanted me, and I was utterly useless until I found my sisters. Unable to do anything but bleed out onto the living room floor, I screamed soundlessly in my mind, hoping someone would hear my pleas.

My cries turned to sobs by the time Jace and Marco appeared in my living room. I was crying on the floor, picking glass out of my hands. Jace cupped my face. His rage poured into me; it gave me the strength to gather my thoughts and speak.

"Who did this?" he demanded.

"Two men and a woman," I said, hating what I was about to do. It wasn't all a lie, and not what I wanted, but I knew the Butcher would kill Elsie if I didn't cooperate. "I couldn't see them, Jace. I can't tell you what they looked like because I can't see! I couldn't tell if they were Hunters or just psychopaths getting back at John."

"Why would anyone seek revenge against him?" Marco asked.

"Lawyer," Jace and I said simultaneously.

"That'd be a little bit too coincidental," Marco grunted. He disappeared. A few seconds later he reappeared. "The Thompsons are out cold but unharmed. The dog is alive but needs those hands of yours to pull through, Jace. The young girl is gone; they took her."

"They spared your life." Jace said carefully touching my arm. "The Butcher was sending a message, Gwyneth. He wants you to fear him. But remember, you're safe until we find your sisters. He doesn't want you to die."

"Not yet anyway," Marco grunted.

"Jace, they're going to hurt me as much as they can without killing me. They'll hunt others of your kind down until they get what they want." Thinking of my memory where the old man grows young, I replied, "He kills to defy death. I'll grant him immortality if he lets Elsie go. It will be simple."

"It doesn't work that way," Jace said. "Anyone who steals you must be willing to kill you for their heart's desire. If they aren't willing to end your life, you don't have to grant their wish."

"They've killed for centuries, Jace. I sincerely doubt he will hesitate to end my life to ensure he gets what he wants. *Please,* heal me. I give you permission to heal me. Give me back my Elysian."

He sighed like I'd given him everything he'd ever wanted and taken everything away at the same time. Jace whispered my name as he brushed the hair away from my face. "Close your eyes, dearest. This will not be pleasant."

He spoke out soundless language. The longer he spoke, the louder the distant ringing in my ears became. I struggled to breathe when the shape of Jace's mouth formed. The white and black in my sight began to twirl furiously. As my world spun into a gray blur, I focused on Jace.

He stroked my cheek. He kissed me like it would be our last. His passion trickled onto my lips as he stole my breath. He broke the kiss only to place the gentlest kisses on both my eyes. As soon as his lips made contact, my eyes burned. As Jace spoke in his soundless language, I screamed out in agony.

An explosion of sound blasted me as he spoke. As he spoke, a melody became apparent but was sung louder than anything I'd ever heard. It felt like I'd been deaf and was suddenly given back my hearing only to be screamed at. He refused to stop even though I begged him. I heard myself scream so loudly that my ears bled.

Jace's body ignited into flames, but he never let go. His heart was broken, but he warmed a cold, dead part of my scarred soul. I reached out, trying to find another soul to connect to. The power I'd refused to believe in grew. I didn't know how to control it, but it didn't stop me from embracing countless human lives.

I saw the destinies lying out before them, ever changing but real just the same. I didn't see them as shadows; their bodies were no longer important. Instead, I saw their threads of life, intertwining with each other. They grew from the dozens to the hundreds. The more I strained to reach each thread of life, the more quickly they pulled away from me like they were afraid.

My world was still painted in black and white. I was soaked in sweat. Utter exhaustion imprisoned my body. I wanted to sever the pain, the guilt, the abandonment I deserved...

Yet Jace looked to me like I was an extension of his soul. He belonged to me and me to him. He was weak but managed to feel imposing. He spoke to me in my mind. Although I didn't understand what he was speaking, I found myself growing tired the louder his voice became. Soon his deep, soothing voice grew darker. The longer he spoke, his vehemence became more apparent.

"Anger feeds my power," he whispered, apologetically.

He stroked my smallest finger with his thumb as he screamed into the night. Shades of gray mixed with shades of color, some not visible to the humans flashed before my eyes. Just as quickly as the colors invaded my mind, they vanished. I saw nothing, not even a single shade of gray.

Chapter Twenty-Seven

The shriek of a hospital alarm woke me. Feeling about as good as being beaten by a sledge hammer, I couldn't fathom trying to move my mouth much less speak or open my eyes.

"I know you can hear me, Gwyneth. Perhaps you don't care about your body right now, but you survived the transformation," Jace whispered in my mind. "It's going to take me a few days before I'm at full strength, so I couldn't speed along your injuries. Just another day, dearest, and you'll see. Your foster parents are safe; they don't recall anything. Marco fed them a story that Elsie had run away while they were sleeping. He told them that you tried to stop her, but it ended in a fight, which is why you are at the hospital. Now close your ocean eyes and dream."

Sleep washed over me quickly. What felt like seconds later, I was awakened again. This time it was by someone stumbling into my hospital room. I couldn't see. Bandages covered my eyes. However, I knew the person was injured because I heard the uneven step of a limp.

"Med time," the person said. His voice was so familiar.

The intravenous line that was hooked up to my arm tugged a bit as medication was administered. Soon I was cocooned in a blissful, medicated haze. It wasn't long before I wondered why my tongue felt so large in my mouth. I giggled.

"You need drugs because we can't have you alerting Jace, now can we? He can sense when your anxiety spikes—so these muscle relaxers should do the trick in keeping you calm."

His voice sounded *so* familiar, but my mind was groggy. I couldn't think straight.

"Jace is tired," I agreed. "He doesn't need to worry about me right now. He's a mess."

"Do you know your name?" he asked.

I laughed; of course I knew my name. I told him not to ask such silly questions. It made the man chuckle. He was pleased at my reaction. I was pleased. I had heard that laugh many times before, yet, it sounded slightly different, like I was hearing with newfound hearing.

Tugging on the bandages covering my eyes, he instructed me to sit very still. He peeled them off. Brilliant light momentarily blinded me. I expected to see the world in an explosion of color. But I was confused. My surroundings—the bed, floor, and nightstand— everything but the man—were still shades of gray. At least it was more than my black and white vision. I saw clear edges of shapes, definition, and depth. That pleased me. I clapped.

On the other hand, the man was painted in pale, dull colors. His skin was a pale tan. His hair was a light brown, and his eyes were light green. He wore faded blue jeans and a gray jacket. A shaggy beard covered his face. I grinned; for the first time in my life, I saw my best friend, Hector. For some reason he looked familiar, but I couldn't place it. In addition to the splash of color, I noticed his fragrance. He smelled like fresh spring rain.

"Hector," I said, giddily. "You've come to visit me!"

He set a vase of lilies on the stand beside me. He always brought me that flower in honor of my sister.

"A few colleagues of mine, Zalen included, have been watching your house in shifts," Hector said. His voice was harsher than I recalled. I couldn't hear the affection in it.

Something wasn't allowing me to think clearly. Something was off with Hector, but I couldn't pin-point it. He handed me an object. I brought it up by my face and studied it. It wasn't until I closed my eyes and slipped my fingertips over its shell that I realized what it was—my cell phone that the lady stole from me! The only thing I could think of saying was *you're welcome* but it didn't feel right. Hector told me I needed to remember a phone number.

"Your library card number," Hector said, staring at me as if this was the most important information he'd ever given me. "If you dial the numbers of your library number, you will reach me."

"Or I can just punch in the number five on speed dial," I offered, trying to be helpful.

"Find your sisters, Chronicler," Hector ordered. He stood up and walked out the door. He paused but never looked back at me. "You're useless to me until then. Call me once you do, or I'll kill the kid, just like I killed your sister."

"You murdered Lily?"

"How else do you think I grew young?" he asked sarcastically. "Call me when you find the other Fates, and we will make our trade then. You get the kid if you grant me what my heart most desires. If you undermine me, I'll track down your lover-boy and kill him just so I can live another lifetime. It'd be my pleasure to end the life of the deity who shattered my leg and sentenced me to a lifetime with this limp. I think it goes without saying that no one is to know about our little talk."

***

My oldest friend. My would-be brother. The person who'd I'd come to rely on over the years had murdered my family. Whatever happened, I knew that he always had an eye out for me—I just thought it was in my best interests.

I rubbed sleep from my eyes, wondering if my previous life was this disorienting and cruel. I sighed and focused on the gift Jace bestowed upon me. I gazed at my gray hand. Like the objects around me, I was painted in black and white. I gazed out the window. The sun kissed the horizon.

"To see the colors of a sunset," I said, longing to view the scene the way it was meant to be seen.

"Seeking a little color?"

Leaning against the hospital door frame stood a

preposterously attractive young man. He took my breath away the moment our gaze locked. His chest failed to move until I gasped. In a world still in black and white, Jace was my splash of color. His chocolate-brown eyes matched the color of his hair perfectly. It was a few inches long, and the flecks of gold shimmered in the light. His skin was lightly tanned. His burgundy shirt clung to his chest like it was sewn on. His blue jeans hung on his hips perfectly. He smiled, and his dimples revealed themselves. I opened my mouth to speak but couldn't get a word out.

The rock walls imprisoned me, but the straw roof allowed light to seep through. An elderly woman hung from rusted shackles. Her gray hair lay in chucks at the floor. Vomit, urine, and a lovely scent of lilies hung in the air. Her breathing was labored, she neared death. I kneeled on my hands and knees in a pool of urine. My clothes were soaked in sweat.

"Give me what I desire most, or I'll kill the Prophet."

My head shook as I gazed up to the young man with piercing light green eyes. Hector circled me, careful not to touch the pool I kneeled in. His brown curly hair looked almost black in the dim lighting. The scent of rain lingered around him.

"Time is slipping away, Chronicler," Hector said, as he tossed a spear back and forth in his hands. "Your sister is hanging on by a sliver of her thread."

He walked gracefully over to her. Yanking what was left of her hair, he spat in her face. Her chest rose as if she was struggling to breathe, but a weak laugh came out. "Utter destruction would be had by all, including the humans."

He beat her, but I was too weak to stop him. A testament of my age. I was no longer young and strong. My nails were yellowed. My skin clung to my bones, like the mouthless ones, my Scavengers. My body warmed thinking of them taking me from this world. I wanted death but refused to leave this life knowing all hope was lost.

"Blood will be spilled, and no new life will be had amongst our race without us three," the Prophet said before passing out. I glanced down at her hand. She made the slightest movement with what fingers she had left. Slowly, she made three snipping movements.

"Our sister will cut soon, Butcher," I whispered. My voice hung in the air as if I'd sung.

Hector laughed, "I've killed enough of you to know there has already been blood spilled. Give me what I ask, and I'll end the genocide."

An impossibly beautiful young man crashed through the roof. Jace's body was engulfed in flames. My captor threw a spear. Jace dodged the blade, but it scraped his cheek. He slammed his foot down on my captor's leg and held it there while the man screamed.

"This will never heal, Butcher," Jace promised, and then rushed over to me. He never opened his mouth, but I still heard his screams in my mind. His misery ripped through me like it was my own, when he lifted my frail body in his arms. My life was draining into death's embrace.

Marco appeared. But it was too late; the injured Hunter vanished into thin air with Zalen. Our gaze locked before they vanished.

I looked up at Marco. His penance for past sins was my sister's doing, not mine. But, we both knew the Cutter would never have uttered a single word to him about our past if it hadn't involved us. Regret erupted inside him.

"Our past is not forgotten but has been long forgiven, Reaper."

Marco snorted, refusing to believe me. He grabbed Jace's shoulder.

292

Within a blink of an eye, I was lying on the ground outside the burning building. My feet brushed against the ground as my savior, Jace, held me in his warm arms.

"Tell that to your sister. She won't be particularly pleased to be on this side of her scissors. You smell like death already," Marco snorted, and vanished.

Jace gently lowered me to the ground. "I've never asked anything from you, until now. Please, grant me what my heart most desires."

"Anything," I said, looking into his chocolate brown eyes.

"Give me a second chance to make this right," he begged, as smoke seeped from his skin. "Give me a second chance to be with you like we once were."

"You wish for my immortality," I said, stroking his thumb with my gnarled hand. My old body scarcely obeyed my command. I wanted to rest, needed it. The thread of my life was unraveling while his was as strong and youthful as ever. It was cruel in more ways than one.

Jace held my face in his hand, comforting me. "I want your immortality and for you to have what you once had before she took it from you and the humans."

"You only get one request, and you have to be willing to kill me for it," I said, and guided his hand over my chest. The knife skimmed my skin, but it was enough to tear it open.

"Living as an immortal in this body would be more like a curse than a gift," he said. The regret in his eyes was already evident. "I want you to have the opportunity to be what you once were, before she took it."

"Reborn as what I once was?" I asked, tracing his thumb since he refused to return my gaze. Smoke rose around us. It seeped over the wheat grass while every building around us went up in flames.

293

"Playing with your fate is dangerous." His voice burned apologetically. "But I can feel the life leaving your body. I've never asked for you to grant me anything, dearest. Grant me this."

"Choose one."

"Then I chose you," he said, and the regret in his eyes was already evident. "I want you to have the opportunity to be what you once were, before she took it."

"My body is aged, and my soul is broken." My voice hung in the air as if I'd sung it.

"So give me a taste of your kiss, and let me be reborn into a life of eternal passion." he said, speaking in the same melody.

"I'll be reborn as human," I said more seriously. My smallest finger stroked his thumb—connecting our souls. "Take my Elysian as promised. The others will be looking for someone to follow; they will look to you even if there are others who challenge you. Return it to me so I may defy death once again in my human form."

"I'm not a ruler," he insisted.

"You must learn," I insisted.

"I don't care about the others, only you matter to me," he said.

"Then you must find me and return the Elysian to me," I whispered. "You must heal me, Jace." The very essence of my spirit– the Elysian pumping through my veins - started to drift into his soul. "Follow your heart. It brought us together once before."

Countless souls of humans and deities pulled away from me as the

294

Elysian drained from my body. I felt disconnected and disturbingly alone. Jace broke the connection before I was completely disconnected from him. I didn't have to ask why he didn't take it all—I saw the truth in his eyes. He couldn't bear it. "I can't steal everything that makes you who you are. I can't take it all. I can't take all the essence of your soul."

His chocolate brown eyes didn't radiate with vengeance as he pressed a knife to my chest. They glistened with tears. His dark brown hair shimmered, like gold had been melted into each strand. The sight would've been utterly breathtaking if sand and sweat hadn't dried into his hair as well. A bloody gash under his left eye interrupted his otherwise perfectly tanned skin.

Burnt oranges, soft yellows, and deep reds surrounded the sun as it neared the horizon. My time was quickly slipping away. A hint of scorched wood piggybacked the wind while smoke crawled over the blood-soaked dirt.

I reached up with my gnarled, weathered hand and gently stroked his face. Hiding in the sheer beauty of his eyes rested his tortured soul—screaming for forgiveness. His tears trickled onto my aged skin as he shoved the blade deeper through my chest. I struggled to breathe. My vision darkened at the edges.

I barely held back tears when he whispered how nothing compared to the splendor of my soul. I never took my gaze off his eyes while he walked over to me. He didn't stop at the bed's edge; he crawled onto it and lay beside me, waiting with a lifetime of patience for me to remember how to breathe. I whispered his name. My angelic voice hung in the air like I'd sung a thousand words of adoration.

"It's you," I whispered.

His hand found mine. His life's thread wrapped around his thumb. My own twirled around my smallest finger. I tugged on his gently, with my fingertip. Our touch connected our souls, making us one. His love for me surpassed centuries. He'd do anything for me; even end my life if required.

His affection crawled over my skin like a fire. Blue flames glistening over his skin as his lips met mine. My feelings for him acted like a catalyst for the fire burning in his soul. He tucked me safely against his body, protecting me from the rest of the world.

Gazing into his chocolate-brown eyes, I knew I could do it—I could kill someone in the name of love. The Butcher gave me a choice: find my sisters and then grant his wish, or he'd kill everyone I loved.

If I was destined to die for someone's deepest desire, it would be for the man who had the most captivating chocolate eyes I'd ever gazed upon. I refused to willingly lay down another deathbed. So I came up with a plan that I hated, but it was necessary.

Everyone would be safe, except for me...

Years ago, I fell in love with a young man; the same one I was falling for all over again. Jace and I lay together on a blanket next to an old tree overlooking Bakker's Cemetery. My family's tombstones were decorated with three lilies again. I sniffed it. It smelled like rain, like Hector. He would always be watching, ready to steal what was never meant to be his—eternal youth. There was no need to ask him; he smelled Hector's scent, just as I could now.

"Lily had to be a goddess if the Butcher grew young after killing her," I said, clutching the flower.

"Marco has several theories about that," Jace said but didn't elaborate. He draped his hand around me and slid closer to comfort me. He encouraged me to ask questions to the answers I sought but didn't pry. His patience was more resilient than any other person's I'd met. He simply twirled my hair around his fingers and waited.

"The unseeing past and unspeakable future are once again surrounded in death's embrace, is what the girl said. We touched and three distinctive sensations came over me," I said, recalling the memory of the Cutter sitting on broken glass with the Prophet hiding in the shadows. "Rage erupted inside the Prophet. The Cutter's derangement tore at her sanity. Calmness encased my soul; I had to be patient if I was to find my revenge."

"Before humanity lost their immortality, you rarely saw your sisters," Jace said, lifting me onto his lap. He took my hand in his and kissed it lightly. A blue flame leapt from his lips to my hand. A blue flare twirled on my hand as it danced in the breeze. "That changed after Analee's wish. Close proximity to each other kept you ageless. Distance was your enemy; it stole your youth. A few seconds apart turned to minutes. Soon days drifted by before melting into years."

"You'll find a new meaning to life, but I must warn you—there will come a time you regret feeling an ounce of love," the Prophet said. "It will blind you, making you susceptible to foolish decisions. Your enemies will use it against you."

"Love is foolish," I agreed. But certainly it couldn't have repercussions as devastating as my sister predicted.

"Love makes you blind," she said.

She had no idea what I saw with my eyes. As Chronicler, I saw into people's past. Their history predicted untold futures. As a Fate Sister, I could meddle with anyone's destiny. I laughed, "Fine, I'll lay down my sword, as it were, if you show me a meaningful life."

As I watched the blue flame dance in my hand, I prayed Jace would forgive me for what I planned to do. Nevertheless, I couldn't stand back and do nothing while people I loved suffered. I was done having others fight my battles. I'd be damned if anyone else was going to perish because of me. It was high time I fight my own battles, no matter what the cost. For years, I'd been combat training. But now, I needed to step up my game. I need a tactile strategy. Something sharp and pointy would do.

Twisted Games

Book # 2

Fate Trilogy

Love is just another word to describe poison.

It's potent and deadly.

Prologue

All traces of my enemy's blood washed off my skin when I dove underneath the ocean's crest. I swam down until I couldn't see the moon's glow. Eclipsed in darkness, my memory guided me to a labyrinth of caves—Niran Caverns. When I broke surface, I treaded water in a pool. Light shone through the cracks of the earthy ceiling. Dew collected on the iridescent rock walls. The rocks changed colors, depending on the season. In the summertime, they were dark violet, whereas they turned turquoise in the winter. They frequently altered hues since the seasons of Elysia could change in minutes rather than years. Currently, the rocks were lavender in color. It complimented the Prophet's midnight-blue dress.

My sister, the Prophet, stood on the cave's ledge. Her wavy, russet-colored hair spilled onto her narrow shoulders. Her willowy figure made her appear fragile, but she didn't have a matching personality. Her delicate facial features were beautiful, except for the *thread of life*—symbolized as a scar—that twirled around the corner of her eye. Sometimes I pitied her for the facial deformity, but it caused her no concern. Only we goddesses, the Fate Sisters, could see the threads of life.

My younger sister, the Cutter, sat beside her. She kicked the water and giggled as the water splashed me. Even though it was annoying, I admired her ability to keep her childlike happiness. Her black hair fell haphazardly over her eyes, for it was chopped sporadically. She never could decide what length she wanted her hair to be, so she cut it every length.

Swimming to the edge, I complained for the umpteenth time about having to swim to the Niran Caverns. If we widened a gap on the stony surface we wouldn't have to get wet every time we entered our underground home! I hated being wet and cold.

Mimicking our older sister's response to my complaints, the Cutter said, "One day, you'll find comfort the remote entrance offers, as well as its isolated refuge."

I coughed to cover my chuckle. Encouraging the Cutter to taunt our older sister was not wise. The Prophet's wrath rarely outshined mine, but she was fierce. The Prophet grabbed my hand and helped me out of the water. When I was on dry land, she turned my wrist over and inspected it. She acted like she could still see the blood on my skin.

"You cannot continue to fight them, Chronicler! It alters their destiny," the Prophet said, dropping my hand.

"It is my *right* to alter their destiny, especially when *they* challenge *me*," I said, squeezing my dress. Water dripped down my legs and pooled at my feet. "The last fool blitz-attacked me with a three-pronged sword."

"You wacked Poseidon?" the Cutter asked excitedly.

Shaking my head, "The infamous trident *has* influenced weaponry design, but it wasn't Poseidon who challenged me."

"You egged on the less powerful gods when you vowed to grant their deepest desire if they were willing to kill you," the Prophet said, dismissively.

The *Elysian* flowing in my veins is the source of my *crafts*, or supernatural abilities. One of my crafts allows me to grant someone's deepest desires. For this inane reason, I've fought countless melees.

It was also well known that I'd only grant their desires if they were willing to kill me. "It's not like I make it easy for them."

"What happens if you die?" the Prophet asked.

"Then I'll be dead and you'll be in charge of everyone's fate," I said, shivering as I stood in the puddle of water.

I rubbed my arms and hoped she got the hint that I was miserably cold. Turning away, the Prophet led us to our living quarters. The Cutter tagged long and jumped on every crack in the

3

stones. She sang merrily about breaking backs.

Smoke rose from the blazing fire pit in the common area. It scudded along the ceiling and seeped into the cracks in the stone. On the surface above, the smoke mixed with ash and steam created from a nearby archaic volcano.

"You can't tell me I have to stop fighting," I said as I warmed my hands by the flames. This argument was far from over.

My older sister looked at me like I was a child, a look I reserved for humans and young deities. She opened her mouth to speak, but stopped when the light behind her eyes flashed, and I knew she was seeing into the future. A few seconds later, she rubbed her temple and frowned. The image must not have been a pleasant one.

She kneeled down beside me and held my hand. She traced my thread of life, a scar that wrapped around my smallest finger, went up my arm and my shoulder before it branched off into three distinct lines on my back.

"If you swear to put down your weapons, I promise that you'll find a new meaning to life." She spoke these words as if it were the deepest darkest secret she'd ever shared. "You'll learn what it really means to love another."

I'd fallen for others before, but it certainly hadn't been life altering.

"I wouldn't agree to her proposition, Chronicler," the Cutter said in a singsong manner as she poked the fire with a stick.

Coals tumbled out of the fire pit. The Prophet grabbed the

Cutter's stick and scowled at her. The Cutter rolled her eyes and stuck out her tongue. Not discouraged from playing, the Cutter held up her fingers beside the fire. The light cast shadows onto the walls. The Cutter giggled with delight when she made a shadow-bunny hop.

"You'll find a new meaning to life, but I must warn you—there will come a time you regret feeling an ounce of love," the Prophet said. "It will blind you, making you susceptible to foolish decisions. Your enemies will use it against you."

"Love is foolish," I agreed. But certainly it couldn't have repercussions as devastating as my sister predicted.

"Love makes you blind," she said.

She had no idea what I saw with my eyes. As Chronicler, I saw into people's past. Their history predicted untold futures. As a Fate Sister, I could meddle with anyone's destiny. I laughed, "Fine, I'll lay down my sword, as it were, *if* you show me a meaningful life."

Chapter One

If I closed my eyes and listened to Jace's heartbeat, I could pretend that I wasn't trapped in an icy prison. I could pretend that I hadn't been betrayed. I could hold onto the hope that my crown would be waiting for me when I returned to Elysia. But, I couldn't escape my reality, no matter how hard I tried.

Fantasy would have to wait, for even with closed eyes I saw the painful truth. I'd been banished to the Bastille Island—a remote, snow-capped, mountainous prison.

"Just a little longer, dearest," Jace whispered, sensing my distress. He rubbed his thumb over my little finger as he walked me to the mountain's edge. Icebergs floated in the bitter cold water fifty feet below us. "When the sun meets the sea, you'll see a flash. That is when you'll need to jump. The current will bring you back to Elysia, if you survive the fall."

"Then you'll be trapped in this arctic hell!"

In order for me to be free, someone had to take my place on the Bastille Island. There was only one code here: someone must stay to pay the price for the *crime.*

"Your sister promised to wait for your arrival," Jace said. Before I could argue, he told me his decision was non-negotiable. I would die if I stayed on the island much longer. "I'm immortal. I'll survive. You won't, not anymore. It's that simple."

"You're immortal, not invincible."

"What I am is in love with you," Jace said. "I'd die a thousand deaths if it meant you didn't have to suffer."

Unable to bear the sorrow in his chocolate brown eyes, I looked at the horizon. Faint blues and a splash of lavender were the only colors decorating the skyline. White snowflakes twirled around the glaciers, shimmering in the falling sun's light. The frosty air froze me from the inside out with each breath. I clutched Jace's shirt and cherished the warmth from his body heat. I memorized the way he felt in my arms. Nevertheless, our time was ticking away. The sun was only seconds from kissing the horizon.

"If you'll still have me after you get the answers to all the questions you didn't ask last night, I'll watch over you until the end of time." Jace said.

I might have only shared one year with him, but it'd been the greatest year of my life. He lifted my chin. My frosty lips instantly warmed when I tasted his affection. The good-bye kiss rendered me defenseless. He could ask anything of me and I'd give it to him.

I wanted to promise him my heart; I wanted to tell him how I felt. However, when I took a breath of air, all the poetry vanished from my tongue. How could I explain how deeply I cared for him in a few, short words?

A sunburst flashed. Heaven kissed Hades. Our time had run out. Before I jumped, I told him that I would find a way to free him.

Reading between the lines...

This trilogy wouldn't have been possible without the help of countless people—friends, family, and a horde of editors. Thank you all for listening to me babble on end about my "book ideas." I'd like to give a special thanks to my parents—because of your own crazy obsession with all that is science-fiction; I found my own love for the paranormal realm because of you. Thank you a million times for encouraging me to be the person I am today. And to my brothers: Thanks Ryan, for always (unknowingly, of course) giving me new material to work with. And to my "Little Brother David," the spark to modernize classical mythology came from you.

To Angelique Verver who brought the imaginary gods who were hijacking my imagination to "real-life.," and to Josh Wilcoxon and Joe Holman who captured their immortal essence on film.

To Megan, Keenan, Stefannie, and Shelby—you are all extraordinary and genuine. I didn't imagine you all being so eager and enthusiastic to work with. Without you, I'd be a strange woman talking to the imaginary people in my head. Seeing you four transform into "the characters" was one of the most exhilarating moments of my life. To Graham Turner, Steve "smiley" Barnard, Olivia Otim, and Kerry Schultz. They gave the characters their voices that were buried within the passages of the novel. "Walkin' a Line," compliments the novel on an otherworldly level. It speaks volumes to the teenage-version of me who is forever trapped in my mind

And finally—to the everlasting adoration from my very own Prince-Charming who inspired the passionate story of this ageless tale. Thank you, for showing me what unconditional love feels like, Dusty. Without you, it would be impossible to describe undying love…

About the Author

Sarah J. Pepper specializes in paranormal romance—think *Happily Ever After* but with a twisted, dark chocolate center. Real-life romance isn't only filled with hugs, kisses, bunnies, and rainbows. True-love can be more thoroughly described in times of darkness and tribulation. It's in those harsh moments where you see what a person is truly capable of—both the good and bad. Sometimes prince-charming isn't always on time, and the glass slipper is a little snug. However, it doesn't mean Charming is not Mr. Right, and who says every shoe is the perfect fit?

www.sarahjpepper.com

www.facebook.com/sarahjpepper.author

@sarahjpepper

www.ingramcontent.com/pod-product-compliance
Lightning Source LLC
Chambersburg PA
CBHW052018240626
47153CB00006B/1867